J
Alvar. J

"Gorgeously detailed and with heart-wrenching conflict, *Across the Dark Water* is a breathtaking read sure to please new fans and old. Jennifer Lynn Alvarez's fantasy world is richly developed with a cast of characters readers will be sure to love, both winged and human. I read it as fast as a pegasus can fly and am already longing for more."
—Mindee Arnett, critically acclaimed author of *Onyx & Ivory*

Praise for the Guardian Herd series

"From page one, Jennifer Lynn Alvarez weaves an epic tale of a doomed black pegasus foal named Star, whose race against time will lift the reader on the wings of danger and destiny, magic and hope. It's a world I did not want to leave, and neither will you."
—Peter Lerangis, *New York Times* bestselling author in the 39 Clues series and of the Seven Wonders series

"Perfect for fans of *Charlotte's Web* and the Guardians of Ga'Hoole series."
—ALA *Booklist*

"Chock-full of adventure and twists, making it difficult to put down. Readers will be clamoring for the next book."
—*School Library Journal*

"Alvarez's world is lush with description and atmosphere."
—*Publishers Weekly*

"Will prove popular with both animal-lovers and fantasy fans. A good choice for reluctant readers. The clever resolution will get kids psyched for more tales from the Guardian Herd."
—ALA *Booklist*

"Filled with fantastical action, and rich with description. A well-paced and engrossing story. Alvarez has created a series that will be beloved by readers."
—*VOYA*

Praise for *Riders of the Realm: Across the Dark Water*

"A story with both wings and heart, Across the Dark Water
is a breathtaking ride into a rich and dangerous world. Animal lovers
and thrill-seekers alike will cheer for Echofrost and Rahkki at each
of the many twists and turns. Clever, epic, and wildly imaginative!"
—Kamilla Benko, author of *The Unicorn Quest*

"An epic adventure that moves at the speed of flight.
Thrilling, compelling, and completely enchanting. I fell in love
with the Storm Herd, and one particular winged steed that
Pegasus himself would fall for!"
—Kate O'Hearn, author of the international bestselling Pegasus series

"Exhilarating! A well-woven tale full of loyalty, bravery,
danger, and love. Readers will be delighted!"
—Lindsay Cummings, *New York Times* bestselling author
of the Balance Keepers series

"A riveting, richly imagined epic tale of loyalty, bravery, and friendship
that will make your heart (literally!) soar—a pulse-pounding adventure!
Jennifer Lynn Alvarez is a true master of her craft."
—Kristen Kittscher, author of *The Wig in the Window*
and *The Tiara on the Terrace*

"Getting swept up in Jennifer Lynn Alvarez's rich world of flying steeds,
Landwalkers, giants, and spit dragons was the most fun I've had all year.
It's like *How to Train Your Dragon* meets *Watership Down.*
But with pegasi. A fantastic read!"
—John Kloepfer, author of the Zombie Chasers series
and the Galaxy's Most Wanted series

"Honor and courage soar on every page of Jennifer Lynn Alvarez's books!"
—Jenn Reese, author of the Above World trilogy

"A beautiful tale of loyalty, adventure, and bravery. Readers will want
to soar through the clouds with Echofrost and befriend kindhearted Rahkki.
Across the Dark Water is a captivating opener to the Riders of the Realm trilogy."
—Jill Diamond, author of the Lou Lou and Pea series

RIDERS
of the
REALM

1

ACROSS THE DARK WATER

BY
JENNIFER LYNN ALVAREZ

HARPER
An Imprint of HarperCollinsPublishers

Also by Jennifer Lynn Alvarez
The Guardian Herd: Starfire
The Guardian Herd: Stormbound
The Guardian Herd: Landfall
The Guardian Herd: Windborn

Riders of the Realm: Across the Dark Water
Text copyright © 2018 by Jennifer Lynn Alvarez
Interior art copyright © 2018 by David McClellan
All rights reserved. Printed in the United States of America.
No part of this book may be used or reproduced in any manner whatsoever without written permission except in the case of brief quotations embodied in critical articles and reviews. For information address HarperCollins Children's Books, a division of HarperCollins Publishers, 195 Broadway, New York, NY 10007.
www.harpercollinschildrens.com

Library of Congress Control Number: 2016949951
ISBN 978-0-06-241539-4

Typography by Catherine San Juan
18 19 20 21 22   LSCH   10 9 8 7 6 5 4 3 2 1

First Edition

FOR DAVID, SLAYER OF GIANTS

AND FINDER OF LOST THINGS

TABLE OF CONTENTS

"A promise born is a promise dying.
Let actions speak where tongues are lying."

—Ancient Sandwen proverb

⊙ SANDWEN CLANS ⊙

Humans

BRIM CARVER—animal doctor of the Fifth Clan

KOKO DALE— age fifteen; head groom of the Kihlari stable of the Fifth Clan Sky Guard

MUT FINN— age fifteen; leader of the Sandwen teens, kids too old for games but too young for war

TUNI HIGHTOWER—Headwind of Dusk Patrol, member of the Fifth Clan Sky Guard. Kihlara mount: Rizah

HARAK NIGHTSEER—Headwind of Day Patrol, member of the Fifth Clan Sky Guard. Kihlara mount: Ilan

BRAUK STORMRUNNER—Rahkki's brother, Headwind of Dawn Patrol, member of the Fifth Clan Sky Guard. Kihlara mount: Kol

UNCLE DARTHAN STORMRUNNER—rice farmer of the Fifth Clan, supplies free rations to the queen's Land Guard army. Uncle to Brauk and Rahkki on their mother's side.

RAHKKI STORMRUNNER— age twelve; farmer's apprentice of the Fifth Clan

DAAKURAN EMPIRE—across the bay from the Sandwen Realm is the empire, a highly populated land of commerce and academics. Common language of the empire: Talu

SANDWEN CLANS—seven clans of people each ruled by a monarch queen. Clan language: Sandwen

REYELLA STORMRUNNER—past queen of the Fifth
Clan, assassinated by Lilliam Whitehall, mother of
Rahkki and Brauk Stormrunner. Kihlara mount: Drael

GENERAL AKMID TSUN—commander of the Land Guard
army

PRINCESS I'LENNA WHITEHALL— age eleven; eldest
daughter of Queen Lilliam of the Fifth Clan

QUEEN LILLIAM WHITEHALL—Leader of the Fifth
Clan, prior princess of the Second Clan. Also referred to
as *Queen of the Fifth*. Kihlara mount: Mahrsan

QUEEN TAVARA WHITEHALL—leader of the Second
Clan, mother of Lilliam Whitehall, I'Lenna's grandmother

Sandwen Clan Divinities

GRANAK—"Father of Dragons," guardian mascot of the
Fifth Clan. Sixteen-foot-tall, thirty-three-foot-long
drooling lizard called a *spit dragon*

KAJI (sing.), **KAJIES** (pl.)—troublesome or playful spirits

THE SEVEN SISTERS—the royal founders of the seven
Sandwen clans

SULA—"Mother of Serpents," guardian mascot of the Second
Clan. Forty-two-foot-long jungle python

SUNCHASER—the moon

C∕◦ KIHLARI ◦◦

(KEE-lar-ee) (pl.), Kihlara (sing.)

Translation: "Children of the Wind"

Tame pegasi of the Sandwen Clans

DRAEL—Queen Reyella's Chosen stallion. Small bay with black-tipped dark-amber feathers, fluffy black mane and tail, white muzzle, four white socks

ILAN—white stallion with black spots, black mane and tail, dark-silver wings edged in black

KOL—shiny chestnut stallion with bright-yellow feathers, yellow-streaked red mane and tail, white blaze, two white hind socks

MAHRSAN—Queen Lilliam's Chosen stallion. Blood-bay with sapphire-blue feathers edged in white, black mane and tail, jagged white blaze, four white socks

RIZAH—golden palomino pinto mare with dark-pink feathers edged in gold, white-and-gold-mixed mane and tail

ᴄᴏ STORM HERD ᴏᴄ

Wild pegasi from Anok

DEWBERRY—bay pinto mare with emerald feathers, black
mane and tail, thin blaze on forehead, two white hind
anklets

ECHOFROST—sleek silver mare with a mix of dark- and
light-purple feathers, white mane and tail, one white sock

GRAYSTONE—white stallion with pale-yellow feathers each
with a silver center, blue eyes, silver mane and tail

HAZELWIND—buckskin stallion with jade feathers, black
mane and tail, big white blaze, two white hind socks

REDFIRE—tall copper chestnut stallion with dark-gold
feathers, dark-red mane and tail, white star on forehead

SHYSONG—blue roan mare with dusty-blue feathers edged
in black, ice-blue eyes, black mane and tail, jagged blaze,
two hind socks

GORLAN HORDES

Giant Folk

Living in the mountains in three separate hordes—
Highland Horde, Fire Horde, and Great Cave Horde. They
stand from eleven to fourteen feet tall. Language: Gorlish,
a form of sign language

RIDERS

◦⌒ of the ⌒◦

REALM

◦⌒ **1** ⌒◦

ACROSS THE DARK WATER

SANDWEN

Mill

Darthan's
Farm

Barn

Rice Fields

FIFTH
CLAN

Ruk

Horse Arena

Fort Prowl

Kihlari
Training
Yard

Kihlari Barn

Rain Forest

Leshi Creek

FOURTH
CLAN

Lake

To the
THIRD CLAN

Beach

Jungle

Brim's
Hut

Fallows

Horse
Pasture

Farmland

Supply
Barn

River Tsallan

Jungle

Sandwen Clan Travelways

SIXTH CLAN

Southern Mountains

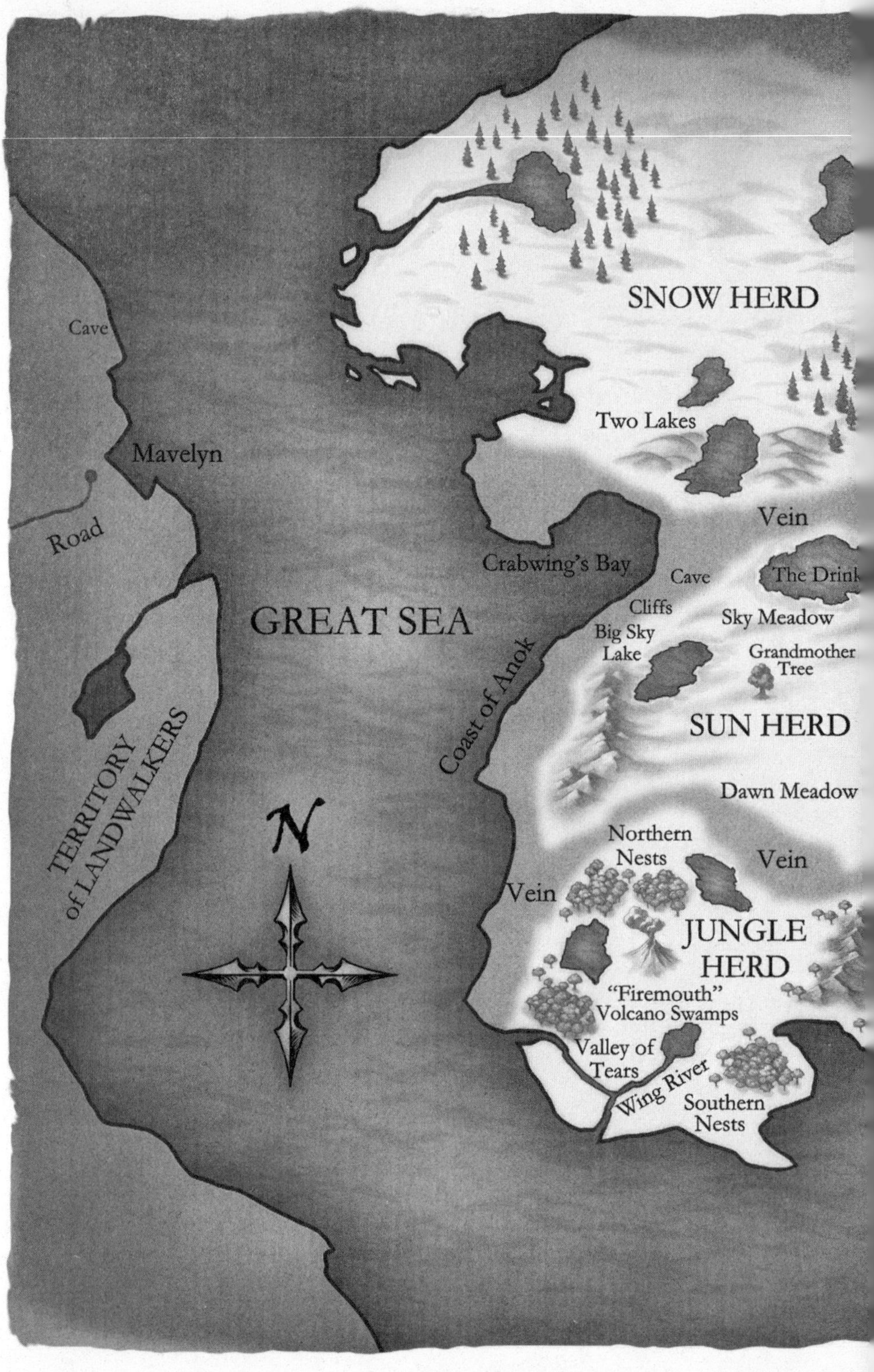

SNOW HERD

Two Lakes

Vein

Cave

The Drink

Cliffs

Sky Meadow

Big Sky
Lake

Grandmother
Tree

SUN HERD

Crabwing's Bay

GREAT SEA

Cave

Mavelyn

Road

Dawn Meadow

Northern
Nests

Vein

Vein

JUNGLE
HERD

"Firemouth"
Volcano Swamps

TERRITORY
of LANDWALKERS

Valley of
Tears

Wing River

Southern
Nests

Coast of Anok

N

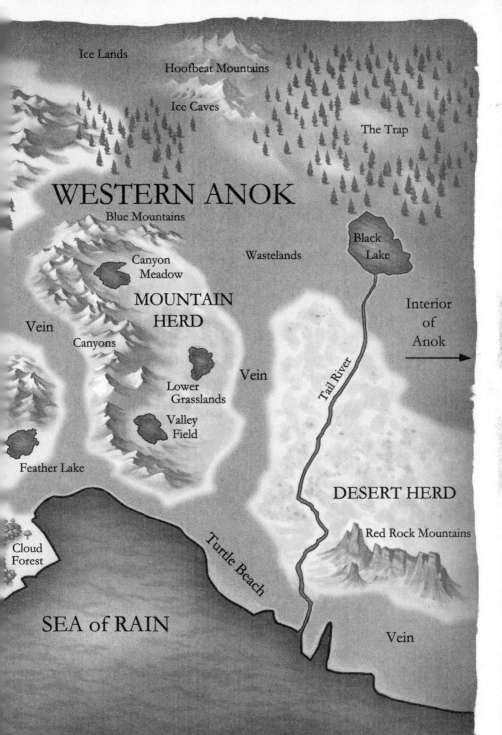

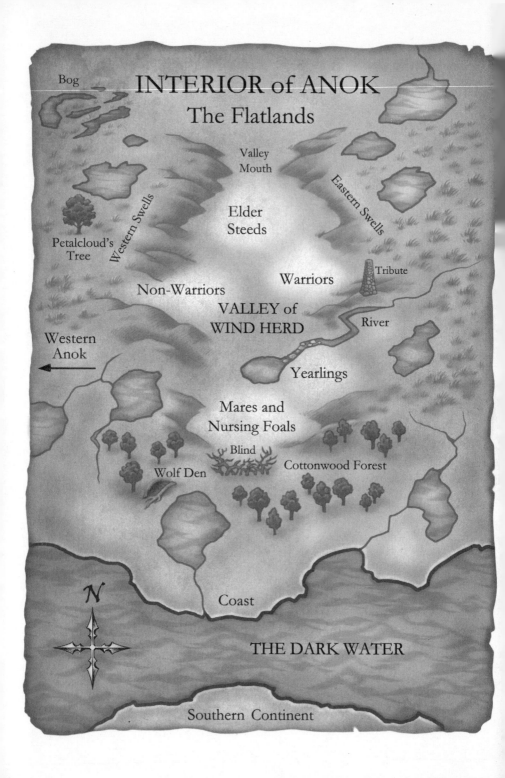

RIDERS of the REALM

1

ACROSS THE DARK WATER

1

RAHKKI

EVERY SANDWEN CHILD DREAMED OF RIDING A winged horse, though most never would, and one would rather not. Rahkki Stormrunner of the Fifth Clan threaded between the trees, hunting for new fighting beetles. Spotting a crumbling log that looked promising, he shoved it with his boot. It splintered, and a small green snake whipped out and into the brush. Rahkki wiggled the rotting trunk and listened for the hissing song of a scarab. But it was the cry of gibbons that filled his ears. A family crashed through the trees overhead, whooping as they swung from branch to branch. "Tshh," Rahkki hissed. "Quiet."

The gibbons paused midswing and cocked their heads toward him.

Rahkki's scalp tingled. The little apes were angry, clearly chasing something, and they didn't like trespassers.

The largest adult rounded his lips and hooted. The entire family had halted their pursuit to stare at the young boy. If they rushed him . . . Rahkki shivered, imagining their sharp teeth in his flesh.

Then, with a sudden chill, a huge shadow blanketed Rahkki and the log.

Whoosh! The apes fled, making the trees shake, and Rahkki wondered what had scared them off. A dragon? A horde of giants? A panther?

Not wanting to find out, he bolted, running as fast as he could toward his clan's territory. The huge shadow passed over him, then another, and Rahkki heard the rhythmic flapping of wings. He slowed and a wide grin spread across his face.

Overhead, glittering feathers, shining hides, and polished armor blocked out the sun—it was his brother's squad of Riders, flying back from patrol. Eighty winged horses, each ridden by a Sandwen warrior, glided in formation, their hooves striking the clouds. There were a total of three squads in the Fifth Clan's Sky Guard, and Brauk Stormrunner was the Headwind of his. The flying steeds were called *Kihlari*, which meant "Children of the Wind," and they were sacred in the Sandwen Realm.

"Land to skies, Rahkki!" his brother shouted down to him. "How many times have I said it? Don't run in the jungle." Brauk waved his squad to continue on without him and guided his stallion lower. "Is there something after you?"

"Nah," Rahkki yelled back. "Just gibbons."

"Gibbons are something. Hold on, I'll pick you up."

Rahkki grimaced. "It's fine, they're gone. I'll walk back to the fortress."

Brauk's Kihlara mount, a muscular chestnut named Kol, angled between the Kapok trees and touched down beside Rahkki. Snorting, the stallion dropped his muzzle toward the boy and lipped at his pockets for treats. Rahkki patted Kol's steaming neck, then glanced up at his brother. "You're back early."

"Yeah, there are giants afoot." At the word *giants*, Brauk leaned over and spit on the ground. The Fifth Clan and the Gorlan hordes had been at war for a thousand years over stolen farmlands. "What are you doing out here alone?"

"Hunting for beetles to sell at the Clan Gathering."

Brauk tossed him a weary look. "We need real coin, Brother, not the few jints you'll get for a couple of wild beetles. Come on, give me your hand."

Rahkki stared at his brother's extended arm, his cheeks burning. Brauk knew his secret—that he was afraid of heights—but that didn't stop his older brother from forcing him to ride Kol, probably even encouraging it.

Brauk cursed him in Talu, the language of the Daakuran Empire across the bay. "*Sa jin*, Rahkki, don't make me drag you home."

So Rahkki threw up his hand, and his brother lifted him easily onto Kol's rump. "Yah!" Brauk hollered. The chestnut galloped forward, wings flapping, and then glided off the soil, leaving Rahkki's belly floating behind him. Gripping Brauk's waist tight, Rahkki closed his eyes as the stallion gained altitude. His brother chattered about the giants. "They're sharpening spears, preparing to fight," he said. "We're reporting this straight to the queen."

Brauk's deep rumbling voice soothed Rahkki. The boy opened his eyes and watched the trees shrink below them. They flew so high that the forest appeared like a child's play set, or a Daakuran painting. Huge drifting clouds layered the sky above them and a warm breeze ruffled their hair.

Rahkki balanced on Kol's back, watching the stallion's giant yellow-feathered wings push down on the wind. When a flock of parrots crossed their path, the stallion cranked back his neck and whinnied at them, sending the poor birds into a frenzied dive. Rahkki knew he was safe; Kol was an excellent Flier, and Rahkki knew how envious other kids felt when they saw him flying, but no amount of *knowing* could quell the sour clench of his stomach each time he looked down.

Finally, Fort Prowl came into view. The high-walled stone octagon sat on top of a hill that was surrounded by the Fifth Clan village, farmlands, and stables. This was the home of their queen, her private guards and servants, her Borla—a clan wise man and healer—and the queen's three princess daughters. The clan's land soldiers and Sky Guard Riders lived in seven of the eight forty-length towers.

Brauk tugged on the reins, and Kol descended quickly, leaving Rahkki breathless. Brauk's patrol had arrived already and landed in the courtyard. Moments later, Kol crested the fortress walls and touched down beside them. Rahkki leaped off the stallion's back so fast that several Sky Guard Riders laughed at him.

"Tie Kol up and wait for me," Brauk commanded, tossing him the reins. Rahkki was his brother's stable groom, and it was his job to take care of Kol, but today was his last day. The boy stiffened, unwilling to think about tomorrow. With the Gorlan giants preparing to attack and the Clan Gathering fast approaching, Brauk needed Rahkki now more than ever. But Brauk didn't have a wealthy family or a sponsor like the other Riders. He had no means to buy new weapons or hay for his stallion—the private inheritance they'd received after their mother died was gone, spent. So the boys had decided that Rahkki would accept an apprenticeship on their uncle's rice farm and send his wages to Brauk. It was settled and there was no sense dwelling on it.

Rahkki led Kol to the hitching post, tied a slipknot, and then followed his brother into the fortress to eavesdrop on his meeting with the queen.

❧ 2 ❧

BLOODBORN

"CALL THE DRAGON," QUEEN LILLIAM SHOUTED. "I won't fight the giants without a good omen from our mascot."

From his position in the Great Hall, Rahkki and the other snooping grooms had been unable to overhear the Sky Guard's meeting with the queen, but the result of it was clear enough when she shouted for their guardian mascot—Granak, the Father of Dragons. The queen would offer the gigantic lizard a fattened sow. If he ate it, they'd fight. If he didn't, Lilliam would consider that a terrible omen. She'd keep the warriors home.

Rahkki flattened himself against the wall as Lilliam's advisers tromped out of her command chamber, their faces grim. General Akmid Tsun, the leader of the Fifth Clan Land Guard, had been called last into the chamber when the meeting started. Now he was the first to exit, his scarred body sheened in sweat. Once outside, he whistled for his soldiers. The rest of Lilliam's advisers filed out behind him, including Rahkki's brother.

As Brauk passed, Rahkki leaped into his shadow, following closely. When they were out of earshot, Rahkki's questions exploded. "What happened? Why is the queen calling Granak? Are the giants that close?"

Brauk's golden eyes were full of thoughts, but none of them for Rahkki. He pressed on, heading toward Kol at the hitching post. Then Brauk spotted Harak Night-seer, the second of the three Headwinds, coming out of the queen's private quarters. "Ay, Harak, there you are," Brauk called, coming to a halt.

Harak whirled around, his eyes narrowed and twitching. "Yeah, Stormrunner, what do you want?"

"Follow me, I'm calling a meeting of the Headwinds."

"Now?"

Brauk frowned at the lean warrior, just a few years older than he. "Yes, now. We can't wait, can we? Not with the Gorlan hordes on the move."

"Are the giants scouting or hunting?" Rahkki

whispered, tugging on his brother's tunic.

Brauk shrugged him off, focusing on Harak. "You got something better to do?" he asked his counterpart.

They glared at each other, Harak breathing out his nose, Brauk rolling on the balls of his feet. Rahkki closed his eyes. *Don't fight. Please don't fight.* Eight years of his brother's squabbles surfaced in his mind—the smack of fist on flesh, the cursing, the dripping blood. Brauk hadn't been so easy to set off when they were younger. As princes of their clan—bloodborn descendants of the Seven Sisters who'd founded the Sandwen Realm—they'd been wealthy and content. The past Queen of the Fifth, Reyella Storm-runner, was their mother, and she'd loved them ferociously. But the brothers had been Reyella's *only* children and, being males, they could not rule. This had left their mother's crown without an heir and vulnerable.

Eight years ago, a bloodborn princess from the Second Clan named Lilliam Whitehall had pounced on Reyella's weakness. She assassinated the boys' mother and took her throne, becoming the Fifth's new monarch. And since Sandwen queens didn't marry or identify the fathers of their children, the orphan princes lost all privilege and purpose. After that, Brauk's love of sport had taken an aggressive turn, and he'd begun scrapping with any man, animal, or reptile willing to brawl. Rahkki opened his eyes just as the tension between the two Headwinds dispersed.

"Right," Harak said, exhaling. "Now is fine, yeah, but Tuni's not here. She flew to the trading post to fetch her mum."

"Bloody rain, she couldn't wait?"

Harak shrugged.

Brauk fiddled with the bright Kihlara feather tied to his wrist, one that had molted off his beloved stallion. "We'll meet tonight then, after Lilliam feeds the dragon. She won't let us fly unless the feeding goes well anyway."

Harak led them out of the hall, and the three headed back the way the brothers had come. Rahkki skipped alongside them, feeling important until Brauk slowed and faced him. "What are you doing, Rahkki?"

"Nothing."

His brother leaned over him. "You're following me. You should be tending Kol."

Rahkki swallowed; he didn't want to miss anything. Soon he'd be living on a distant farm with their uncle—he dreaded it, but most of all he dreaded losing his brother. They'd shared a room in the fortress for the last eight years, but starting tomorrow, Rahkki would sleep alone. His eyes grew hot. "Yes, I'm following you."

Harak rolled his eyes. "I'm off, yeah. I'll see you love-birds later." He grinned, showing his sharp teeth, and left them.

Brauk ignored the slight, keeping his eyes on Rahkki. "Don't be sad," he ordered his younger brother.

"Okay," Rahkki said, as if it were that simple.

Brauk crossed his arms and every muscle beneath his tanned skin flexed. He was twenty-one, tall, and fierce. He had the same black hair and golden eyes as Rahkki, but their similarities ended there. Rahkki was the short-est twelve-year-old in the clan. Brauk said he was strong for his size, but unless Rahkki planned to fight against nine-year-olds, that wasn't helpful. His brother graced him with a rare smile. "I'll see you tonight, okay? Now tend to Kol; he flew hard today."

Rahkki nodded. Early this morning, before Brauk's Dawn Patrol had flown out, he'd cleaned Kol's stall, picked his hooves, and mixed a new bag of grain, but he was anx-ious to do more. If the giants were about, then no Sandwen was safe.

"Clean my tack too," Brauk added. "All of it. The sad-dle especially, and check my weapons. Today's your last day; make it count."

"I will."

"And don't worry about those stinkin' giants." Brauk spit on the stone floor. "We'll drive them all the way to the Daakuran Empire if we have to."

"I'm not worried," Rahkki said, and he wasn't. Dragons, giants—nothing upset him more than leaving his brother.

"That's the way," Brauk said, striding off to attend to more important matters.

Rahkki felt cold in Brauk's sudden absence, but also determined. As he jogged toward Kol, he decided that his brother would have the cleanest Flier, the most polished tack, and the sharpest sword in the Sky Guard by end of day. Rahkki licked his hand and slapped the wooden hitching post, making his thoughts an oath. Buoyed by his important responsibilities, he untied the stallion and led him toward the Kihlari stable down the hill.

When they arrived, Rahkki threw open the double doors. Happy nickers erupted from the winged horses—all of them knew and liked the boy. Up and down the aisles, individual grooms rushed to complete chores, preparing the Day Patrol steeds to fly out and rubbing down the hungry and tired Dawn Patrol Fliers. Some kids nodded to Rahkki, others ignored him.

Mist from the jungle rolled through the barn,

shrouding the mares and stallions as if in fallen clouds. Rahkki heard hooves dancing and wings stretching. He smelled oil and leather and feathers. The Kihlari barn was his favorite place in the Realm.

Rahkki locked Kol in his stall and then fetched a soap bar, liniment, and rubbing cloths from the tack room that was shared by all the Riders. Soon he had Kol washed and dried in the bathing pit. Rahkki rested a moment and wrapped his small arms around the stallion's sparkling chest. Kol's hot breath steamed down his neck, and the orphan prince felt his eyes grow hot again. He wasn't just losing Brauk tomorrow; he was losing the winged horses too, his best friends in the world.

C⟶ 3 ⟵O

LEAVING ANOK

ACROSS THE DARK WATER OCEAN, FAR FROM Rahkki's home, a wild pegasus mare angled her wings and sped through the clouds. Behind her a battle raged in the Flatlands of Anok between two immortal pegasus stallions: Star the Healer and Nightwing the Destroyer. She dared a glance back and saw dark smoke and bright, flashing lights. Then a horrific noise stung her ears, like a thousand trees falling. It was starfire—the supernatural power that black pegasus foals received on their first birthdays—Nightwing and Star were destroying each other with it. The earth shook and the land below her hooves fractured, creating fissures in the soil that spread like cracked ice. A family of deer spooked and bounded madly toward the forest. Echofrost swallowed, her heart racing.

A year ago, Nightwing had woken from a four-hundred-year hibernation and returned to Anok. He'd come to kill his rival, a young black stallion named Star, and to enslave the five herds of pegasi. A shudder rolled through her as Echofrost remembered the battles and deaths that had followed. She'd learned to sharpen her hooves and fight, and how to spy—and she was only two years old.

But when the final battle erupted today, Echofrost and her band of rebels escaped early through an underground tunnel with the plan to find a new, safer home. Echofrost was the last one out, and her friends were waiting for her on the southern coast. *Unless they left without me,* she thought. She tossed her white mane. *No, they wouldn't!* But Echofrost had been abandoned before, and anxiety made her fly faster. Another explosion rocked her ears, sounding closer.

As Echofrost glided toward the beach, high winds plucked out her loose feathers, and they fluttered behind her like chaotic purple butterflies. But with each wing-length she put behind her, her heart lightened. Her captivity was finally over. The days of being bitten and kicked by Nightwing's Ice Warriors had ended.

Now she and the buckskin stallion named Hazelwind would lead the one hundred and forty pegasi rebels across the Dark Water ocean to the continent south of them. She had no idea what they'd find there: two-legged Landwalkers, dangerous predators, or creatures yet unknown. But she couldn't wait to see it. It would become her new home, if she and the others made it there alive.

It was afternoon when Echofrost spotted Hazelwind and the others. They were gathered close together on an expanse of scrub grass, but they weren't grazing. They were scanning the cloudless sky and prancing. The chestnut stallion named Redfire spotted her first. "There she is!"

Immense relief flooded Echofrost at the sight of the pegasi. She tipped her feathers and descended, landing lightly. Redfire trotted toward her, his copper-colored coat reflecting the sunlight into her eyes. She threw up her wing. "I think you're visible from *space*, Redfire." Then she stared at the group of bright-feathered pegasi standing in the open, her earlier relief forgotten. "Couldn't you all have found better cover?"

Hazelwind cantered toward her, his hooves flicking up the sand, and everyone moved out of his way. "Taken cover? Where would you have suggested?" He fanned his jade-feathered wing, indicating the miles of short coastal plants and small gray rocks. The wind whipped his mane forward, and his thick black forelock covered one eye.

Echofrost shut her mouth. She didn't know where, but really, anywhere was better than here. "I don't know," she mumbled, looking up and studying the horizon for their enemies.

"You're here now; that's all that matters," said Hazelwind.

Anger, grief, and longing exploded in her chest. Hazelwind had been her best friend . . . once. She turned away from him, not wanting to think about the past. Hazelwind took a hard breath, and Echofrost knew he still didn't understand why she was mad at him. Well, she didn't understand it either, but this wasn't the time to reflect, so she stuffed the feelings back down where they couldn't disturb her.

The pinto battle mare named Dewberry trotted between Echofrost and Hazelwind, her voice slicing the tension. "Where are the others?" She glanced north toward the Flatlands.

"Yes, where's my sister?" Hazelwind asked. His sister was Morningleaf, and she was younger than Hazelwind but more widely known. She was Star's closest friend.

"She and Brackentail stayed behind to watch Star's final battle with Nightwing." Echofrost scented the wind and smelled rain. She was already thinking about what came next: leaving this continent behind and crossing the Dark Water.

Hazelwind stomped his hoof, striking the wedge-leafed plants that grew out of the sandy loam. "If I'd known we'd have to wait for my sister, I'd have taken the time to find better cover," he said. "When will they arrive?"

"They won't. She's decided not to come with us at all."

"What? Why not?"

"Did you really believe Morningleaf would leave Star?" asked Echofrost. "After all she's been through to keep him alive?"

Hazelwind's wings unfurled and drooped at his sides. "I did."

He was sad, and Echofrost understood why. Nightwing had murdered Thundersky, his sire, and now his sister was staying behind. But anger pinched at her sympathy. He wasn't the *only* pegasus who'd lost family. Dire wolves had fatally injured her twin brother, and her dam, Crystalfeather, was stuck in the Flatlands, waiting to see which immortal stallion would kill the other. Even Echofrost's dear friend Shadepebble was staying behind because of her one short wing. She flew well, but not well enough to journey across the dangerous Dark Water ocean.

Echofrost raked her eyes across the rebel pegasi, noticing how each seemed deep in thought for the friends they'd lost or left behind, and what was happening back in the Flatlands. They were each as bereft as Hazelwind. In fact, they were a wretched group, and it wouldn't do. They wouldn't survive the hardships ahead with these mournful attitudes. "Listen," she whinnied, arching her neck. "We're free."

She let the word *free* linger. It floated over their heads and then drifted toward the ocean, but it helped them. The pegasi pricked their ears forward.

Echofrost pranced, drawing their attention. "We're *never* coming back here. Let go of the dead. Let go of your fears. It's difficult, I know, but our future waits across that ocean." She faced the beach, and the wind blew her white mane in a tangle across her silver face. "We're free," she repeated, savoring the word. "No one can tell us what to do. Not ever again."

The pegasi rallied. Their captivity was over, so they bucked and lifted into the sky, ramming each other like foals. Echofrost glanced at Hazelwind and lost her breath at the sight of him, standing so tall and steadfast with his long black tail whipping in the breeze. So like his sire, Thundersky. She missed their once-easy friendship.

Then she tore her eyes away. Each time she looked at him, bad memories of her brother's death bubbled to the surface. She forced them down again, as fast as she could, not wanting to sort them out. But eventually, she knew she'd have to, because while most bad memories would be staying in Anok, some would be traveling across the ocean, flying side by side with her.

4

STORM HERD

THE JOURNEY ACROSS THE DARK WATER BEGAN immediately. "Formation!" Hazelwind whinnied, and his loud bray sent the pegasi scurrying into position.

Dewberry took the spot in front of Echofrost because she was full-grown and much stronger. The pinto's muscles trembled eagerly, and her eyes sparkled as she gazed south across the sprawling black sea. "I'll never return to Anok," she said.

Echofrost understood. She and Dewberry were anxious to leave the place of so much death and destruction and start a new life. Her thoughts flashed to her twin brother. Dewberry had loved Bumblewind too, and Echofrost had thought they'd one day join as mates. But he was in the golden meadow now, with all the fallen pegasi, and it would be a long time before Echofrost saw him again. At least she hoped it would be a long time because, for all her grief and sadness, Echofrost's heart thrummed with hope. "Our future lies ahead," she said to Dewberry.

The pegasi rebels buzzed their feathers, ready to migrate south. "We need a name for our herd," Hazelwind said, tossing a protective glance at the steeds who'd volunteered to leave Anok. The group was made of pegasi who hailed from each territory—from the freezing Snow Herd lands to the steep ranges of Mountain Herd, and from the lush meadows of Sun Herd to the dangerous territory of Jungle Herd, and all the way to the unforgiving terrain of Desert Herd—and each steed was strong, young, and fierce. They were the perfect group to travel across the dangerous sea and begin a new herd on an unknown continent, but they needed a name.

"How about Storm Herd?" said Dewberry.

"Or Cloud Herd?" suggested a blue roan named Shysong.

Graystone, a furry white pegasus from the north, spoke up. "What about Smoke Herd?"

The stallion from the desert named Redfire tossed his dark-red mane. "Storms are strong and powerful and often accompany a change in season. I think Storm Herd suits us best."

"I like it," said Echofrost, and the rest of the steeds nodded their agreement.

"It's settled," Hazelwind neighed. "We'll call ourselves Storm Herd. Now, let's fly!"

The Storm Herd pegasi galloped across the shell-laden sand and then reared up, leaping one by one off the beach and gliding into an angled formation, like migrating geese. The biggest steeds took the headwinds and the others drafted. They would trade places when the leaders grew tired.

The wind cooled as the shore receded. Echofrost glanced at the waves that rolled smoothly below, curling and white frothed. This sea was called the Dark Water because the sand on the beach and the ocean floor was black, making the water so opaque that it was almost impossible to see what was swimming below the surface.

"Don't fly too close to the water," Echofrost warned, but the wind swept her words away. She peered south. The longer their journey took, the more dangerous it would become. There would be no food or fresh water available. They would have to land on the surface of the ocean to rest, and their paddling legs would attract blue sharks, and maybe worse. And they would have to face bad weather unprotected. The safest tactic was to fly as fast as possible. That meant maintaining a consistent altitude, staying calm, and speaking little.

Storm Herd flew in silence for the rest of the day, conserving their energy. Their wingbeats synchronized as they traded positions effortlessly, the lead pegasus dropping back and a fresh one bearing the headwind, without a need for words. This was how they migrated twice a year, and the familiar system soothed them. They chose an altitude about fifty winglengths above the surface of the Dark Water, and with the help of a southern tailwind to boost their speed, Anok's shoreline soon faded from sight, leaving them surrounded by black water, a hazy sky, and an endless, shimmering horizon.

But as the yellow sun dropped faster and faster in the west, the ocean winds picked up force. The rain Echofrost had scented earlier had morphed into a storm, and heavy clouds gathered, swallowing the sky. Echofrost curled her wingtips, gripping tightly to the current. What had her friend Morningleaf told her about crossing the sea? Was it to fly slowly in turbulence? Just then the clouds rumbled, spitting cold rain, and the waves tumbled. Sea spray stung her nostrils and static filled the air. The instinct to seek shelter rattled Echofrost because there was nowhere to hide.

"Steady," Hazelwind neighed as if reading her mind, but he was addressing all Storm Herd.

"Is that lightning?" asked Dewberry. Just then a bolt of light crackled across the sky, answering her question.

"Fly on," Hazelwind brayed.

Thunder boomed, followed by more lightning. Echofrost's heart lurched, and rain dripped down her forelock, blurring her vision. The air thickened with moisture, and clouds piled upon clouds overhead, billowing in dark clumps. Below her hooves, the waves sloshed. Echofrost cast a wary eye at the horizon where the sun was quickly vanishing.

"Spread out," Hazelwind commanded, casting his eyes toward the sparking clouds. Each formation of pegasi surged away from the other, hoping to create smaller targets for the lightning. A cross breeze slammed into Echofrost. She gasped, choking on ocean spray. The herd flew just a winglength above the water now, their fear of the sea far outweighed by their fear of the storm.

Echofrost squealed in shock when a hot bolt of light

shot through the grouping of pegasi on her right and struck the water, highlighting a dozen lean shapes coasting beneath the waves. "Sharks!" she whinnied.

The sun vanished in the west, and darkness descended like a closed eyelid. Ahead of her, Redfire echoed her alarm, and then another pegasus repeated it, and the news about the sharks carried through Storm Herd.

More lightning shattered the darkness. The sky changed from black to shocking white and then back to black again, burning Echofrost's eyes. The quick sharks darted away and then slowly returned. Hazelwind's hoof splashed the waves when a blast of wind tossed him toward the surf. "We need to get out of this weather. Now!" Echofrost whinnied.

"She's right," neighed Redfire, "but how?"

"We can't avoid it," said Hazelwind. "We have to go through it."

Graystone balked. "Fly *through* the storm?" he asked.

The pegasi tensed. They were each weary from struggling against the wind currents, but above the murderous clouds, the sky was safe and calm.

Echofrost eyed Graystone, noting his heavy body. He'd been an Ice Warrior in Nightwing's army, but a sympathetic one. He'd risked his life to help her smuggle steeds out of the Flatlands, but as strong and powerful as he was, northern steeds like Graystone didn't fly well in high altitudes.

Redfire answered him. "You can do it, Graystone. Lift your nose and power straight up. Don't look down."

Graystone nodded, but Echofrost saw the fear lurking in his eyes. Fresh thunder rocked her ears and she missed Hazelwind's order to go, but she didn't need to hear it. She was bound so tightly to her new herd that instinct rocketed her after them. As they darted up and through the swirling clouds, lightning flashed, followed by rumbling thunder. Whatever happened next, Storm Herd would endure it together. Powered by fear and hope, Echofrost raced through the storm, heading toward the heights that were clear and safe and dry.

5

THE SOUTHERN CONTINENT

FIVE DAYS PASSED AFTER THE TERRIBLE STORM, and the pegasi were still traveling. They hadn't lost any herdmates, and that was a relief to Echofrost. The herd landed and floated on the sea when they were tired. The strongest of them kicked at the blue sharks that hunted them patiently from the depths. They drank the rain that fell from the clouds, but they were starving and weary. Headaches plagued Echofrost and her dry tongue swelled, filling her mouth.

The herd had fallen into an unspoken pattern of leadership. They decided most things as a group, but sometimes it was best if one steed, like Hazelwind or herself, made the quick decisions. Echofrost wasn't sure why anyone listened to her, a two-year-old mare, except that she had risked her life spying on Nightwing. They trusted her.

"I hate this ocean," Dewberry said, breaking into Echofrost's thoughts.

No pegasus had spoken since dawn, and the sun now blazed directly overhead, but the fact that Dewberry was still strong enough to speak bolstered Echofrost's glum mood.

Then Dewberry spoke again. "Look at those trees."

Echofrost saw the trees too and sighed. "It's just a trick of the eyes, Dewberry." They'd spied land several times in the last two days, but when they flew toward it, it evaporated. Redfire had explained the mystery to them yesterday—they were hallucinating, seeing things that weren't there.

"The trees are so tall," said Dewberry.

They *were* exceptionally tall, which was strange. The pegasi didn't normally hallucinate the exact same image. Echofrost watched the swaying branches, and instinct drove her toward them. Hazelwind and the rest followed. She knew the forest would disappear as soon as she reached it, but Echofrost didn't care—it looked beautiful to her.

Briefly she closed her eyes and heard a cheerful whistle, a bird. It reminded her of Dawn Meadow, where she'd

29

been born. More birds joined the first and insects chirped. A breeze whispered through the leaves. *What a sharp hallucination*, she thought.

Then a loud grunt startled her. She opened her eyes and saw that Graystone had succumbed to a wing cramp and fallen. He lay in a crumpled heap.

Why wasn't he sinking into the ocean?

Echofrost glanced around her. All the pegasi were hovering over Graystone and staring at him, their faces perplexed.

"It's like he hit solid ground," said Dewberry.

"It *is* solid ground," rasped Hazelwind. "We made it."

Shysong burst into tears.

"We made it?" Echofrost whispered. She fluttered toward land but misjudged and struck a tree, becoming entangled in its branches. An excited whinny rippled up from her chest. This was no mirage—this was a real forest. Birds jetted out of her way, but one stood on his branch and stared at her with an outthrust chest. He was red and yellow, with a blue beak and green breast. Echofrost reached out her wing to touch him. "Hello," she nickered.

He pecked her hard on the muzzle and then flew away

in a whir of color. Echofrost looked around, stunned at the bright birds, towering trees, and shoulder-high plants. To the east were three steaming volcanoes and a mountain range with peaks so high that they disappeared into the clouds. The surrounding terrain was a mixture of lowland marshes, open fields, and rain forest. This place was like nowhere she'd ever traveled.

They'd reached the southern continent.

Echofrost disentangled herself from the tree and glided down to join her friends. Leaves protruded from her tangled mane, and a fat, furry caterpillar clung to her forelock. Upon landing, her hooves sank into the marshy grass, and the soil felt delicious after so many days of flying and swimming.

"I smell freshwater," said Redfire. He whirled and galloped toward it. Pegasi from the desert knew everything about water, so Echofrost and the Storm Herd steeds followed him.

Graystone had regained his bearings and joined them. "Am I dead?" he asked. "Is this the golden meadow?"

Echofrost let him lean against her. "I hope not, because there are bugs here." She flung the lumpy caterpillar out of her forelock.

Shuffling across a low hill, the herd trod single file into a shallow ravine, following Redfire. Echofrost gaped. Everything appeared larger than it had from the sky. The tallest trees reached the clouds, gigantic boulders lined the shores of the creek, and water reeds stood taller than Echofrost. As she measured herself against her new environment, she felt small, as if she'd shrunk while crossing the ocean.

When the herd reached the creek, they raced forward and plunged their muzzles into the cool water.

"We survived the Dark Water," Redfire announced. "All of us."

Echofrost nodded, pleased. The hardest part of their journey was over. This southern continent had plentiful foliage for grazing, and settling here appeared to be a simple task.

"This land reminds me of the jungles in southern Anok," said Redfire. As an ex-captain in the Desert Herd army, he'd traveled the neutral Vein between herds and seen many territories.

But Shysong, who hailed from the jungle, shook her mane. "No, there are enough differences here to worry me."

"How so?" Redfire asked.

"Well, besides the birds and plants that I don't

recognize, have you noticed how big everything is?"

Dewberry sidled next to a fern leaf that was as tall as she. "Yeah, I noticed."

"Big plants mean more food," said Hazelwind.

"It also means bigger grazing animals, which means . . ."

"Bigger predators," Dewberry finished.

Hazelwind stiffened. "We'll set up patrols and explore this place, but for now we have shelter in this ravine. Let's rest and graze, and then we'll fly out and see what's here."

The pegasi relaxed, just grateful to be on land, and Echofrost felt content. So far her mission to found a herd on a new continent was unfolding well.

Hazelwind trotted to her side, startling her. "I can't believe we made it," he said. The warm breeze tossed his mane forward, and his long black forelock fell across his left eye, almost reaching his muzzle.

She longed to lean against him, but resisted the urge. They hadn't spoken much on their journey, and she didn't want to start right now. She was still confused and tired and hungry. When he tried to nuzzle her, she pulled away.

"Echofrost—I, what's wrong?" he asked her. "Is this about your brother?"

She grunted. "Let's not talk about the past."

Hazelwind flicked his ears forward. "All right."

She wondered how she could be so attached to Hazel-wind and yet so angry with him at the same time. She stamped her hoof, frustrated with herself. She'd forgiven her enemies in Anok; why was it so much harder to forgive her friend?

"We need to scout this land," Hazelwind said, chang-ing the subject.

"True, but it's almost dark and everyone needs rest. Let's go at first light. Would you mind assigning sentries to guard us?" All Echofrost wanted right now was to sleep.

"Not at all." He trotted away, forming patrols and deciding shifts.

Echofrost found a patch of grass on the ravine's bank and curled onto her side, but rest would have to wait. The blue roan mare named Shysong approached, her eyes bulging. "I smell smoke—do you?"

Echofrost sniffed the breeze. "No. Do you think it's a forest fire?"

"I thought maybe it was, so I flew up to look. It's just a few thin streams. Nothing dangerous, unless . . ."

"What?"

"Unless it's Landwalkers. The elders say they can tame fire."

Echofrost startled. She'd heard stories about the two-legged beasts, but she'd never seen one. They lived across the Great Sea. They didn't inhabit Anok and there were no tales about them living in the south. "It can't be Landwalkers," Echofrost said. "And you know that extreme heat can cause old, rotting trees to combust, right? There are lots of old trees here."

Shysong nodded. "That's true."

"Anyway, Landwalkers live in the west." But even as she said it, Echofrost realized she couldn't be sure. Listening to legends had bored her as a filly and she'd paid little attention to them, but surely if Landwalkers were known to live in the south, someone would have said so *before* they crossed the treacherous ocean to get here.

But even if they lived here, Echofrost didn't believe the frail creatures posed much threat to pegasi. They carried weapons because they had no claws or fangs. And one slice from a sharpened hoof would tear their hairless hides wide open. It was said that a pegasus outweighed a Landwalker adult by six to one. Besides all that, they couldn't *fly*. Echofrost yawned. "We're warriors, Shysong, we have nothing to fear. Our troubles are behind us. Rest now, tomorrow we'll find our home."

"All right, good night." Shysong tucked her black-edged feathers across her back and cantered away.

Echofrost closed her eyes, and exhaustion pulled her into a deep, dark slumber.

6

SMOKE

IT WAS DAWN, AND THE SUN HAD JUST CRACKED the horizon. Echofrost woke feeling disoriented and anxious. Most of Storm Herd was already awake and flexing their wings, ready to explore. They gathered into their migrating formations. Echofrost smoothed her feathers and then trotted to her place behind Dewberry.

"Fly low," Hazelwind neighed. "We don't want to alert whatever lives here that we've arrived."

The breeze brushed a chill down Echofrost's spine. *Whatever lives here.* His words sounded ominous.

Storm Herd lifted off and flew south, traveling deeper inland. The climate was hot and moist, but pleasant enough. They soared over open terrain that rose and fell in gentle swells, and then glided into a broad-leafed forest. Echofrost cruised between the massive trees, enjoying the cool shade. Green vines twisted around the trunks, and large, bright flowers decorated the jungle floor. Monkeys leaped from branch to branch, screeching at them, and odd-shaped insects scurried across the leaves, each chirping louder than the next. The ancient trees towered a hundred winglengths above them and higher, lifting toward the very sky.

Shysong hovered near, nickering at something funny Redfire was saying, and Echofrost relaxed. The full night's sleep had restored Storm Herd's spirits, and yesterday's uncertainty seemed silly in the pale light of morning.

Dewberry suddenly whipped her tail in alarm. "There's a creature down there, walking ahead of us," she hissed. "Something big." She hurtled forward, almost throwing Echofrost out of her wake. The silver mare flapped faster to catch up. Dewberry led Storm Herd toward the animal she'd spotted. "See the trees shaking?" she asked, breathless.

The pegasi broke their formation and hovered above the rain forest. A very large creature was traveling through, snapping twigs and cracking trees.

"It must be *huge*," Shysong said with a trill in her voice.

The Storm Herd steeds stared at the tumbling forest, watching the upper branches sway as the beast pushed through them.

Seconds later, a gigantic, muscular reptile trudged into an open basin and halted, squinting in the sunshine. Drool dripped from its mouth, creating huge puddles at its clawed feet. Its scales were black, iridescent. As it turned its neck, the scales twisted, reflecting a rainbow of colors that flashed and then disappeared. Bright fresh blood splattered its chest.

"What is that thing?" Dewberry rasped.

The lizard tasted the air with its forked tongue, and more saliva leaked in a long stream from its jaws. A nearby pond caught its attention and it stomped across the clearing, its heavy steps vibrating the soil. The long black tail whipped back and forth, flattening shrubs and grasses and knocking down small trees. Its ribs expanded, creating a whoosh of noise, and the jungle animals went silent.

"It looks like a spit dragon," Shysong answered. "But I've never seen one that large or that color."

The reptile paused to drink, revealing sharp, serrated teeth. Its eyes, dark and rounded, looked nothing like the slanted eyes of a reptile. "What's a spit dragon?" Echofrost asked.

"They live in the rain forest, but in our territory they're small and green colored," Shysong answered. "They stand no taller than our knees, but we've always avoided them. They have nasty tempers, and their drool is toxic."

"Can they run fast?"

"Oh yes."

The black, wingless dragon finished drinking and continued across the basin. Shades of blue, green, and purple flitted across its bumpy scales.

"What do they eat?" Redfire asked.

"Anything they can catch."

"That dragon is big enough to eat us," Dewberry nickered. "This isn't a safe place to raise foals."

Echofrost gaped at her. Why was Dewberry concerned about foals—Storm Herd didn't have any. She was about to point this out when it struck her that their mission was to *settle*—and that meant starting families. *By the Ancestors, I haven't thought that far ahead.* Her belly whirled. "Dewberry is right; let's keep going."

Echofrost and her friends blasted across the basin.

"There's smoke ahead!" Graystone neighed.

Echofrost craned her neck and spotted gray tendrils rising in the distance. This was what Shysong had been worried about yesterday.

Pegasi avoided smoke, fearing even to fly above it. Echofrost couldn't imagine anything more threatening than fire, but the lines of smoke ahead were not thick enough to suffocate them.

Hazelwind had come to the same conclusion. "Stay true to course," he ordered.

The herd crested the edge of the rain forest and Echofrost lost her breath.

Sprawled ahead of them were hundreds of stone structures. They dotted the base of a green foothill. Rock-lined pathways ran between them, crisscrossing one another, and the foliage on either side had been cut short. Each stone den had a small outdoor enclosure that corralled goats, young pigs, or chickens. The smoke Shysong had seen was rising from holes cut in the rooftops, which meant that fires burned within.

Across the hillside, the dead hides of animals hung on stakes, and Echofrost's stomach lurched. She recognized deer, snake, and boar skins.

"What is this place?" Dewberry nickered, flicking her ears.

No one answered at first; they just hovered, staring.

Then two creatures emerged from a den. One appeared to be a wolf, or a coyote, though it seemed too short-haired to be either. The other was thin, mostly hairless except for its head.

"It's Landwalkers!" someone rasped, and Echofrost sucked for air. Could it be? She squinted at the thin two-legged being. Echofrost had imagined them looking like apes, but this creature had yellow hair and a tall forehead.

She watched it walk to a depression dug into the ground that was full of dry grass and wood. The creature sat there with the wolf-like animal following, wagging its tail. The Landwalker was clumsy, just a cub. Its hands fidgeted and then a spark flew and fire erupted in the small pit.

Storm Herd recoiled, stunned. In spite of the legends that warned otherwise, Echofrost had imagined the Land-walkers as common animals, just a bit smarter. Perhaps she'd been terribly wrong about that.

Her eyes moved on, scanning the rest of their territory.

Where the terrain was flattest there stood a huge herd of land horses, mostly black with a few browns and pintos, and a white one mixed in. Wooden sticks created a barrier around them, trapping them inside. But the horses stood peacefully in their pen, grazing on the trampled grass.

Beyond the horses, the land was striped in neat rows, and from these rows grew plants at regular intervals. "I think that's where they grow food," Hazelwind said, following Echofrost's gaze. "The legends are all true. They've tamed fire, land, horses, and—it seems—wolves."

The wolf-like creature whined and rolled on its back, letting the Landwalker cub rub its belly. Echofrost tensed, waiting for the animal to bite, but it didn't. Dread filled her. *Even the young were powerful.*

Just then the Landwalker cub looked up and spotted the pegasus herd flying overhead. Her eyes rounded, and her screeching cry slaughtered the peaceful morning. *"Kihlari! Kihlari!"*

Echofrost didn't have to understand her words to know that the cub was sounding an alarm. "Keep flying!" she whinnied.

Landwalkers and their wolf companions poured out of their homes. Some took up the alarm, screaming excitedly and pointing. The pet wolves howled. The land horses spooked and galloped in wide circles inside their pen. An elderly adult Landwalker ran to a platform that housed a huge, shiny-gray object. He beat it with a rod, and a terrible clanging noise blared out of it and reverberated for miles.

"I think they're calling for more Landwalkers," Dewberry whinnied.

"Fly faster!" Echofrost neighed.

One adult retreated into his den and then returned carrying a bowed contraption. Soon he was shooting barbed sticks at the pegasi. One struck Shysong in the wing. "Ouch!" she whinnied, and blood dripped from the wound.

"They're attacking us!" Echofrost's heart thudded louder than the rushing wind. *How did their weapons reach the sky?* Again she'd underestimated the Landwalkers.

The pegasus sprinters dug into the current and flew faster. Echofrost hurtled forward on Redfire's flowing wake, and this followed down the line of pegasi. The Landwalker male shot another round of his lethal sticks, but the weapons fell short as the pegasi soared away.

"More trouble ahead!" Redfire brayed. They approached a tall hill that had been carved flat on top. At the height of it stood a massive structure that could house hundreds of Landwalkers. It was eight-sided with walls constructed of thick mossy stone. Eight towers girded its sides, and a tall, spiked gate stood closed. Inside the walls were smaller structures and open spaces, and in these exposed areas Landwalkers rushed about, seemingly called by the clanging alarm. They stared up at the pegasi with their mouths agape. "*Kihlari!*" they shouted, pointing at Storm Herd.

"Bank left," Hazelwind neighed, changing course to avoid the huge den that housed so many dangerous Landwalkers. But his new course took them past the hill to a sprawling wooden structure that was stretched across flat ground.

As they approached this den, Echofrost noticed sixteen Landwalkers scurrying to grab the ends of four long, braided ropes. They pulled hard, four to a rope, their muscles straining; and the ceiling split in half and began to open. Each lashing was attached to a corner, and as the Landwalkers pulled, the ceiling opened wider. Echofrost saw creatures moving inside, veiled in shadows, and her gut twisted.

"Something's in there," Shysong warned.

Echofrost panted, feeling dizzy. Then she heard a shocking but familiar sound: the call of an over-stallion to battle. She blinked, thunderstruck. "Who's calling pegasi to fight?"

Hazelwind caught her eye, looking equally baffled. The challenging bray hadn't come from their group. Echofrost scanned the sky. It was empty except for the Storm Herd steeds. Then she peered down again, and suddenly she knew.

The sound had come from within the wooden den.

The Landwalkers gave a final pull, and the ceiling slid wider apart. Then, up from the darkness sprang an army of foreign pegasi with their legs coiled tight, their eyes narrowed, and their wings pumping.

Sitting astride their backs were Landwalkers, riding them like horses and looking as fierce as their winged mounts.

Echofrost sputtered, breathless.

Then Dewberry's sharp whinny pierced the silence. "FLEE!"

7

FLYING FREE

RAHKKI SHOVED OPEN HIS BEDROOM DOOR AND skipped down the tower stairs two at a time. Today he was supposed to start his apprenticeship on the rice farm, but the clanging of alarm bells had woken him from a thick sleep. Off-duty land soldiers and Riders poured out of their rooms and into the stairwell, shouting.

What's happening?

It's the giants!

Nay, it's just a drill.

No one knew for sure, that was clear. Rahkki had thrown on his tunic, but forgotten his boots, so he slid into the courtyard barefoot. Around him, his clansfolk stood frozen, as if under a magic spell, their eyes turned toward the sky. He peered into the gray dawn. Over a hundred Kihlari soared overhead, riderless. He blinked in disbelief. Winged horses didn't fly without their Riders.

"Which clan is that?" one soldier asked another.

The woman slowly shook her head. "There are no *people* on those Kihlari and they're not branded—they're not from any clan."

"But—" The first speaker broke off because there was no obvious explanation for over a hundred free-flying horses.

Queen Lilliam burst from the hall that led to her private quarters. "Where is General Tsun?" She was wrapped in a Daakuran silk dressing gown, her hair disheveled, her belly extended with her unborn child. Her daughters tiptoed along behind her, and Rahkki glimpsed I'Lenna, the crown princess, but Lilliam spotted the girls too. "Back to bed," she snapped, and the girls retreated. Quickly, her eyes swept the courtyard, then the sky. She gasped. "Are those our Kihlari?"

General Tsun appeared beside her. "We don't know where they're from, my queen."

Lilliam's dark-blue eyes glittered, her mouth set in a firm line. Four hundred years ago, the first flying horses had mysteriously appeared on Sandwen shores. As lovers of horses, the Sandwen people had tamed them and divided them among the seven clans, naming them Kihlari.

But not much time passed before they realized that their new winged pets were braver and more aggressive than warhorses. The Sandwens trained them for battle. Once the Fifth Clan was equipped with a flying army, their Sky Guard easily beat the flame-haired Gorlanders out of the lowland valleys and into the mountains for good.

No wild Kihlari had been spotted since. All were bred and foaled at the Sandwen's Ruks. Until today.

"Those Kihlari are worth thousands of dramals," Queen Lilliam said. She shoved her general's thick chest. "Catch them. Don't let them get away."

"The Sky Guard is already airborne, my queen. They'll bring the winged steeds down."

Rahkki peered at the Kihlari stable and spotted his brother and Kol hurtling out of the split ceiling. Beyond them, one of the foreign steeds, a blue roan, was struggling to fly. An arrow, shot up from the vicinity of the Fifth Clan village, had struck her wing.

"*Mushkas*, idiots!" The queen had also spotted the wounded creature. "Who shot that arrow?"

"It's a wing shot," reported General Tsun. "The villagers don't want the herd to escape either."

Lilliam braced, angling her thin arms. "I can't sell wounded steeds."

"Yes, my queen. I'll quiet the villagers." The platinum-haired general bowed his head to her and departed.

She was about to move on when her gaze landed on Rahkki. They stared at each other across the courtyard and he winced at a flash of memory—Queen Lilliam's cold hands around his throat. He'd been four years old when she'd snuck into Fort Prowl, killed his mother, and then gone after him—and that awful evening remained a muddy blur in his mind. But then another memory struck him: his mother's rounding belly. She'd been pregnant too when Lilliam had assassinated her. Rahkki bent over and sucked for air.

Lilliam smirked at him and strode back to her quarters.

The clansfolk closest to Rahkki threw him apologetic glances and went about their business. They'd loved his mother, and the tension between the Stormrunners and the Whitehalls hung heavy in the clan, but Queen Lilliam was their monarch now. Though she was untrained, inexperienced, and insatiably greedy, Clan Law demanded loyalty to her. If only Reyella Stormrunner had birthed an heir, a daughter. But there was nothing to be done about that now, and so nothing was.

Rahkki recovered himself and passed through the fortress gates, which had opened to release the Riders. Down the hill from Fort Prowl, the grooms had slid open the Kihlari stable ceiling and the Sky Guard had exited, soaring toward the riderless herd.

Soon they disappeared from view, leaving Rahkki wondering—Where did the strange Kihlari come from? Why didn't they wear halters or saddles? And why weren't they branded?

His mind answered for him: *Because they're wild.*

Rahkki's lips curved with pleasure. *Wild Kihlari?* There was no such thing; the elders said so. The Sandwens had tamed them all. Yet an entire herd had just glided past. And if *they* existed, then what else lived out in the woods, in the world? Instead of frightening Rahkki, his thoughts excited him. Suddenly his bleak future seemed full of possibilities, and he let his imagination fly, like those wild winged horses, soaring into the endless blue.

8

KIHLARI

THE STORM HERD STEEDS BLASTED TOWARD THE clouds, their feathers a blur. Behind Echofrost, she heard the whoosh of wings and the snapping of jaws. She glanced over her shoulder and saw the foreign pegasi racing toward her, their tails lashing and their ears pricked forward.

The Landwalkers kicked their mounts in the ribs and jerked on the long straps connected to their mouths, turning the pegasi right or left. Bright stones decorated the pegasi's manes and tails, and each steed had a symbol burned onto his or her right shoulder. Dark curiosity glittered in the foreign steeds' eyes, and Echofrost felt the same curiosity for them. She had not expected to find pegasi living outside of Anok. "Who are you?" she whinnied.

A fiery chestnut stallion flying in the lead answered her. "I'm Kol, and we're the Kihlari Fliers of the Fifth Clan Sky Guard," he neighed. "And *you're* trespassing."

Echofrost understood him, but barely. His accent was thick and slow, so unlike any in Anok.

"Come to me," he drawled, "and I'll tell you more."

Her blood surged.

Hazelwind dropped toward Echofrost and glared back at the chestnut. "The Landwalkers are drawing their weapons," he brayed. "Scatter!"

The Storm Herd steeds splintered off in different directions. Hazelwind flew beside Echofrost.

The Landwalkers swung braided ropes over their heads, and a red-haired female screamed instructions to the others. "Don't shoot. Lasso them."

"They're too fast," a male shouted back.

"We can't risk hurting them," she answered. "Look, those villagers already shot one, trying to ground her. Just be careful."

The Landwalker noises meant nothing to Echofrost, but she understood that they were speaking to one another—not like the howling of wolves or the chuffing of bears, but in a *real* language. She bent her wings and flew faster. "They're communicating!"

The Storm Herd steeds surged higher. "Hide in the clouds," brayed Graystone.

Echofrost found a large puff of mist and flew inside it, instantly shivering as her wings beaded with moisture. Hazelwind dived in next to her. "They don't mean to kill us," he said.

"Then what?"

"I don't know. I think they're trying to catch us alive."

Echofrost heard an agonized squeal. She nose-dived out of her cloud, followed quickly by Hazelwind.

"There!" she whinnied. Below the clouds, some of the foreign pegasi, the *Kihlari*, as they called themselves, had formed a circle. In the center Echofrost saw a roan mare with dusty-blue feathers edged in black. "They've got Shysong!"

The Storm Herd steeds hurtled toward the circle. Several lashings were looped around Shysong's neck and legs. The mare bucked and kicked, but the Landwalkers steered their mounts out of her reach, keeping an equidistant circle around her body.

"Get out of here," Shysong neighed to her friends when she saw them coming. "Save yourselves!" Tears streamed down her face.

Echofrost ignited. "I won't let them take you, Shysong.

No pegasus will endure captivity again, not while I'm alive. I promise." She rammed the closest enemy pegasus, a palomino pinto mare. The golden steed faltered, and her rider lost her balance, almost falling off. But the red-haired female righted herself quickly and spoke to her mare. "Steady, Rizah!"

Echofrost flew closer and bit into the woody rope that was tied to Shysong at one end and to the golden pinto at the other. She snapped it in half.

"Back off," whinnied the foreign mare. She kicked Echofrost in the flank and sent her spiraling toward land.

Hazelwind and Graystone teamed up, trying to bite the remaining lashings that held Shysong. Redfire battled the chestnut stallion named Kol, and Dewberry darted quickly in and out, kicking the foreign steeds.

The Landwalkers unstrapped clubs from their backs and swung them at the Storm Herd pegasi. The female aboard the pinto mare shouted, "Careful, don't damage them!"

Hazelwind snatched a Landwalker male by his arm and dragged him off his mount.

"Bloody rain, they're attacking us!" the male shouted. He whacked Hazelwind in the knee with his club. Hazelwind whinnied and let go. The green-eyed rider fell toward land, screaming, "Ilan, help me!"

His mount, a white stallion with black spots, charged after the falling Landwalker, coasted beneath him, and then caught him on his back, dropping his altitude to absorb the speed of the fall without breaking his rider's bones.

Once safe, the Landwalker wrapped his legs around the steed's ribs and stroked his neck. The stallion nickered with pleasure, and Echofrost faltered. These pegasi *liked* their riders. Then the pair charged toward Hazelwind with murder in their eyes.

Every instinct told Echofrost to retreat, but she couldn't. She'd promised Shysong that she wouldn't be captured—yet there the roan was, trussed up like a fly in a web.

Dewberry blasted across the sky, wings pinned, eyes blazing. "Playtime is over," she whinnied. And then she flew in a fast circle, kicking each foreign steed in the flank. Redfire and Graystone rallied and joined her. Hazelwind and the rest attacked from the rear, and Echofrost helped, striking steeds from above. The rebel pegasi from Anok charged in full force, and one by one, the rest of Shysong's lashings fell away.

But the Landwalkers urged their steeds forward

and tossed more ropes at the Storm Herd steeds. One fell around Echofrost's neck and then tightened around her throat. She reared back, and it clamped tighter, like the constricting grip of a snake. She opened her mouth to scream, but the noise came out a strangled gasp. The Landwalker who'd caught her yanked hard, pulling her closer. She saw up close his short white teeth and green eyes, and his grimace of effort. Sweat rolled down his whiskered chin. He was the one who'd fallen off the black-spotted stallion. As he tugged Echofrost closer, his eyes glowed with triumph.

Echofrost couldn't breathe, and she became dizzy, confused. *I'm panicking*, she thought.

Hazelwind charged toward her and whinnied to the spotted stallion. "Why are you helping the Landwalkers catch us?" The wind carried off his words, and the clouds drifted overhead, spurting warm rain.

"Don't talk to him," Echofrost rasped. "Just get me loose."

Hazelwind bit through the rope holding her, and she was free.

The Storm Herd pegasi pulled away from the Kihlari steeds. They'd released Shysong too, but her injured wing had begun to swell. She quickly lost altitude.

The chestnut Kihlara named Kol turned his head and brayed toward land, calling for reinforcements. Then he stared at her, his black eyes gleaming. "You won't escape us."

Her belly flipped.

"Look! More are coming," Graystone whinnied. Echofrost glanced toward the huge wooden den with the retractable ceiling in the far distance, and she saw hundreds more Kihlari pouring out of it.

"Retreat," Redfire brayed. The Storm Herd pegasi, including Shysong, gathered and fled.

"Stay together," Echofrost neighed, but she didn't look back. None of them did. They flew in a tight group like they had when they crossed the Dark Water, but unease tugged at Echofrost's heart.

Storm Herd was outnumbered, and the Kihlari steeds were large and energetic. They had clean, glossy coats and plump, well-fed muscles. By comparison her group looked ragged, dirty, and starved. They were in sorry shape for battle, that much was clear.

"They're gaining on us," Dewberry whinnied.

"Fly higher," ordered Redfire. "As high as you can. I doubt the Landwalkers can breathe well in the heights."

Hope surged, because Echofrost believed Redfire was

correct. She'd noticed the Landwalkers' shallow breathing when they'd reached the level of the clouds, but she'd been too busy freeing Shysong to consider the implications. The Kihlari army had a weakness—and it was their riders. The Landwalkers slid off their mounts easily, had small, inefficient lungs, and their pegasi would abandon a fight to save them if they fell.

As she and her friends glided toward the sun, flying higher and higher, Echofrost glanced down. Several Landwalkers went limp and fell, and their mounts dived down after them. "It's working!" she whinnied. The Kihlari army halted and hovered, realizing their riders could fly no higher.

"They've stopped following us," Redfire whinnied.

But Echofrost's uneasy feeling returned. She scanned her herd, counting them, and then dread seized her. "Where's Shysong?"

Storm Herd paused, hovering in place. "She was just behind me," neighed Dewberry.

Echofrost peered far below, where the Kihlari were circling. She squinted at them through the swift, wet winds that tousled her mane, and her vision grew sharper as she focused. The winged army was gliding toward land, but they had a blue roan pegasus with them. They'd thrown new lashings around her legs and neck, and they were dragging her away. Echofrost's heart sank—it was Shysong. The one mare she'd promised to keep free was captured.

9

BREAKDOWN

"WHERE DID THOSE PEGASI COME FROM?" GRAY-stone asked, wheezing for air. "And how did they get here?" The Storm Herd pegasi had retreated to the southern mountains and were hiding under a massive overcropping of limestone. Colorful parrots swooped through the surrounding trees, feeding.

"There are no legends about pegasi living in other lands," Dewberry said. The battle mare appeared tired and thin to Echofrost, except for her distended belly. Storm Herd needed to find a home and settle, to regain the muscle and fat they'd lost crossing the Dark Water.

Hazelwind unfolded his jade wings, drawing everyone's attention. "There is one legend."

All eyes turned to him.

"The Lake Herd pegasi who'd once lived in the interior of Anok disappeared four hundred years ago. My sire believed a massive tornado destroyed the herd, but some elders claim they fled during the first reign of Nightwing. So it's possible they landed here."

Echofrost lashed her tail, agitated and concerned about Shysong. "No. I don't believe it," she whinnied. "A pegasus from Anok would never allow a Landwalker on his back. Those steeds came from somewhere else."

Hazelwind stamped the ledge. "None of this matters right now. I mean, it matters—but we don't know the truth. All we know is that we need to get off this continent before the Landwalkers try to catch us again."

"What about Shysong?" Echofrost asked. "We can't leave her behind."

"We can't save her either," said Dewberry.

"We have to try."

"We can't lose track of our mission," Hazelwind interrupted. "We must spread our kind out of Anok; otherwise we risk extinction from destroyers, plagues, and disasters. You each knew that when you agreed to this, right?" He stared at the pegasi, and they nodded. Hazelwind continued. "So we owe it to those we left behind to finish what we started. We can't lose sight of our goal over the life of one captured steed." He stood beneath the overhang in the shadows, looking dejected. "I don't like it either, but this place isn't safe. We have to leave before more of us are taken."

"But what if they try to ride Shysong?" Echofrost had been captured twice in her life. The first time was when she was a weanling. She'd trespassed into Mountain Herd's territory with her friends. A patrol had spotted them and had taken her and another weanling hostage. She'd been tortured and kicked. Yearlings had made a sport of yanking out her mane and tail hairs by the roots. She'd eventually been released, but hatred and fear had haunted her until she'd finally let it go and took sharp control over her life, and her feelings.

The second time she was captured was when Nightwing had enslaved her and all the pegasi in Anok. He'd forced them to live like horses on the ground, and he'd used his starfire power to kill any steed who disobeyed him. But they'd all escaped merely seven days ago, and now one of them was caught again. Echofrost stood, trembling, her feelings unraveling as she remembered the promise she'd made to Shysong: *No pegasus will endure captivity again, not while I'm alive.*

Hazelwind folded his jade wings across his back. "I don't want to leave her behind either, but I think it's best for the herd. We're still recovering, and their army is fresh. We should go."

Echofrost reared and slammed down her front hooves, glaring at Hazelwind as if they were the only two pegasi in the mountains. "We can't just go! Would you leave me behind too?"

He didn't answer, but he held her gaze, and in his eyes she saw the truth. He *would* leave her behind. Of course he would; it was best for the herd—she knew that—but was it right? She grunted, pulling hard for air and feeling dizzy again.

"We tried to save her, Echofrost," said Dewberry in a soothing tone. "But Shysong's injured, and she can't keep up with us. Hazelwind is right. There's nothing we can do, and we risk losing more steeds if we go back for her. We risk failing our mission."

But Echofrost wasn't listening. Her mind reeled with memories from the past, the hauntings of the abuse she'd endured from the Mountain Herd yearlings. She knew what it felt like to be left behind. Thundersky, the past leader of her herd, had not rescued her because she'd willfully trespassed into Mountain Herd's territory to save a friend. Thundersky wouldn't risk a war over her disobedience, and she'd understood his decision, but she'd felt hurt and abandoned all the same.

Her jaw tightened and her teeth sank into her cheeks. Her tail twitched from side to side, and she knew everyone was watching her, but she saw only darkness. The dizzy feeling grew stronger.

Her control was crumbling.

Hazelwind walked forward and touched her wing. Adrenaline shot through her and her vision cleared. She whirled on him. He was so like his sire when Thundersky was over-stallion of Sun Herd: protective of the herd as a whole but *not* of her, and not of Shysong. "I can't leave her with those Landwalkers," she whinnied.

Hazelwind pricked his ears. "Echofrost, please . . ."

"I know it's for the good of all, but it's not good for Shysong."

Hazelwind glanced at Dewberry. The pinto mare shrugged. He edged closer to Echofrost.

She jerked away from him. "Don't come near me."

"What did I do?" Hazelwind blurted. "What's this all about?"

Long-suppressed feelings erupted from deep within Echofrost. This was about everything. *No!* This was about *one thing.* Echofrost gasped as her twin brother's jovial face flashed across her mind, and then the tears finally exploded from her eyes and dripped down her cheeks. "This is about Bumblewind!" she cried.

Hazelwind lifted his head, startled. "What?"

Echofrost turned and flew off the mountain, away from him, away from the shocked stares of her herd. *What am I doing?* she wondered. *I'm losing my mind.* She wanted to be alone, so she flew faster and faster, gliding away from her outburst. But her temper cooled quickly and regret washed over her. She landed on steep terrain near a rain-fed river. A bright-red bird cawed at her, and lizards scurried across the wet rocks. The water rushed by, masking her sobs as her body quaked.

Then the rustling of wings broke into her thoughts. She glimpsed emerald feathers and knew it was Dewberry. "What do you want?" Echofrost asked, wiping her eyes.

"Nothing," said Dewberry. She stood beside Echofrost for a long time. Finally she spoke. "Your brother was my best friend." Then she shook her black mane. "No, he was more than that. Much more."

Echofrost shuddered. "I know," she whispered.

"I wasn't there when he died either, but your brother

couldn't be saved. That isn't Hazelwind's fault."

Echofrost groaned.

Dewberry waited a moment and then continued. "I blamed myself too, for not being in the den. He died without me there." Her eyes filled with tears. "Maybe I could have helped him, but Hazelwind said it happened fast. His injury was just . . . too severe."

Dewberry let out her breath and thoughtfully stroked her belly with her wing. "But the truth is, me being there wouldn't have changed a thing. It was his time, that's all, but Bumblewind will live on with Storm Herd. And I'm sorry we couldn't tell you until the next day, I truly am; but it wasn't safe for you, or any of us, to tell you in the valley with Nightwing so close. And I'm sad to say it, but Shysong can't be saved either. The Kihlari and the Landwalkers outnumber us. If we tangle with them, we'll lose."

Echofrost knew Dewberry spoke reason, but she didn't want to hear it. She wanted Storm Herd and Hazelwind at least to consider saving the mare.

Dewberry rubbed her eyes with her wings. "And I don't think it's Hazelwind you're mad at."

"What? Yes, I am."

"No," said Dewberry, gently shaking her head. "No,

you're not." She turned and flew back to the Storm Herd steeds.

Echofrost could see them in the distance, huddled together on the side of the mountain. They were invisible from the sky, because of the limestone overhang, but she stood at their level, just on a different ridge, and so she saw them well.

Embarrassment crept through her, making her feel hot. She'd had a fit, like a foal, and in front of everyone. Her wings sagged at her sides. She watched Hazelwind through lowered lashes. His jade feathers glinted in the sun as it dropped lower. He stood with Graystone and Redfire. They were talking, probably about her. Hazelwind glanced her way, and she couldn't read his expression at this distance, but Dewberry was wrong. She *was* angry with Hazelwind. Not just for burying her brother without telling her, but for deciding so quickly to abandon Shysong.

But if the Storm Herd steeds agreed with him, what could she do about it?

Echofrost gathered herself and flew back to her friends. She landed and silently picked at the plants that grew out of the rocks. "So what's next?" she asked Hazelwind, and the tension uncoiled from Storm Herd.

"We'll fly east from here," he answered. "And we'll keep going until we feel safe. Even if we have to cross another ocean."

Echofrost nodded.

"We'll rest until full dark, and then we'll leave," said Graystone gently.

"All right," said Echofrost.

Hazelwind approached her, but she turned her back on him. He halted and advanced no farther. Dewberry tossed her black mane, looking disappointed.

Everyone left her alone until the glow of evening had faded, but by the time the Storm Herd steeds readied to leave, they couldn't find her.

Echofrost was gone.

10

THE PLAN

ECHOFROST TROTTED THROUGH THE LOWLAND jungle of interlocking trees and dewy plants, her ears pricked for danger. She'd drifted away from her friends while they rested and grazed, and then she'd flown away without saying good-bye. Now she was down the mountain and loping through a rain forest almost as dense as the Trap in northern Anok.

Glancing over her shoulder, she halted, listening. It was dark here; the tree branches blocked the moon, which glowed like a giant eye in the sky. She heard the sharp calls of animals, monkeys probably, and leaves rustling, but no wingbeats. No one from the herd was following her.

Echofrost exhaled and walked forward. Damp plants

slid over her hide, wetting it. A pack of bats whooshed overhead, spooking her. It'd be difficult for a spit dragon, like the big one she'd seen in the valley, to sneak up on her in the jungle, but Shysong had said most jungle predators ambushed their prey. She clamped down her tail and broke into a trot. She would fly if a predator appeared, but she didn't want Hazelwind to spot her, so for now she traveled under the cover of the forest canopy.

The scent of smoke and burning wood drifted toward her from the Landwalker settlement. Every instinct told her to run, to turn around, but she ignored her feelings and drew ever closer to the Landwalkers . . . and to Shysong. Hazelwind and the Storm Herd steeds could leave if they wanted. She'd certainly tried to change their minds but had failed, and so she'd rescue Shysong by herself. She had a plan—well, the seed of a plan anyway.

As she journeyed farther from her herd, each strange noise sent a jolt through her heart, causing her to halt and scent the wind for trouble. It was spring here, and huge flowers bloomed, their petals splaying open even at night. Their sweet fragrance cloyed at her nostrils, and she pranced now, overwhelmed by the foreign scents. Spongy soil retracted beneath her hooves, moist air filled her throat, and life thrived in every viable space, from the insect-laden brush to the bat-filled sky.

She was almost to the Landwalker settlement. She emerged into a clearing, and the moonlight reached her, setting her aglow.

Clickety-clack

Clack

Clickety-clack

Echofrost froze. What was that sound? She flexed her wings. The low clicks and clacks vibrated her eardrums, rhythmic and steady. Whatever it was, the creature wasn't hunting; it was making too much noise for that, but it was coming toward her. Echofrost scooted into the shadows.

Soon the grasses parted and a line of gigantic ants stomped into the clearing. Echofrost flinched and disgust bloomed in her stomach. The lead ant circled its antennae and snapped its pincerlike jaws, and the others followed it in a perfect line, each the size of a large hare, without variation. They matched one another's steps, pace for pace. If they were aware of her, they ignored her.

Echofrost held her breath as the ants passed her in a steady stream, like a bright river of blood. The moonlight illuminated small hairs that dusted their otherwise hard-shelled bodies. Sensory spikes edged their long legs, and their eyes were solid black. She wondered if they were venomous like the fire ants that lived in the southlands of Anok.

Squinting down, she noticed several ants carrying pieces of an animal over their heads. She saw tufts of spotted tan fur, like the hide of a fawn. She decided they must be poisonous; otherwise she doubted they could have hunted an animal larger than themselves. Echofrost backed farther away, and her hoof clunked against a rock, making a loud vibration through the air and soil.

The ant line halted, and hundreds of glittering copper heads turned toward her. She froze. Their antennae swiveled, and their legs shifted.

Ancestors, help me, thought Echofrost. There were hundreds of them, and if they chose to swarm her, they could easily kill her. She quietly flared her wings, ready to fly away.

But the leader of the ants, who was far in the distance now, resumed walking and so did the rest of the line. Echofrost waited until the last ant was long gone before she emerged back into the clearing. Hazelwind was right; the pegasi didn't belong on this continent. She hoped to free Shysong quickly and catch up to Storm Herd, but the plan forming in her mind depended on too many factors she couldn't control—like where Shysong was being held, if she was guarded, and what sort of Landwalker weapons Echofrost might have to face.

She was about to trot off when a shape leaped at her. Echofrost reared back, and it just missed her throat. Growling filled her ears. She kicked off and hovered near the treetops. A black panther snarled up at her. He jumped again, trying to snatch her feathers in his claws.

She flattened her neck and bolted. *It's time to get out of this jungle!* The panther chased her from the ground with his green eyes turned up, hoping to yank her out of the sky. She flew faster, and a family of gibbons screamed at her, like they were laughing. Sweat erupted and dripped down her silver hide. She rose higher than the trees, leaving the hungry panther behind, and rocketed toward the Landwalker camp.

Soon Echofrost soared over the final edge of the jungle and coasted down toward the Kihlari den. Beyond it, on the top of the hill, was the massive, eight-sided structure that housed their riders. Echofrost hovered a moment, thinking. Once the Landwalkers spotted her, there would be no turning back.

She sniffed the air until she located Shysong's scent. It was coming from the huge den that housed the Kihlari. As Echofrost had expected, her friend was trapped inside with the foreign pegasi. She inhaled, and her plan sharpened. She could not approach the structure that held Shysong without being seen by the Landwalkers. And she couldn't fight hundreds of Kihlari steeds on her own. There was only one way to help Shysong—Echofrost had to let the Landwalkers capture her too. If she could infiltrate the Kihlari den, maybe she and Shysong could work together to find a way back out.

Echofrost flapped her wings, hovering between two fates—saving Shysong or abandoning her. The truth was, she wanted to flee, to leave Shysong behind, but she couldn't. Why? She closed her eyes and the Mountain Herd yearlings appeared in her mind; she felt their hard blows, remembered them tearing out her mane, laughing at her. She faltered, almost falling out of the sky, and anguish roared through her. She'd fought so hard to live free—the thought of subjecting herself to Landwalkers was unthinkable!

But the promise she'd made was not just to Shysong. *No pegasus will endure captivity again, not while I'm alive.* No—she hadn't fought so *she* could live free; she'd fought so that *all* pegasi could live free.

Echofrost rattled her feathers as fire and determination shot through her veins. She would not abandon

Shysong the way she'd been abandoned. Echofrost braced her heart, shoved aside her better judgment, and glided into view.

The land horses noticed her first and whinnied in excitement. They lived on the lush lower plain just north of the Kihlari den, and now Echofrost noticed more animals too: horned buffalo of varying sizes, small boars, and goats. They were all trapped and housed by the Landwalkers in separate pens. Armed sentries guarded them, and it was one of these males who glanced up, saw her, and shouted, "Ay! A wild Kihlara!" His voice drew more Landwalkers out of the shadows, and they ran toward Echofrost.

She hovered low in the sky, watching the chaos below. More shouts echoed throughout the rock walls of the Landwalker fortress, and the two-legged creatures spilled out and stared up at her. Her heart quaked, but she flared her wings and landed, her hooves touching down with a whisper.

The Landwalkers slowed as they approached, and one spoke softly to her—a male by his look, but a young one. He was slim and short, just a cub. His hair was raven black and cropped close to his head, unlike the Kihlari riders, who had longer hair. His eyes were the color of fresh honey.

"Careful, Rahkki, it's wild," said a taller, older Land-walker who closely resembled the younger one. Echofrost recognized him from the sky battle earlier today. He rode Kol, the big chestnut stallion who'd warned her that she wouldn't escape.

The short-haired cub whispered to the taller version of himself, and Echofrost guessed they were brothers. "She's a *braya*, Brauk, a female."

The sound of the cub's voice set Echofrost's feathers on edge. Would these Landwalkers hurt her? Would they pen her with Shysong, or elsewhere? Her resolve began to melt as she considered all the unknowns.

The taller brother inched closer. "Whoa, braya," he said.

Echofrost tensed, reminding herself that she'd cho-sen this, but that did nothing to quell the rapid slam of her heart as the Landwalker approached with his back hunched, trying to make himself appear small and harm-less. He outstretched his arm.

As she watched, he flicked his wrist. Too late she noticed the rope in his hand as he flung it over her head.

She blinked and pulled back; the rope tightened. She whinnied in shock. *I can't do this*, she thought.

Six more Landwalkers tossed ropes that tangled around her neck and hooves. They each held tight, and she couldn't stop herself from struggling. The Landwalkers shouted to one another in excited voices and then gave a mighty tug, yanking her off her hooves. She hit the ground and rolled onto her side.

The Landwalkers swarmed her. They bound her wings and legs. She whinnied, and they slipped something between her teeth. She tried to close her jaw but couldn't. They'd gagged her! She'd allowed this capture, but she had to show the Landwalkers right away that she would not be bullied. She kicked at them, but they darted out of her range, forming a circle around her. She moaned and grunted, trying to stand.

The short-haired Landwalker cub who'd first spoken to her crawled close and placed his hand on her cheek.

"Get away from her, Rahkki," said his older look-alike.

Echofrost understood they were speaking to one another, but she couldn't understand their long, rolling words.

"Don't fight, braya," said the short cub.

She glared into his golden eyes and saw herself

reflected there, bound and gagged. The cub's hand was gentle as he stroked her face, and she recognized that he was trying to calm her, but his repulsive touch fanned embers of rage instead. Echofrost flared her nostrils and drank in his scent—memorizing it.

"Shh, braya," he whispered.

Echofrost made a silent vow to kill him first when she and Shysong escaped.

"She likes you, Rahkki," said the female rider with the dark-red hair. Her comment made the other Landwalkers laugh. They sounded to Echofrost like the monkeys in the trees.

"Nah, Tuni, I don't think that's love in her eyes," said the green-eyed warrior who rode the spotted stallion called Ilan.

The young cub continued stroking Echofrost's cheek, making her stomach roil. She struck at him with her front hoof, but he leaped to safety.

"She reminds me of Sula, the guardian mascot of the Second Clan," Rahkki said. "She's as still as a stone but strikes as fast as a viper."

The green-eyed male turned up his lips, showing his teeth. His long golden hair fell around his shoulders like a shining mane. "You could join the Sky Guard with this one, Rahkki. You already named her, yeah? Sula. It suits her."

"Rahkki's going to be a farmer now, Harak. You know that," interrupted the red-haired female called Tuni. Echofrost squinted at her, remembering that she rode the palomino pinto mare.

Harak spit on the ground. "Farming is for land lovers."

Echofrost strained harder to understand their language, but it sounded like senseless babbling to her.

"Well, this wildling is terrified," said Tuni. She turned to the Landwalkers who were holding Echofrost's ropes. "Take Sula into the barn for the night."

Echofrost groaned as the Landwalkers lifted her body and carried her toward the wooden structure they called a *barn*. "Your new home, little viper," Harak said. His words sounded like growling to Echofrost. His green eyes reminded her of the panther.

She trembled as they carried her into the Kihlari den. Was Shysong inside as she suspected? Could Echofrost free them both? When Star had formed the United Army in Anok to battle Nightwing's forces, she'd trained as a spy and she'd learned how to assess her enemies for weaknesses. But so far these Landwalkers, who tamed animals, fire, land, and pegasi, appeared to have few. She'd need to study them from the inside to understand them, and to discover how to beat them.

I chose this, Echofrost reminded herself as the door of the barn opened and she entered the Kihlari den. Hundreds of pegasi turned their heads to stare at her, and her heart thrummed. *I'm in complete control*, she said to herself. *Complete control.*

As the door shut behind her, cutting off the night air and her view of the sky, Echofrost turned off her thoughts and faced the truth.

She was terrified, and maybe this was a mistake.

11

THE WILDLING

RAHKKI FOLLOWED THE SKY GUARD RIDERS AS they carried the wild Kihlara mare into a box stall. They removed her gag and rushed out, leaving her to chew off her bindings because no one was in the mood to get kicked to death tonight. Two men worked together to drag netting over her walls so she couldn't fly away. Several braver warriors had plucked a few of her purple feathers as trophies. Rahkki's brother, Brauk, was one of them.

"Why'd you take those?" Rahkki asked, watching his brother twirl the feathers.

"Because a wild Kihlara hasn't been spotted in four hundred years. This is rare stuff," Brauk answered. Then he lowered his voice so the other Riders couldn't hear. "If I make charms of this plumage, I bet I could sell 'em for forty jints apiece at the Clan Gathering. The merchant kids'll pay smart."

Rahkki believed that was true. "Where do you think that wild herd came from?" he asked.

"Don't know, don't care," Brauk said, jabbing his little brother. "I don't question opportunity when it comes my way; I just take it." Brauk sniffed the feathers and then tucked them into his boar-hide pouch.

The other Riders scattered to calm their mounts, and Koko Dale, the lead groom for the stable, appeared from the tack stall. She was fifteen, three years older than Rahkki, and she was as fierce as the winged steeds under her care. She approached Sula's stall, ready to attend to the new flying horse, her eyes wide with wonder. But Brauk waved her off. "I'll take care of her," he said.

Koko tossed Rahkki and Brauk a disappointed frown and returned to her evening chores.

Rahkki leaned against the stall door, drinking in the scents of the barn. Rows and rows of stalls filled it, each housing a tame Kihlara steed. Their hot breath and warm scents drenched the air. The breeding stock and the foals were stabled at the Ruk, which was located near the horse pens. This barn was for the Sky Guard Fliers only, the prized winged warriors of the Fifth Clan.

But Rahkki noticed that the Kihlari were nervous. Each steed stood with its head high, its ears forward and nostrils flared. They peered over their stalls, trying to glimpse the two wild mares in their midst.

Brauk had named the blue roan Firo, for her sparkling blue eyes. *Firo* meant "bright" or "fire" in Talu. The seven Sandwen clans often named their animals in Talu because the words sounded exotic to them—and Rahkki thought Firo suited the roan mare just fine.

Just then the silver wildling that he'd named Sula whinnied sharply. Nickering erupted among the Fliers, punctuated by piercing squeals and earsplitting brays. Rahkki listened intently to the noise. He'd long believed that the winged horses spoke to one another in a real language, even though the noises they made sounded quite similar to horses. But his older brother, Brauk, thought that was ridiculous. "Kihlari can't speak," he often argued, and then thwacked Rahkki on the head.

"Hand me that rake," Brauk said, and Rahkki obeyed. His brother used the rake to lower an empty water bucket into Sula's stall.

She sprang toward the long wooden handle and bit it.

"She's quick," Brauk said, laughing as he often did, without mirth.

Rahkki nodded, wondering at the wild steed. She was lean and dirty, but beneath the filth, her coat was silver gray, like the even color of a *sawa* sword. Her white mane and tail hung tangled and mudstained. She appeared intelligent, like most Kihlari, so why had she come back here and landed in plain sight? Didn't she know she'd be captured? Especially after the Sky Guard army had trapped the roan mare and then chased her and her friends into the clouds.

Rahkki glanced at Firo. Perhaps Sula had come back to save her friend? But Rahkki knew his clan would never set either mare free. Even untrained, they were too valuable. They would breed the mares, sell them, or train them.

But this silver braya had determined eyes—Rahkki saw that as plain as the moon that chased the sun. He studied her—looking past the mud, the mess of tangled hair, and the bent purple feathers to her conformation. Her head was fine, her eyes wide set, and her bones were straight and strong, her legs unblemished. "Sula's a warrior," he said to Brauk.

His brother snorted. "If you say so. She looks like a starved chicken to me."

Rahkki shrugged, but they both knew he had an eye for spotting well-bred Kihlari, usually as soon as they were born. He'd chosen the copper chestnut named Kol for Brauk. At first the clan had mocked Rahkki for choosing such a big-boned colt for his brother, believing that Kol would be slow in battle. But as he grew, it turned out that Kol's physical conformation was perfect for flying, and his oversize lungs powered his huge muscles efficiently. Kol was fast, strong, *and* big—a rare combination for a Flier.

Studying this wild mare, Rahkki guessed she was two years old, maybe three. He imagined her in the sky and saw agility in her bones. To him, agility was worth more than size or speed, or both. Not every Rider would agree with him on that, but Rahkki had fled from Mut Finn enough times to appreciate the merits of agility. Mut was a Sandwen teen who was too old for games but too young for war. To relieve his boredom, he harassed whoever crossed his path. And Rahkki had escaped the abuse of Mut more than once simply by dodging him.

Brauk filled Sula's water bucket and then poked at her with the rake.

Rahkki flinched. "Don't do that."

"I want to see her move."

The little Kihlara ignored Brauk, but Rahkki saw her

pulse thumping in her neck. "She's waiting for us to leave," he said to his older brother.

Brauk replaced the rake against the wall. "Looks like her herd ditched her."

"No, I think she came back here on purpose, for her friend." Rahkki nodded toward Firo, who was sleeping in the next stall. Brim Carver, the clan's animal doctor, had already come and gone. She'd dosed Firo with strong medicine, and then she'd yanked out the arrow that their overzealous clansman had shot into her. After that, Brim had stitched the wound closed and predicted that the mare would heal just fine. Rahkki noticed that Firo was as dirty and skinny as Sula, but not as well built for flying.

"Right," Brauk said, tugging on Rahkki's ear. "The mare has *friends*." He drawled the word *friends* and shook his head. "That roan is probably her foal; instincts drove her back here. Or she's just stupid. But animals don't have *friends*."

"Sula's too young to have a foal," Rahkki said. *And she's not stupid.* The mare's eyes were as clear and dark as a rainless night.

Brauk tossed fresh hay into Sula's stall, and his sudden movement spooked her. He leaned on her door, thinking.

"I don't know. Maybe that herd isn't wild. Maybe they got loose from one of the other clans."

Rahkki pointed to the mare's right shoulder. "She's not branded; none of the wildlings were, and that doesn't explain why there are so many of them." The seven Sandwen clans each valued the Kihlari steeds as precious. They didn't just *lose* them.

"Well, she's worth some dramals, maybe even a full round. The other one too—if I can have them ready in time for the summer auction at the annual Clan Gathering."

"You're going to sell them that soon?" Rahkki asked, his voice rising. "They just got here."

"Land to skies, Brother! Of course I'm selling them that soon. You're looking at weapons, hay, armor, and food for the Sky Guard. As soon as I plump their bones and knock the spit out of 'em, they're gone."

Rahkki's heartbeat sped a notch. He knew the Sky Guard was underfunded, but the truth was, Rahkki was excited about the wild brayas, and he wanted them to stay. "I doubt Queen Lilliam will let you keep the profits," he said, his voice a whisper.

Brauk's eyes darkened. He was one of three Headwinds who led the Sky Guard, and part of his job was to help fund the army. "We'll see about that," he said.

Tuni Hightower, the female Headwind who rode the golden palomino named Rizah, stood a few stalls down the row, feeding her mare a handful of grain to quiet her nerves about the strange steeds in the barn. Tuni rubbed her eyes. "Come on. The wildling mares need their sleep." She extinguished the wick of her lamp and walked outside, followed by the rest.

When Rahkki passed Tuni, she smiled at him. Her long red hair was unbound, and it flowed around her face like a shimmering waterfall. She was twenty-one years old, the same age as Brauk. "Did you hear about the giants, Rahkki?" she asked. "The Gorlan hordes have banded together in the mountains."

"I heard," he said.

"We could really use another Rider, even an inexperienced one like you. If you buy one of those wildling mares, you could scout the hordes for me. You don't have to fight."

Rahkki paused. No one in the clan knew how poor he and Brauk were, even though Rahkki thought it was obvious. Didn't Tuni notice his worn clothing, his cheap goat-hide boots, and his knife-shorn hair? He couldn't afford to purchase a haircut, let alone a precious Flier. "I start my farming apprenticeship today," he reminded her.

Brauk shook his head. "Nah, it's almost dark. You can go in the morning. I'll explain to Uncle. These wild steeds took up the entire day."

Rahkki grinned because he was getting one more night with his brother.

Tuni faced the Riders. "Is everyone out?" she asked, raising her voice.

"All out," Brauk shouted.

Tuni slammed the barn doors and locked them, leaving Sula and Firo in darkness.

12

TRAPPED

AS SOON AS THE LANDWALKERS WERE GONE AND their footsteps had faded, Echofrost attacked her lashings, biting them off her legs and wings. When she was free of them, she spread her feathers and flew straight up. She needed to find Shysong and get her out of here. But Echofrost struck a web of ropes that crisscrossed over her head. Her neck became entangled, and she flapped harder but couldn't break through this new barrier. She landed and yanked her neck free of the ropes.

Calm down, she chided herself. Spies *act*; they don't *react*. Flaring her nostrils, she drank in the scents—in front of her was a pile of freshly cut forage, and behind her was the container of water the Landwalker had lowered into her pen. Nearby, she smelled wood, animal hides, and the faint, clean odor of the foreign pegasi.

She swiveled her ears. At least three hundred Kihlari stood in separate enclosures in this den, but they were preternaturally silent. When the Landwalkers had carried Echofrost inside, she'd counted twenty rows of twenty enclosures like hers, but one section lay empty. They were called *stalls*, she believed, because a Kihlara mare had whinnied, "Don't put that filthy braya next to my stall."

Now Echofrost nosed around her prison, examining it for weaknesses. She kicked the sides; they were solid. She knocked over the bucket of water, and the liquid spilled around her hooves. She pawed at the cut forage, destroying it. She heard the soft shuffling of hooves as the Kihlari began nickering to one another:

Who is she?

Where did she come from?

What happened to her friends?

"Shysong?" Echofrost's loud bray silenced the whisperings.

"Your injured friend is asleep in the stall next to yours," neighed a stallion, and she recognized his voice. It was Kol, the shiny chestnut who'd threatened her in the sky. His stall was located next to hers.

"I can't smell her," Echofrost said. Now that she was inside the barn, she was overwhelmed by all the strange odors and so she couldn't place Shysong's.

"*We* can smell her," answered the stallion with a snort. "And you too."

Echofrost flattened her ears. This stallion let Land-walkers ride on his back; who was he to judge her and Shysong?

"Where did you come from?" he continued.

Echofrost said nothing. She was thinking.

"Answer me!" he brayed.

"Are you the over-stallion of this herd?"

He paused. "Herd? We're not *horses*, wildling."

The surrounding Kihlari nickered, amused.

Echofrost felt her ears grow hot. Didn't all pegasi live in herds? She felt confused, unsure; but she was the stranger here, not them. She'd have to study their ways. "Tell me what you are and I'll tell you where I came from," she bargained.

The stallion pranced closer to the wall they shared. "I already told you, we're Kihlari. We guard the Fifth Clan of the Sandwen people, and I'm Kol, the leader of Dusk

Patrol and first colt of Mahrsan, the Queen's Chosen stallion. My Rider is Brauk Stormrunner."

Echofrost's mind swirled with all the strange titles and names he spoke; but she detected the pride in his voice, and she understood that—titles aside—he was an over-stallion by heart and by blood, and she would have to watch herself with him. "Why do you let the Landwalkers ride on your backs?" she asked.

"What's a Landwalker?"

She pricked her ears, listening closely because of his odd accent. "The two-legged creatures, the ones who tamed you."

Kol snorted. "Without a Rider, how would I fly?"

"You don't need a Rider to fly," Echofrost countered. "You saw me doing it."

Quiet tension drifted onto the Kihlari as they absorbed that.

"It's just not permitted," explained the spotted stallion named Ilan. His rider was the green-eyed Landwalker, Harak. "We don't go up unless our Riders take us."

Echofrost detected the same deep pride in Ilan's voice that she'd heard in Kol's, and she decided it was best not to judge the foreign steeds. It would set her at odds with them unnecessarily. "That makes sense," she said, though it actually made none.

"It's your turn," Kol neighed. "You promised to tell us where you came from."

"I come from a faraway land," she said, offering as little about Anok as possible.

Kol slammed his hoof against his stall floor. "Tell us something we don't already know."

Echofrost lashed her tail, growing impatient. "I crossed an ocean to get here."

"Which ocean?"

Her gut twisted. She didn't want to tell the Kihlari anything that might indicate in which direction Anok lay. No, she couldn't trust any pegasus who was friendly with Landwalkers. Anok was free of the two-legged pests, and after seeing that the legends about them paled in comparison to the truth, she feared that they and their winged mounts might invade her homeland if they knew where it was.

So Echofrost lied. "The ocean is west of your lands. My friends and I crossed it and came here, looking for a new territory." Echofrost had never told a lie before, and she hated the taste of the false words in her mouth.

Kol was silent for a long while.

He knows I lied, she thought.

But when he spoke, she realized that he didn't know. "Why did you leave? What happened to your land?"

"It . . . it became inhospitable," she said, thinking of Nightwing the Destroyer.

"And then you flew here? Is this better?" he asked.

Echofrost considered Nightwing's treacheries: burning Morningleaf's feathers with his silver starfire, turning hundreds of pegasi to ashes, stealing newborns from their dams, and murdering the five over-stallions of Anok. She studied the walls that trapped her, the pile of fresh food at her hooves, and the overturned container of water in the corner—and she answered. "Yes, this is better, but that's not saying much."

"I didn't know that wild Kihlari existed," Ilan whinnied. "Do you really live in herds, like horses? Who feeds you?"

Echofrost gaped at him across the aisle of stalls. "We feed ourselves. We graze."

The tame Kihlari murmured to one another, seeming shocked by that information.

"Well, you're safe now," Kol said to her in a tone so casual that it took her breath away.

"Safe?" she whinnied. "My friend and I are *captured*."

Kol nickered. "You're not captured; you're *rescued*. Do

you know what's in that jungle? There are three hordes of Gorlan giants that live in the eastern mountains. They eat flying horses and people, and that's not the worst of it. There are spiders that attack in armies, plants that will devour you alive, the drooling dragons that mash trees, and the tiny ones called *burners*. The burners live at the volcano, and they can fly—and breathe fire."

"Breathe fire?"

"Yes, annoying little beasts."

"I didn't know about all that." Echofrost had only seen one spit dragon, some oversize ants, and a panther. "What's a . . . Gorlan giant?"

Kol shuddered. "A Gorlan is neither animal nor human. They're over twice the size of a Sandwen and ten times stronger. There are three hordes of them near Mount Crim. They speak with their hands and ride elephants, and they hate us. If they catch you, they'll eat you."

Echofrost's gut clenched.

"Be glad you're rescued and get used to it," Kol finished. "The Sandwen clan will never let you or your friend go."

Fury slithered through her veins. "Why? What will they do with us?"

A golden palomino mare interrupted. "I'm Rizah," she

said, greeting Echofrost. "You have nothing to fear." She paused. "The clan will most likely sell you."

"*Sell*? What does that mean?"

A mare down the row answered. "It's like trading. They'll trade you for something valuable, like land or sacks of coin."

"Trade me to who?"

"To a young Rider or another clan."

Echofrost bit her cheek. *Never*, she thought. She felt exhaustion sinking into her bones and her eyelids drooping. "Please tell me," she said, "is my friend safe? I can't see her, and she's not answering me."

"She's safe," Rizah nickered. "She's been given strong medicine to help her sleep. You can talk to her tomorrow." Rizah abruptly changed the subject. "Did you know you have a name now?"

"My name is Echofrost."

Kol and many of the listening Kihlari steeds nickered out loud.

"No," said Rizah. "That's your wildling name, but now you have a Sandwen name: *Sula*. I heard Rahkki call you that."

Echofrost's heart thudded. "You can understand the

Landwalkers?" It would be *so* helpful to know what they were saying.

"No. We don't catch most of what they say, but there are Melds, people who can translate between us and the Sandwens," said Ilan, the spotted stallion. "They've helped us understand the clans, but there hasn't been a Meld around here since I was a foal."

Rizah interrupted with a sharp glance at Ilan. "Yes, but you can never trust a Meld, Sula. Some are honest. Some translate the Sandwen language word for word, but others twist it to manipulate us."

"How can you tell the difference?" Echofrost asked.

"Sandwens fidget and sweat when they lie," she answered. "So to answer your question more simply, we don't understand their language except for a few words. But when a word is repeated over and over again to the same steed, we know it's their name, and the Stormrunner brothers have named you Sula."

After that, the conversation drifted to other things, and Echofrost's eyelids drooped as she sank onto her bedding. The foreign words, sights, and smells overwhelmed her senses. *Shysong and I must escape before they sell us,* she thought. *Maybe tomorrow we'll get our chance.* She imagined Hazelwind and the others flying east, leaving her and Shysong behind, and she felt like she had when Mountain Herd captured her long ago: alone and without help.

Echofrost closed her eyes and saw visions of the giant black spit dragon tromping through the rain forest. She cleared her mind and slid quickly into sleep.

⟆ 13 ⟆

PLAYING STONES

RAHKKI FOLLOWED CLOSELY BEHIND THE THREE Headwinds of the Sky Guard army: Tuni, Brauk, and Harak. Tuni had just locked up the Kihlari stable for the night, leaving the wild brayas to adjust to their new home.

Now, as the four of them headed back to Fort Prowl, the octagonal fortress on the hill above the stables, Rahkki's feet kicked up dust because there'd been no rain today. He shuffled through the dirt spray, thinking. He was happy about getting an extra night with Brauk, but he wasn't happy about leaving for the farm in the morning. When he'd agreed to the apprenticeship, his clan hadn't had two wild Kihlari locked up in the barn!

Tuni's voice caught his attention. "Are all three Gorlan

hordes working together?" she asked Harak.

Rahkki glanced up, curious about the giants. His clan's farmland had once belonged to the Gorlan hordes, but when Rahkki's people drove the giants off it a thousand years ago, they'd sparked a grudge that continued to grate.

"Nah, we only saw the Fire and Highland hordes," he said. "Their warriors banded together on Mount Crim to share soup." Then he spit on the ground. "Stinkin' giants."

Rahkki found it difficult to believe that the giants could farm at all. They were thickheaded, stubborn, and stronger than gorillas; and the idea of them hoeing soil and planting delicate seeds was laughable.

Brauk paused, rubbing his chin. "If they shared soup, then that means those two hordes are working together."

Rahkki shuddered at the word *soup*. The legendary broth simmered at the center of each Gorlan horde encampment in huge black caldrons that spanned fifteen lengths across. The giants tossed in whatever they caught during the day—including Sandwen children, some said. The pots were never emptied or cleaned; the broth could steep for years, decades even, before misfortune struck and the soup had to be tossed. Each horde ate solely from its communal pot, and it was a great dishonor to be without soup. So when the giants shared theirs with other hordes, it was an unmistakable sign that they had banded together.

"It will take the Gorlanders five days to march here from Mount Crim," Tuni said. "We have plenty of time to make a plan, but the queen . . ." She shook her dark-red hair.

"She's useless," said Brauk.

"She's our ruler," Harak hissed. He was twenty-eight, the oldest and most volatile of the Headwinds.

The group fell silent as they crossed the Kihlari training yard and climbed the steps that had been cut into the side of the hill. At the top loomed Fort Prowl, their home. When they reached the iron gates, Harak spoke their credentials and they entered, but Brauk halted so fast that Rahkki bumped into him. "Shh," Brauk said. Tuni and Harak stopped too.

Rahkki glanced past the Headwinds, and his belly twisted. Across the flagstone courtyard was Queen Lilliam. She sat astride her winged stallion, Mahrsan, and was surrounded by her personal guards. By her flushed cheeks and wind-tousled hair, Rahkki guessed she had just returned from a flight. Dismounting, she spotted them and her gaze arced across the courtyard like an arrow.

Tuni, Harak, and Brauk dipped their heads.

Lilliam strode closer to the Headwinds, leading Mahrsan, who was hot from flight. "Are the wildling mares bedded and grained for the night?" she asked, her eyes landing on Harak.

"Yes, my queen," he answered.

Her eyes lingered over his glossy blond hair, green eyes, and sun-darkened skin. The corners of her lips flickered. "Cool my stallion out for me." Lilliam handed him the reins.

"Yes, my queen." Harak smiled and walked away, taking Mahrsan on a long walk.

With a curt nod, Lilliam dismissed Tuni and Brauk, and ignored Rahkki. She strode away with her back straight and with no evidence of the waddle that was common in the final month of pregnancy.

Once the queen had disappeared into the inner chambers of Fort Prowl, Rahkki let out his breath.

Tuni flashed him a compassionate smile, and her daring brown eyes reminded Rahkki of his mother.

"You okay?" she asked.

He nodded.

She pointed at Brauk. "We start training those wild mares tomorrow, right?"

"Right."

Her eyes drifted back to Rahkki. "It's too bad you're leaving in the morning; you could help us train them. You'll hate farming, you know." Sky Guard Riders like Tuni couldn't imagine a life stuck on the ground,

"Farming suits me just fine," Rahkki answered. He wasn't sure if this was true, but even if he *wanted* to join the Sky Guard, he couldn't afford a Kihlara Flier, not even a skinny, untrained one like Sula.

Tuni brushed her finger across Rahkki's cheek. "Good night, Sunchaser."

That brought a smile to Rahkki's face. Sunchaser was the moon spirit, and he was always brooding because he lived in the dark. "Good night, Tuni."

Brauk and Rahkki climbed the stairs to their small room. While they dressed for sleep, Rahkki chattered about the move to the farm as if he was okay with it. This would be his last night living with his brother. He stopped short when Brauk leaped across the floor, snatched him up, and tossed him onto his bed, imitating the roar of a Gorlan giant.

Squealing, Rahkki brandished a pretend dagger.

They wrestled, and Brauk allowed Rahkki to pin him. Then he twisted free, hurled Rahkki down again, and sat on his chest. "Let's play stones," Brauk said.

Rahkki thrashed under his brother's weight. "Really?" Brauk never wanted to play stones with him.

"Yes," Brauk answered, "but quick, before I change my mind."

Rahkki's heart raced, and Brauk turned him loose. He fumbled with his satchel and pulled out the wooden playing board and the small, smooth stones, placing four in each shallow cup on the board.

"Losers go last," Brauk said, pointing at Rahkki.

"But I haven't lost yet," he protested.

"Ah, but you admit to its inevitability." Brauk grinned, leaning forward. He wore only trousers, and the lamplight highlighted each muscle in Brauk's chest and arms. As his brother took up a handful of stones for his first turn, Rahkki stared at him, wondering if he'd look like Brauk when he grew up.

"Come on, what are you waiting for?" Brauk asked after finishing his turn.

Shaking off his thoughts, Rahkki sat down on his brother's mattress. He couldn't remember the last time they'd played a game, any game. He grabbed a handful of stones and worked his way around the carved-wood board. Then it was Brauk's turn again.

"Is rice farming hard work?" Rahkki asked as they played.

Brauk shrugged. "Don't know, really."

Uncle Darthan invited his nephews over for supper once every ten days or so. He and his sister, Reyella, had been close when she was alive, but evenings on the farm were quiet. The brothers ate. Darthan smoked his pipe. Sometimes he told clan stories by the outdoor fire pit, but only on clear nights, in case the dragons were hunting.

"I wish I could stay and help you train those wild mares," Rahkki said.

"Maybe if I run into trouble I can borrow you." Brauk pushed on Rahkki's foot with his. Rahkki smiled and pushed back.

They ended up playing three more rounds of stones before Brauk started yawning. "Will you visit me?" Rahkki asked.

Brauk pulled away. "This isn't good-bye."

Tears filled Rahkki's eyes. It felt like good-bye.

"Don't start," Brauk warned. "That crying stuff is for tots, right?"

Rahkki nodded.

"You're just going to Uncle's farm, not to the empire. I can get to you fast if I take Kol. Don't wait on me though.

The Gorlan hordes are on the move, and Lilliam can't make a decision. I've got things to do. You understand?"

Rahkki packed away the game. "I understand," he said, and smiled to prove it.

Brauk extinguished the oil lamp beside his bed.

As Rahkki scooted off the mattress to find his own bed in the dark, Brauk snatched his wrist.

"What is it?" Rahkki asked.

Brauk squeezed tighter, his breath hitching. Then he yanked Rahkki close and embraced him, hugging the air out of him. Rahkki felt his brother's hot tears drop onto his short hair, and Brauk's breaths were shallow, as though he were the one being squeezed near to death.

"I'll miss you, little rat," Brauk said in a tight breath.

Rahkki's lungs felt ready to burst, so he couldn't answer, but he relaxed in Brauk's arms. Soon the two were fast asleep, piled like puppies on the cot, the way they'd slept when they were small children.

14

THE PRINCESS

RAHKKI WOKE BEFORE DAWN. ONCE HE WAS away at the farm, Brauk would have to oil his own leathers, file Kol's hooves, mix his grain, and polish his weapons by himself. Rahkki would miss being his brother's groom, and he'd miss living in Fort Prowl.

His mind drifted to the wild mares, and he knew he had to see them again before he left. Sliding out of bed, Rahkki tiptoed across the room, being careful not to wake his brother. He lifted an overripe banana off the small, square dining table beneath their window. Outside, the sky lightened from black to gray as he packed his satchel and a backpack and left the room, peeling the banana. He had to shove hard on the stubborn door to close it, then he descended the circular steps of the inner tower.

Each floor had a landing and a dusty exterior window to let in sunlight, but it was still too early for them to provide much illumination, so Rahkki felt his way down the steps with one hand on the wall. It was difficult to believe that everything he owned fit into two small bags. Even sadder was his purse. Eight jints clanged against each other at the bottom of it—enough for a few pounds of dried fish, or a packet of spices, or a pair of used sandals—but not enough to feel secure. He reached the end of the stairwell and leaped over the final four steps, landing lightly on his feet. Uncle Darthan would feed and clothe him now, as was expected in an apprenticeship.

Rahkki exited the tower and approached the iron gates.

"Ay, who goes?" asked a posted guard.

"Rahkki Stormrunner, off to begin my apprenticeship."

"You can't wait until the morning bells ring?" the guard asked, irritated.

"Uncle wants me to start at dawn, not after." That was a lie and Rahkki felt bad for it, but he wouldn't have time to visit the wild mares if he didn't leave now.

The guard grumbled and logged Rahkki's departure

with a mark in his book. While Rahkki waited, he stared up at the tall double gates and the walls that were thirty lengths high. The fortress seemed overengineered for the small Sandwen people who lived inside, but it wasn't built to contain them. It was built to keep the Gorlan hordes, their saber cats, and their massive elephants out. The Fifth Clan had paid royal engineers from Daakur to construct the fortress six hundred years earlier, and it had withstood countless raids and sieges since. The guard closed his book and unlocked the smaller wooden gate that allowed single individuals quick passage in and out of the courtyard.

Rahkki jogged down the wide laddered trail that led from the mossy fortress to the Kihlari stable. Already he could smell the scent of the winged steeds in the air, and his heart thumped faster. He seemed the only person awake as he skipped through the dark training yard, his eyes fixed on the barn. The jungle surrounding the Fifth Clan settlement was quietest before dawn, as though inhaling a long breath before the explosion of noise that would announce the arrival of the sun and the wakening of the clan.

Thwack!

Something struck Rahkki in the back of the head and

he flew forward, striking the ground so hard it knocked the breath out of him. The missile rolled into his line of vision—a coconut.

"Where are you going so fast?" asked a deep voice. And Rahkki heard snickering.

He sat up, unable to speak. But he knew that voice. It was Mut Finn, the Sandwen teen who never had anything better to do than make trouble. He and two friends came around from the side of the hill.

"I asked you a question," said Mut, sauntering in front of Rahkki. He was fifteen years old and already the tallest male in the clan. Because of his size and bright-red hair, kids joked he had Gorlan blood in him—but never to his face.

Rahkki would normally run, but Mut was standing between him and Sula, and Rahkki wanted to see that wild mare again. He lurched unsteadily to his feet. "I left something in the barn," he answered, wheezing. But why was Mut out this early? His gang was breathing hard and dressed in black. Rahkki guessed they'd been out teasing droolers, the smaller dragons.

Mut smirked, eyeing Rahkki's bags. "I think I left something in your purse."

Rahkki blanched. It was time to run.

But Mut's long arm snatched him before he could take off. He ripped Rahkki's purse off his belt and opened it, feeling around inside.

Rahkki grimaced and his gut burned with helpless anger. He'd fought Mut before, when the teen was a head shorter, and *that* hadn't gone well. Now that Mut was man-size, fighting him was useless.

"There they are." Mut grinned, pulling out Rahkki's coins. "My eight jints. I knew I'd left these somewhere." He pocketed the last of Rahkki's money, grinned, and tossed the purse on the ground. "Thanks, Stormrunner," he said with mock politeness. Then he and his gang ran off, as swift as shadows.

Rahkki picked up the torn, empty purse. *That's it*, he thought. *I've not a coin to my name.* He laughed without humor, sounding exactly like his brother, and stuffed the purse into his satchel. Fuming, he arrived at the wooden doors of the Kihlari barn. Rahkki knocked softly and waited, looking around. The horse pasture and the homes of his clansmen bordered the Kihlari training yard. A few of his people were awake, tending immature fires and feeding livestock.

"Who is it?" whispered a voice from the other side of the door.

"It's me," Rahkki answered.

Koko cracked open the door and peeked out. "Bloody rain, what yuh doin' 'ere so early?"

"I came to see the wild brayas."

The head groom yanked him inside. "Well, aren't yuh two sneaks a pair," she said, crossing her arms.

"What?" Rahkki didn't understand Koko sometimes due to her odd accent. Her parents lived alone on the coast as hermits, and they'd raised Koko there, outside of the clan for most of her life. But when Koko outgrew the beach and returned to the Fifth Clan a year ago, she'd quickly secured a job in the Kihlari stable. Within months she was running it. Now she lived in a loft above the tack room that held the saddles and bridles, so she was never far from her charges. But sometimes, like now, her accent confused him. "What two sneaks?" he asked.

"Yuh and 'er!"

Rahkki followed Koko's gaze and spotted the queen's eldest daughter, Princess I'Lenna. She was standing in front of the blue roan's stall. He froze as though he were staring down a panther instead of a princess. I'Lenna was eleven, a year younger than he, but she was taller. She wore a yellow silk nightdress and rabbit-fur slippers, and her long, sun-streaked hair hung in an untidy braid. She seemed as surprised to see him as he to see her. Then she smiled, and turbulent feelings erupted inside Rahkki. After all, this girl's mother had murdered his.

Koko snorted, looking from one to the other. "Right. Yuh two chat; I got work ta do."

I'Lenna stepped toward him, her eyes shining. "Hi, Rahkki." Her cheerful tone struck him like a physical force, and he fell back. But she didn't stop; she closed the gap between them. "I couldn't wait to see the mares either," she said. "Just look at them!" She turned back toward Firo's and Sula's stalls, and exhaled in wonder. "They're incredible! I want to ride them, don't you?"

Rahkki swallowed and approached the mares, giving I'Lenna a wide berth. The last time he remembered playing with her was two years earlier. She'd snuck out of the fortress disguised as a villager to play tag in the fallows, the unplanted fields in the lowlands. She'd passed out candy to all the Sandwen kids. Everyone liked her; he remembered that. And he'd liked her too.

"Well," I'Lenna pressed, "don't you want to ride them?"

"They aren't trained," he said.

She narrowed her eyes. "I know that. I didn't mean right now. I'm just imagining."

He studied the mares. The injured blue roan was asleep, no doubt because of the drugs that Brim Carver had given her. The silver one, Sula, was nickering at her friend as if trying to wake her.

"I think they can talk to each other like we do," I'Lenna said.

Rahkki's heart stuttered. Was she serious? His eyes grazed I'Lenna's features. Her expression was sincere, and she rocked on her toes, awaiting his response. Rahkki flushed and lowered his voice. He didn't know anyone else who felt the way he did, that the Kihlari spoke to one another. "I think you're right," he said.

"Really?" She seemed delighted with that.

He exhaled and relaxed. I'Lenna was the crown princess of his clan, the first heir to the throne, but she was also a kid. "No one believes me," Rahkki said. "The Kihlari sound like horses to us, but I think they have their own language." He gestured toward the mares. "I think these two are friends."

"Of course they are." I'Lenna leaned over the stall door and stretched her free hand toward the blue roan.

"Careful," he warned her. "They don't like us."

"Oh, I know," she said. "I already tried to pet *that* one." I'Lenna's eyes drifted to Sula. "She's angry, and I don't blame her. It must be scary here, locked up in a barn after living free."

Rahkki watched I'Lenna watch the mares. "Where do you think they came from?" he asked.

Her eyes widened. "Could be from anywhere, right? Maybe they're a gift from the wind spirits, or maybe they rose out of the foam in the sea, or maybe they're fallen stars."

"Fallen stars?"

"Sure, why not?"

Rahkki finally returned her smile, adding, "Or they could have escaped from a clan Ruk a long time ago and learned to survive in the jungle."

She frowned. "That's possible, I guess, but I've never heard of a clan losing their Kihlari."

"True," he said. Around adults, Rahkki rarely spoke, and he didn't talk with kids much either. Born royal and then cast out an orphan—the clan kids acted awkward around him. But now, talking to I'Lenna about the wild Kihlari, he was reminded of how much he missed playing. "Okay, here's one," he said, letting his imagination loose. "Maybe they were statues in Daakur. They came to life and escaped the empire."

I'Lenna leaned toward him, nodding. "Yes," she said. "What else?"

"Or they flew here from another land, one we haven't discovered."

"Right," she added, "and then they got lost. Now they're trying to get back home, but they can't because they're trapped."

"That would make me angry," said Rahkki.

"Me too."

Rahkki snapped his finger. "What if their land got burned up? What if they're the only survivors?"

I'Lenna took his hand and squeezed his fingers. "Or maybe it's something completely different?"

Rahkki's mind went blank as he stared at the princess's small hand holding his.

"Maybe they aren't really here. Maybe we're imagining them," she continued.

The barn door creaked open. "Princess I'Lenna!" Harak's voice snapped at her like a whip.

She dropped Rahkki's hand and stood taller. "Yes."

Harak strode down the aisle and leaned over the princess, his jaw twitching. "How did you get out of the fortress?"

"I walked." I'Lenna said this with such a straight face that Rahkki snorted back a giggle.

Harak squinted at her, his green eyes hard and cool.

"You know what I meant. Do you have permission to be out? From your mother?"

She shook her head, and Rahkki gaped at her. The guards weren't allowed to let the bloodborn princesses out of the fortress without Lilliam's consent. So how did she do it?

But then he remembered that I'Lenna snuck out of Fort Prowl all the time—and not just to play in the fallows with the other kids. I'Lenna was a thief. She stole candy, lots of it. She smuggled it out of Fort Prowl's larders and hid it beneath kids' pillows, slinking into their rooms at night like a rat.

She'd done it to Rahkki once. He'd woken with a pep- permint stuck to his ear.

I'Lenna also lifted medicines from her mother's Borla, the clan healer. She slipped them to the young mothers in the village. Rahkki knew this because I'Lenna had been caught once and flogged for it, but that hadn't broken her. A few days after her flogging, he'd seen her pocket more remedies from the medical clinic and run off with them, grinning like a gibbon.

And it wasn't because she was defiant or malicious. I'Lenna was trying to help. When Rahkki's mother was queen, she'd dispensed medicine for free—most clans did.

But when I'Lenna's mother took over, she began charging villagers for it. She also collected tithes from the Fifth Clan—like the emperor did to his subjects in Daakur. Her greed was insatiable, probably because she hailed from the Second Clan, the poorest in the Sandwen Realm. But while none of Lilliam's new laws made her a popular queen, stealing medicines and giving them to poor mothers had made I'Lenna a popular princess.

Harak, who was glowering at I'Lenna, seemed to be on the same line of thinking as Rahkki. "You snuck out again, didn't you?"

Princess I'Lenna said nothing. Her back was straight, like an arrow, and her eyes burned through Harak. "I'll return to my mother now," she said. "You may go back to doing whatever it was you were doing, Harak Nightseer." I'Lenna about-faced and exited the barn without a backward glance.

Rahkki made the mistake of chuckling. Harak turned and slapped Rahkki so hard that he knocked him off his boots and into Sula's stall door. "You like what you see?" he asked.

Stunned, Rahkki picked himself up. *Was Harak talking about I'Lenna or the wild mares?*

The Headwind sneered, grinning like a jaguar. "Keep

away from the princess, yeah?"

Rahkki gulped. "Yeah."

Harak tossed back his blond hair, smirking now. "Those wild Kihlari are bonier than you are."

Rahkki said nothing.

The Headwind put his arm around him like they were friends. "I like that one," he said, pointing at the sleeping blue roan. "She has eyes like ice. Yeah? You like her too?"

"She'll make a good pet," Rahkki replied. "The silver one is the warrior."

"Hah, see? You've already picked one out. You belong in the clouds, little farmer, not on land." He poked at Rahkki, laughing.

Tuni Hightower arrived in the barn just as the morning bells rang down from the fortress, and she saw Rahkki cringing away from her counterpart. "Back off him, Harak."

"We're just talking," he said, looking at her with wide eyes.

She huffed and stalked off, calling for Koko, the head groom.

Harak winked at Rahkki, mouthing the words "little farmer," and then he left too.

Rahkki turned to the silver mare that he thought

would make a fine warrior. "Where *did* you come from?" he asked her.

Sula narrowed her eyes and rattled her feathers.

He gathered his satchel and backpack, wondering if he'd ever find out. Then he left the barn and began the long walk to Uncle's farm.

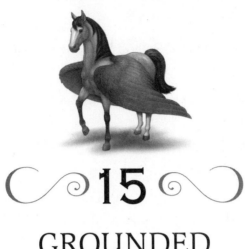

15

GROUNDED

ECHOFROST WATCHED THE YOUNG LANDWALKER cub walk out of the barn, feeling nervous. She didn't like how the yellow-haired one called Harak had struck him. "Shysong!" she neighed. "Are you awake?"

"Huh?" said the mare.

Echofrost guessed she was still groggy from the Landwalker medicine. "It's me, Echofrost. Are you hurt?"

Shysong stood and slid her head over the wall between them. Her blue eyes blinked slowly. "Oh no, they caught you too?"

"Don't worry about that. Just listen, okay? I'm going to get us out of here. I haven't figured out how yet, but I will." She'd thought it'd be as easy as kicking down a wall and

123

storming out of the barn, but the walls were too solid, and the netting over their heads kept them trapped.

"Where's our herd? Did anyone else get captured?" Shysong nickered.

"No, just me. The others . . . they left, I'm sure."

"Good. I'm glad they got away," she said. "The mission to find a new home is more important than you or me."

Echofrost winced. Shysong didn't know she'd come back for her on purpose, and the roan would feel conflicted if she found out. Echofrost decided not to correct the mare's assumption that she'd been captured against her will.

Just then the Landwalker called Brauk peered over Echofrost's stall door. Harak had returned with him, and behind them was another big male who she hadn't seen before. Echofrost took a sharp breath. *Don't move, don't fight—study them*, she reminded herself, but her pulse thumped hard in her throat.

Brauk glanced at the trampled hay and overturned water bucket. "She's not eating or drinking."

"Then she'll be weak and this will be easier," Harak said. He clutched a long stick in his hand, and he twirled it so fast it blurred.

Brauk frowned and turned to Echofrost. "This is a halter," he said to her. "And you're going to wear it."

Opening her door, he reached out and tried to slip the contraption over her head. Echofrost panicked and flew to the back of her stall. Brauk produced a stick similar to Harak's and followed her, brandishing it at her throat. She lunged, jaws wide, and Harak leaped to help Brauk. They struck at her chest, driving her deeper into the corner until her flanks brushed against the wood. Quivering now, Echofrost peered past Brauk, thinking to dart around him. But he saw the flick of her eyes and the collection of her muscles. He smacked her again. "No!"

She recoiled. The pain reminded her of a wasp sting. *No!* A hundred wasp stings!

While she was stunned, Brauk slipped the halter over her ears. She snapped at him, and he clubbed her over the head so hard that her vision flickered.

Echofrost whinnied for help. Her scream pierced the wood walls and rose into the sky, carrying for miles; but there was no answer, only Brauk covering his ears and Harak laughing. In Anok, a thousand warriors would have flown to her aid.

Ilan, Harak's spotted stallion, neighed to her. "Don't fight him, wildling. He's not going to kill you."

"He—he *hit* me," Echofrost sputtered.

"He'll hit you again if you don't calm down. You came

from a herd, right? Think of Brauk as your leader and do what he wants."

"What does he want?" Echofrost snapped as the pain subsided into a dull ache.

"If we're lucky, it's to bathe you," said Kol.

The few Kihlari still in the barn nickered at her, and Echofrost gasped. *They thought this was funny!*

Brauk shifted and pulled something soft over her eyes, making the world go dark. She tossed her head and reared, but the soft hood wouldn't come loose. Then hard pressure cut into her nose as Brauk tugged hard on her halter. She dropped to all fours, confused and blinded, but the horrible pressure immediately stopped. Next she felt Brauk touching her wings and she yanked them out of his grasp. "What's he doing to my feathers?" she whinnied.

The neighboring Kihlari steeds went silent.

"Help me!" Brauk called to his friends.

She heard the extra Landwalkers he'd brought with him rush toward her. Brauk pinched her muzzle in his hand and squeezed. His grip was like the bite of a puma, and her instincts told her to hold still. She felt ropes tighten around her legs.

With a sharp tug, they yanked her off her hooves and she slammed onto the hard floor. Her chest heaved as she absorbed the pain, and Echofrost felt like a weanling again, like when she'd been attacked by Mountain Herd yearlings. Now she squealed angrily and clamped down the feelings that were erupting inside of her—helplessness and rage; they mixed together and lit a storm inside her.

The Landwalkers grabbed her hooves and rolled her onto her back. One sat on her neck while the others held her down. Her fast breaths filled her ears, like she'd dived into an icy pond.

Next they gripped her wings and stretched them out. Then she heard clicking noises, and Brauk's hot breath filled her nostrils, stinking of meat. She couldn't see, couldn't think.

Then just as suddenly as it had begun, it was over. Brauk and his friends leaped away from her and tugged the animal skin from her eyes. They released her front hooves and yanked on her halter, pulling her upright.

She rose, trembling, and glared at Brauk. He held his club high, threatening her. Echofrost remembered Thundersky. He'd expected instant obedience, and as long as he had it, he never hurt her. Echofrost lowered her head, though it crushed her soul to do so. *Don't strike him*, she told herself, her legs trembling. *There are too many of them. The time isn't right.*

But what had the Landwalkers done to her wings? She fanned them, noticing they felt different, lighter. Then she saw the damage and she reeled, inhaling sharply. *Brauk had sliced off the ends of her flight feathers.* She backed away in horror and heard crunching noises beneath her hooves. She looked down. The cuttings from her beautiful purple feathers lay crumpled on the stall floor.

Echofrost panted, and her blood rushed between her ears. She felt dizzy and sick. She whinnied. "No, no!" Violent shudders ran from her ears to her tail.

Brauk stared at her with some compassion in his eyes. "Sorry, braya, but we can't have you flying away."

She couldn't understand his words, so she whinnied to the Kihlari. "He . . . he cut my feathers!" Echofrost expected sympathetic outrage from the foreign pegasi. Brauk had *grounded* her, like a *horse*!

"They'll grow back," said Ilan, who was yawning in the heat. "He just doesn't want you getting away until he knows what to do with you."

Echofrost slowed her breathing and swiveled her head toward Brauk. She'd vowed to kill his little brother when she escaped, but now she changed her mind. Brauk would be the first to die. Blast it! Why wait? She reared to strike him, but Brauk was ready. He slammed his club down on her forehead, making her stagger into the barn wall. Her vision blackened, and she gasped for breath.

Then Brauk pulled hard on her halter, and Echofrost automatically walked forward to relieve the pressure. In a daze of pain and anger, she followed him, glaring at his back. She imagined how he'd feel if she broke his legs, rendering *him* unable to walk. But from the depth of her anger rose knowledge; it floated up like a bubble and popped open inside her mind: Brauk had cut her flight feathers to correct an imbalance of power between them— the fact that she could fly and *he* couldn't. But her feathers would grow back; and when they did, she could fly away, shifting the power back to her. She stored that information for later.

"Good girl," Brauk said. He lowered the stick, dropping his guard.

Echofrost pricked her ears, listening closely to his voice, noticing he was pleased with her because she was following him. Echofrost stored that information away too: obedience made Brauk believe he was safe with her.

Echofrost exhaled and regained control of her breathing. She guessed it would be a full cycle of the moon before she could fly again, and it was too risky to escape overland, what with dragons, poisonous ants, panthers, the

Gorlan giants, and who knew what else roaming in the woods. Besides that, horses were faster than pegasi on land, and the Landwalkers had plenty of horses to use to chase her. She was going to be stuck here much longer than she'd anticipated. How would she ever catch up to Hazelwind and Storm Herd?

Brauk led her past Shysong's stall, and she nickered to her friend. "Did Brauk cut your feathers too?"

"I don't know who did it," Shysong answered, sounding dazed. "I must have been sleeping, but yes, someone cut them."

Her anger swelled, but Echofrost also saw that a poultice had been packed into Shysong's punctured wing. The Landwalkers were healing her, and that much was good. Before she could say another word to her friend, Brauk pulled hard on her halter and led her out the barn door.

They emerged into blistering heat and painful sunlight. Echofrost balked, squinting. Brauk paused, letting her adjust to the outdoors and the flurry of activity around her. Overhead, Riders flew their Kihlari, playing and training. Nearer to her, foreign pegasi crisscrossed the dirt yard, ridden or led by hand.

Her eyes adjusted and she examined her surroundings. Long, wide steps led upward from the training yard to the eight-sided fortress at the top of the hill. To the north, she saw the horse pens and beyond that a cluster of several hundred Landwalker dens. The jungle pressed against the settlement, its branches swishing, full of chattering birds and other branch-dwellers. Sea salt spiced the warm winds, a reminder of the Dark Water that lay to the north. Echofrost swiveled her head and spotted the eastern mountain range that the Kihlari called Mount Crim. That's where the Gorlan giants lived. It was only a day or two away by flight, farther by land. To the left of that were the volcanoes, the dwelling place of the little dragons Kol had called *burners*.

She startled when a large winged stallion whooshed past her, flapping his wings, bringing her attention back to the yard. Contented nickers and a merry jingling sound filled her ears. Echofrost realized the noise was coming from the pegasi and their Riders—from shiny, round objects tied into their hair and tails that rang as they hurried about. She took a breath, feeling confused. It seemed everyone had somewhere to go, something to do, but she sensed no pressing concerns—no predators on the wind, no shortage of forage or water—so why all the activity?

Brauk, sensing she'd got her bearings, make a clucking noise and tugged on her halter. It was easier to follow him than fight him, so she followed, threading between the Kihlari steeds. Their Riders talked and laughed, sharing food and playing rough. They had long hair that twisted down their backs, and some had bright pegasus feathers tied to their wrists. Young Landwalkers had short hair, but all had lethal weapons strapped to their waists and backs.

A huge winged stallion trotted past Echofrost ridden by an older female Rider. "Get out of my way, wildling!" the pegasus brayed. He was gray, and his expression was intense as he clumped along, swishing his tail. He bumped her shoulder hard as he passed her.

Echofrost stepped back and accidentally cut off a cantering mare. The red roan pegasus nipped her flank and whinnied. "Watch where you're walking!"

"You're popular," Brauk said, pulling her forward.

Echofrost reared, unwilling to walk farther into the melee, but Brauk lifted his club, and that threat she understood. She dropped to all four hooves and followed as he wove her through the chaos.

The Landwalker warrior named Tuni dived down from the clouds, riding her golden pinto named Rizah. The mare nodded to Echofrost, and her gold-edged pink feathers caused a layer of soil to swirl up from the ground and into Echofrost's mouth. She coughed as Rizah and Tuni hovered overhead.

"What is it?" Brauk asked Tuni, shielding his eyes from the sun as he looked up at her.

She yelled down to him, her brown eyes glowing. "The Highland horde is moving closer. They've set up a camp at the base of Mount Crim."

"That's not good." Brauk gazed east, toward the mountains.

She nodded. "Especially with the Clan Gathering and the Kihlari auction coming up. The other clans will be packed and traveling here by now."

Echofrost listened to them, wishing she could understand their language. This was one of their strengths—that they could talk to each other—and she stored that information away too.

"Is it just the Highland horde?" Brauk asked.

Tuni's mount reared when a stallion blasted by her, his Rider hollering to another in the distant sky. "Easy, Rizah," she said, patting her mare's neck. Tuni shifted, keeping her balance while answering Brauk. "We only saw the one camp, but since they've shared soup with the Fire horde, I'm sure they're coming down too." Tuni leaned over Rizah's shoulder. "Their scouts are throwing trees at us, Brauk—big trees. They've whittled the trunks into sharp points."

"May the sun fry them," Brauk said, and he spit on the dirt at his feet.

Tuni spit too. Then she glanced at the fortress on the hill above the training yard. "The queen has called another meeting with her advisers. We'll know soon what we're to do." She glanced at Echofrost with approval. "Your braya looks calm."

Brauk's lips curved, showing his blunt white teeth. "A few wallops with this, and now she follows me like a pup." He lifted his club.

Tuni shook her head. "Never mind, I don't want to hear about it. Is the blue roan awake?"

"Yep. She's in the barn."

Pricking her ears, Echofrost tried hard to decipher their words, but their language sounded like nothing but a long stream of noise punctuated by rises and falls in pitch.

"Good," said Tuni. "I'll get to the roan after I finish my runs on Rizah. The auction is in twenty-eight days. We have that long to get them fat, trained, and ready to sell. Did you hear the queen's proclamation this morning?"

Brauk shook his head.

"She's allowing the Sky Guard half the earnings from

their sale." Tuni grinned. "That's a lot of new weapons, hay, and armor."

"We caught them, we should get it all," Brauk said, and then changed the subject. "Have you seen my brother?"

"Rahkki? Yes, I saw him walking to your uncle's farm with his things." Tuni drew in her eyebrows. "Didn't you two say good-bye?"

Brauk's golden eyes darkened. "Yeah . . . I guess we did."

"There's my squad," said Tuni. "Catch you tonight." She pulled back on the leathers that were attached to Rizah's mouth, and the pair shot up toward the clouds. Tuni's red hair, which was decorated with Rizah's pretty feathers, whipped against her back, and Rizah's shining tail fluttered in the wind.

"Come on, girl." Brauk yanked on Echofrost's lead rope.

Her mind reeled, succumbing again to panic. *No!* Echofrost dug her hooves into the packed soil.

Brauk whacked her left shoulder, stinging the muscles there. She glared at him. *Cooperate and he won't hit you. You control this, not him. Just wait.* Echofrost dropped her head and limped along behind him, her shoulder stinging where he'd hit her.

Brauk led her into a shallow depression of sand. "Buckets," he hollered.

Three young Landwalkers emerged from the shadows carrying containers of water. Echofrost spun in a circle. *What are those for?* Seconds later she knew.

It was time for her bath.

⚡ 16 ⚡

HUNGER

FOUR DAYS PASSED AFTER THE HORRIBLE BATH, and Echofrost lay in her stall, taking short, shallow breaths. She was dying, and it was her own fault because she refused to eat the Landwalkers' food—the Kihlari called it *hay*—and she'd only allowed herself a few sips of their water when her thirst became unbearable. She'd assumed the Landwalkers would figure out what she needed: a fresh stream and access to grasslands; but no, Brauk kept pitching dry hay at her hooves until her body began to fail her. And now she was in dire trouble.

And worse, she didn't care. Hazelwind was gone, Storm Herd had left her, she'd made no progress in freeing Shysong, her flight feathers were cut, and she lived in a stall.

She felt hopeless. She missed the wind in her feathers and the clouds below her hooves.

Brauk entered the barn and stood in the aisleway, staring at her and tugging on his long dark hair. He wore it down today and loose, falling below his shoulders, but small sections, he'd braided. Jingling bells, colorful stones, and vibrant feathers were woven throughout the thin plaits—*her* feathers, and Kol's too. They fluttered in the breeze from the open doorway where he stood, and she stared at her cut plumage, transfixed.

"You're gonna die, braya," Brauk said to her, his voice soft.

Echofrost pricked her ears. Why did he talk to her when he knew she couldn't understand him? She usually didn't waste time talking to *him*, but this time she answered. "Take me outside. I want to feed myself."

Brauk stared at her, his expression blank. She knew he heard her voice, but to him she probably sounded like a nickering horse. Since he couldn't understand her, she added, "You look like a big, ugly monkey."

Still no response from Brauk.

Frustrated, Echofrost turned away. Dying in this stall didn't feel like giving up, but taking their food, *that* felt like giving in. Like if she took a bite, she was agreeing to all this. *But you chose to be here,* her body screamed. *Shut up,* her mind shouted back. Echofrost was at war with herself.

She lifted her head and then let it drop back into the straw. This hunger was worse than when she'd flown over the Dark Water. At least on that journey she'd had hope in her heart, fire in her gut, and friends by her side. She wondered where Hazelwind, Graystone, Redfire, Dewberry, and Storm Herd were now. Already at the eastern coast, crossing another ocean, or were they battling spit dragons and Gorlan giants in the jungle?

She stared at the four wooden walls that penned her and then at the wooden ceiling high above that cut off her view of the sky—and she felt numb, like she was buried in ice.

Tuni emerged from the tack room after putting away Rizah's saddle and bridle.

Brauk called her over. "I can't get this braya to eat or drink."

Tuni chuckled. "You met someone more stubborn than yourself?"

Brauk frowned. "If she dies, there go our earnings for the Sky Guard. How's your roan doing?"

"She tried to hold out too," said Tuni, glancing toward

Shysong. "But last night she broke and started eating. I think Rahkki was right about these two steeds. The blue roan is pet stock, but the silver mare has warrior blood. Her will is strong, and she'll make a good Flier, if she doesn't starve to death first." Tuni flicked her eyes toward Echofrost.

"Right. Whatever. Maybe I should just put her down and strip off the rest of her feathers. I could make a hundred charms for the auction, sell 'em for forty jints apiece, maybe fifty. The other clans will pay a lot for wildling feathers."

Tuni shook her head. "At *that* price you wouldn't sell half of them, and I think it's too early to give up on her. Maybe in another day she'll give in. Has the queen seen how thin she's gotten?"

"Not yet. Lilliam's too busy screaming at her council about the giant horde. They broke camp and moved in closer last night. She needs to send us out, and I don't know what she's waiting for."

"The right timing," said Tuni. "I heard that her Borla had a bad dream, a vision. He said he saw the giant hordes on the move with over a hundred captured Kihlari steeds. That's almost half our force. So even though Granak ate the sow, the bad dream foretells defeat. She won't attack until there's a better omen."

"She's afraid to fail, that's the real problem." Brauk kicked the dirt floor. "And I'm running out of time. This braya has to be trained in twenty-four days. How would it look for the Sky Guard of the Fifth Clan to auction off a bony, sour mare who's barely halter broke?"

Tuni touched his hand. "But she *is* a Kihlara, a Child of the Wind. She would fetch a decent price if she were a hundred years old and swaybacked."

Echofrost pricked her ears, catching their excited tones and intense expressions, as if they were arguing. Landwalkers were more like pegasi than she'd ever imagined.

Brauk smiled, but his gold eyes darkened. "I'll wait one more day. If she's not eating by tomorrow, I'm going to put her down."

"Suit yourself." Tuni strode away from him, her back stiff, and then she said over her shoulder, "I bet Rahkki could fix that braya for you."

Echofrost grunted as a hunger pain ripped through her belly.

Brauk watched Tuni stalk off, and then he opened Echofrost's door and shouted at her. "Get up and eat, you stupid horse!"

Echofrost lurched to her hooves and charged him, fueled by rage and pain. She snapped at his leg, but he jumped free of her just in time. Then he grabbed his stick and shoved her into the back of her stall, pinning her with it. "Try that again." He peered straight into her eyes.

Echofrost flattened her ears but held steady. She knew that Shysong had given in and was eating, and it was driving Echofrost crazy. She had to get the mare out before she became as tame and dependent as the creatures that trotted at the heels of the Landwalkers, the ones they called *dogs*.

Brauk slammed her stall door shut and then entered Kol's pen next door. Soon she heard soothing sounds and soft nickering. The powerful stallion adored Brauk; she'd noticed that in the short time she was here. Kol rubbed his head on Brauk's chest, ate treats from his hands, and knelt to let the man climb onto his back. Kol's eyes never wavered from Brauk when he was near.

And Brauk, for all his gruffness with her, was kind to Kol. He spoke to him softly and scratched his hide in ways that pleased Kol, and he didn't yank on Kol's halter. He demanded nothing of the winged stallion, but Kol did everything Brauk asked of him.

She watched the Landwalker cuddle his stallion, stroking his muzzle, and then Brauk glanced past her and Kol to the open barn door. Echofrost followed his gaze. It was dusk, the light was quickly dimming, and thousands of insects screeched in the jungle beyond. Brauk paused for a long time, and then he seemed to make a decision. He glanced at Echofrost. "Land to skies, braya, you know I'm sick of your attitude, but my brother—he *likes* you. Maybe he can help." Brauk snapped his fingers at Kol, and the stallion knelt. Brauk climbed onto his back and rode the stallion out of the Kihlari den with no saddle and only the halter and lead rope to guide him.

Once outside, Echofrost watched the shiny chestnut stallion gallop across the yard, flapping his wings until his hooves lifted off the ground. Brauk whooped and Kol whinnied, and they soared up into the clouds and flew out of her sight. She craned her neck, hunting for any sign of Hazelwind or Dewberry, Graystone or Redfire in the sky—but she knew they wouldn't be there.

Then she noticed something interesting. In his haste, Brauk had forgotten to shut the barn door. Echofrost tensed, staring at the easy escape. She glanced up at the netting over her head. If she could just bite through it! She'd tried that her first few days with no success, but now there was an open door and a crescent moon. The sky would be dark tonight. But where was Shysong? Tuni had taken her out to train her, and they hadn't yet returned.

Echofrost set to work chewing at her netting. If she got loose, then she could find Shysong in the training yard or the horse arena with Tuni. They couldn't fly yet and the jungle was dangerous, but Echofrost no longer thought that waiting for their feathers to grow back was wise. She'd rather face all the dangers of the jungle at once than spend another day with Brauk.

She bit into the fibrous rope and sawed her teeth back and forth.

After several moments soft hoofbeats broke her concentration. She grunted, expecting Kol or Rizah. "What?" she nickered, irritated. She looked up and was face-to-face with Hazelwind.

She gasped.

Behind Hazelwind was Dewberry. Echofrost's spine tingled. *Were they real?* Hazelwind stretched his beautiful head toward her. "I'm here," he whispered.

Several Kihlari heard Hazelwind's unfamiliar voice, and whinnies of alarm rang through the aisles.

Relief flooded Echofrost's heart. "I—I thought you left."

"We did," Hazelwind admitted. His dark eyes scanned her stall and the thick netting over her head. "But we came back." He gave her a meaningful look that made her belly flip. "We've been watching this den from the heights, but this was our first chance to get inside." He grimaced, perplexed. "How do I get you out of there?"

"I don't know." Echofrost could guess the anguish that his decision to come back had caused him. Hazelwind was duty bound, and she knew that stalling the mission to rescue her and Shysong went against the very nature of his soul, his upbringing.

But he'd done it for her! "Where are the others?" she asked quickly.

"They're waiting for us in the trees," Dewberry answered. "The pegasi who were born to Jungle Herd taught us how to build nests. We're safe from predators up there."

Hazelwind nodded. "We thought it'd be easier for just two of us to sneak in and get you out." He glanced at the stalls around her. "Where's Shysong?"

"Outside. We'll have to find her, but this netting is too thick to bite through," she whispered. "And Shysong and I can't fly. They . . . cut our flight feathers."

Hazelwind arched his neck, rumbling. "They *grounded* you?"

"Shh, just open the door."

He grasped at the complicated lock with his wingtips, then turned around and kicked it as hard as he could with both hind hooves. "By the Ancestors!" He shuffled from hoof to hoof. "That door is as hard as stone."

Dewberry tried next, with the same result.

A sharp clicking noise drew Echofrost's and Hazelwind's attention. Standing at the end of the aisle was Koko. She stood on the balls of her feet, her breath coming fast, her eyes locked on Echofrost's rescuers. She had an arrow drawn and aimed at Hazelwind's chest.

Echofrost fluttered her purple feathers. "That's the weapon they used to shoot Shysong!"

Hazelwind turned slowly and faced the girl. He lowered his neck and flared his wings, threatening her right back. Dewberry joined him, spreading her wings wide and striking her hoof against the floor.

Sweat beaded on Koko's forehead. She pulled the arrow

back farther, and closed one eye. "Yuh aren't takin' that braya," she said, her voice cool and calm.

Hazelwind stepped toward her, and Koko exhaled.

"No," Echofrost cried. "She'll shoot you. Just go."

Koko loosed the arrow. Hazelwind dodged to the side, and it grazed a thin line of blood across his hide. His nostrils flared, and he trumpeted a challenge. Koko had already nocked another arrow.

Outside the barn, Echofrost spotted a patrol flying down from the night sky.

"A patrol is landing!" she neighed. "Leave while you can. I'll figure a way out of here."

Another arrow flew, slicing another trail of blood across Hazelwind's buckskin chest. Koko advanced, and Echofrost realized she wasn't trying to kill Hazelwind, just scare him away—but she also believed Koko would kill Hazelwind if he didn't leave.

He seemed to come to the same conclusion. "This isn't over," he blared at Koko.

"She can't understand you," Echofrost whinnied.

"Oh, she understands me well enough," said Hazelwind, glaring at Koko. Then to Echofrost he neighed, "I see how it is. Next time I'll bring more steeds."

Then he and Dewberry lifted off and soared over the

stable girl's head, out the door, and into the blustering heights where the Sky Guard Riders couldn't fly.

Echofrost watched them until Koko slammed the barn door shut, cutting off the glow of the moon. Slowly, Echofrost's heartbeat returned to normal and then expanded with hope. Hazelwind had not abandoned her.

C⁓ 17 ⁓C

THE FARMER

"GET UP, GIRL," RAHKKI SAID, CLUCKING AT HIS uncle's swamp buffalo. He'd been a farmer's apprentice for almost four full days now, and he was busy helping Uncle Darthan prepare a new rice field for the following season. His uncle was farther away, tending the mature plants on the lower plains. It was almost dark, and Rahkki had just one more irrigation ditch to dig before nightfall.

"Get up," Rahkki repeated. He was standing on the end of a trencher, which was like a plow, except that it cut one long rip into the soil at a time. It was hitched to his uncle's swamp buffalo. Rahkki clucked at her, urging her forward. He'd named the beast Lutegar, which meant "lazy" in Talu, but he spoke to her in Sandwen. "Move!"

Uncle Darthan's rice farm was located northwest of Fort Prowl and bordered by the River Tsallan, which was wide and long and dumped into the black-sand ocean in the north. Rahkki's uncle diverted water from the river to irrigate his rice fields, and his crops provided the bulk of the rations for the land soldiers.

But heavy afternoon rains had further drenched the soil today, and Lutegar, who liked to wallow in mud, lay down in her traces every ten steps to roll in it. Rahkki shouted commands at her, waved the whip his uncle had given him, and cursed her to the clouds and back; but she merely swiveled her big ears. He tried to scare her forward with low growls and sudden movements, but Lutegar watched him with fearless eyes.

Now Rahkki abandoned his perch and stumbled toward her. Placing both hands on her gray rump, he pushed. Lutegar bellowed but didn't budge. He pushed harder. She leaned onto her side. Rahkki was dripping sweat, and each time he had to get off the trencher, his feet sank deep into the turned-up soil. His only pair of boots was soaked, the worn leather ruined.

He marched to Lutegar's head. "Up!" he commanded, pulling on her harness. "Please." He grabbed her horns and stretched her neck out straight. She groaned, but her hooves didn't shift, and the sun was dropping fast. Rahkki let go of her horns and walked ahead of her, thinking she might follow him. She didn't. He stopped and stared at her big, flat face. "You would sleep here all night, wouldn't you?"

She blinked her black eyelids.

"Well, that's the problem, isn't it?" he said, leaning against her. "You aren't afraid of anything. You're too big for the dragon to eat and too heavy for a Gorlan giant to carry away."

Lutegar whipped her short tail at a fly.

Rahkki glanced at the rice bed where his uncle worked, pulling weeds, hunched over and concentrating. "You're making me look bad," he said to her.

She groaned softly, as if to say: *You don't need my help for that.*

Stumped, Rahkki walked over and sat on her back. Lutegar didn't like that. She heaved herself up and began walking. "Hey there! That's better." Rahkki squeezed his legs, urging her to walk faster. She turned her head to bump him with her horns, but her neck was too short. She gave a weak buck, but that only made Rahkki laugh.

"You'll have to do better than that to get me off."

Rahkki had ridden horses since he was two. The village kids teased him, calling him Rahkki the Spider because he stuck to unruly horses like a spider sticks to its web. It wasn't the worst thing to be called, Rahkki had decided, except when it was followed up by the older kids catching him and throwing *actual* spiders down his pants.

Rahkki patted Lutegar. "I'll get off at the end of the field," he promised her. "Just keep walking."

The swamp buffalo dug into her work and dragged the trencher, forming a deep ditch. Rahkki stretched his arms toward the disappearing sun. "I am King of Beasts," he bellowed, and his voice rang out over the valley. No one but Uncle Darthan heard him, and his uncle didn't look up from his work. Rahkki wondered what Princess I'Lenna would think of him, riding a buffalo. He shook his head. No, she wouldn't be impressed. She wanted to ride the wild pegasi. I'Lenna was as fearless as Lutegar.

While Rahkki pondered, Lutegar trudged obligingly to the far end of the field and then Rahkki leaped off her wide back. When he turned around to admire their work, his heart sank. The ditch was crooked. Since he'd been riding Lutegar and not guiding the trencher, it had fallen over and zigzagged side to side, chewing up the land so that the destruction was as wide as it was deep. The new ditch now cut into the future bed where the rice would grow—or not. Rahkki stared, wringing his hands.

Just then Uncle Darthan arrived from the lower fields to inspect Rahkki's progress. He beheld the torn-up field, blinking as slowly as Lutegar.

"I'm sorry," Rahkki said.

His uncle pointed. "That doesn't look like work. That looks like play."

Rahkki's jaw dropped. His boots were ruined, he was soaked in sweat and mud, and he was pretty sure he'd ripped a hole in the back of his trousers. "I had no fun doing it . . . I promise."

His uncle frowned. "Maybe you will have fun cleaning it up."

Rahkki glared at Lutegar. The clan liked to joke that he was a Meld, someone who could communicate with animals. But Lutegar was living proof that he could not. "She doesn't listen to me."

Uncle Darthan peered at Rahkki, his sun-darkened face as still as the deep river that flowed behind his hut. "It's *you* who doesn't listen to *her*."

"She's not a Kihlara, Uncle," Rahkki sputtered. "She doesn't have a thought in her head. I can't get to her."

His uncle's lips curved gently. "She's certainly gotten

to you." He pointed at Lutegar's right horn and whistled. The swamp buffalo trotted to his side like a well-trained pony.

"Hey! How'd you do that?"

Uncle Darthan and Lutegar headed toward the barn. "I'll put her up," he said, chuckling like a contented hen. "You get inside." Uncle glanced up at Sunchaser. The pale moon was a thin crescent in the sky. "This is a night for dragons."

Rahkki shivered, realizing how dark it had gotten, and he sprinted toward his uncle's hut. The giant, drooling dragons hunted on dark nights, and they were known to eat boys Rahkki's age. But Rahkki was careful. He slept with his shutters closed, and he didn't bait the dragons like Mut Finn and his friends. Teasing dragons didn't prove anything really, except how fast you could run (or couldn't).

He froze when a voice called out his name. "Rahkki!"

Looking up, he spotted his brother hovering overhead, flying on Kol. The chestnut stallion descended, and the wind from his huge wings whirled Rahkki's hair. "What are you doing here?" Rahkki asked. "What's wrong?"

"I need your help with something. Go ask Uncle if I

can borrow you for a few hours."

Rahkki's heart surged. He didn't care what Brauk wanted him to do; *anything* was better than spending another boring night indoors with Uncle. Uncle was kind, but about as exciting as the plants he grew.

Rahkki trotted to the barn and asked Uncle Darthan for permission to leave with Brauk, and he was surprised by how quickly Darthan agreed. "Yes! And I'll pack you a dinner." He shut the barn door and they returned to his cabin together. "Call your brother inside while I prepare."

But Brauk was already striding into the hut with Kol. The big stallion lowered his head to fit through the doorway.

Darthan broke into a wide grin at the sight of the chestnut. "Your Flier looks good."

"Thanks," Brauk said, puffing at the compliment. "I'm trying a new grain that I bought from the Fourth Clan. It's working—he's shinier than ever." Brauk pointed down. "And look at those hooves! They're smooth as river stones."

Uncle nodded approval as he opened his larder and removed three strips of buffalo jerky, a rice ball, and a scoop of salted seeds. "Your mother would be proud of you," he said.

Rahkki's eyes shifted to Brauk. He didn't like talking about their mother, not with Rahkki or anyone else. "What's done is done," he'd grumble when Rahkki tried to question him about her. Brauk was thirteen—a man— when Reyella was assassinated, and Rahkki wondered how much his brother blamed himself for her death, and the death of their unborn sibling. But tonight Brauk just nodded, letting his uncle's comment pass without temper.

Darthan finished packing Rahkki's dinner into his satchel, which already carried his empty purse, some dried sinew, a few Kihlari feathers, his blowgun, which he used to dart fish in the River Tsallan, and his game of stones. He was grateful when Brauk struck up a new conversation.

"Are you ready for the giants if they come?" he asked Darthan. "You know they're on the move. They'll try to destroy the crops."

Uncle nodded with a wry smile. "I'm as ready as one man can be." Uncle hired extra workers during the planting and harvesting seasons, but otherwise he ran the farm alone, until now.

Brauk grunted. "The queen will send the Land Guard here. She'll protect her—I mean *your* land."

The room went still again. The farm was another sore

subject—but not for Brauk, for Uncle. After Lilliam assassinated their mother and then failed to kill her sons, their uncle had stepped in quickly to protect them. He swore his rice farm, the largest farm in the seven clans, to Queen Lilliam and her Land Guard in exchange for his nephews' lives. Uncle Darthan had transformed himself from a wealthy landowner to Lilliam's indentured servant in the span of a heartbeat.

The queen's greed led her to accept the offer, and all seven Sandwen queens were present to seal the pact at a Clan Gathering. Lilliam later regretted the deal because she'd made it in haste. Brauk and Rahkki had been young and harmless then, but each day they'd grown older and more dangerous, like baby tigers. Rahkki didn't plan to seek vengeance on Lilliam, but he saw that concern in her eyes each time she looked at him.

"This should feed you well," Darthan said, handing Rahkki the packed satchel. "I added an apple for Kol and a slice of honeycomb for you, Brauk."

Brauk grinned, and the tension left the hut. Honeycomb was Brauk's favorite treat, but rare. Only the First Clan kept bees, and they charged richly for the honey they collected.

"I'll have Rahkki back soon," Brauk promised.

"Keep him as long as you want," said Darthan.

Rahkki frowned, and Uncle patted his back. "Just have him back by dawn," he corrected.

Was he imagining it or did Uncle seem eager for him to go? Rahkki thought back over their last few evenings together. Was he annoying? He tried to sit quietly and stare at the fire, like Darthan; but Rahkki enjoyed humming and tossing fat into the flames, making them sizzle and spark. And when that got boring, he tried to be helpful.

The first night he'd fleshed buffalo hides, but that ended when he broke Uncle's carving bone. The next evening he'd made wax dolls using candles, thinking to sell them at the coming Clan Gathering, but his uncle took the wax away after Rahkki had set the curtains on fire. The following night he spiced the stew, not realizing that his uncle had already done so, and that meal had to be fed to the pigs.

But Uncle was never angry about these mishaps; instead he taught Rahkki how to fix his mistakes. Overall, Rahkki thought things were going well, but perhaps Uncle felt otherwise. The man had lived alone for thirty-five years, and maybe he did find Rahkki's humming and foot tapping and fire baiting bothersome.

But Rahkki wasn't about to wait for Uncle to change his mind. As soon as Darthan handed him his cold dinner packed in his satchel, he raced out of the hut with a wave, followed by Brauk and Kol.

The stallion knelt, and Brauk climbed aboard, then snatched Rahkki's hand, lifting him off his feet and dropping him onto Kol's back behind him. Rahkki tucked his dinner satchel over his shoulder and wrapped his arms around his brother's waist.

"Ready?" Brauk asked.

Before Rahkki could answer, Brauk squeezed Kol's sides, sending the stallion flying forward. Rahkki's gut flipped and he looked down, watching the farm shrink beneath his dangling feet.

He gripped his brother's waist tighter, sitting dead center on Kol's back. The stallion's ribs expanded and contracted between Rahkki's legs, and his bright wings hinged at his shoulders, pressing down on the wind. Rahkki felt dizzy as they sailed over the jungle.

"Want to fly higher?" Brauk asked.

"No!" Rahkki yelled this so loudly that their uncle probably heard him.

"Faster then?"

Rahkki leaned against Brauk's warm back. "No, please."

A long chuckle ran through his brother. Rahkki's fear of heights was why he would never ride a Kihlara by himself, and the reason he would not join the Sky Guard, even if he had a full round of dramals to purchase his own winged steed.

Brauk patted Kol's neck and Rahkki noticed a purple feather tied to his wrist. Kol's yellow one hung from his other wrist. "Is that Sula's feather?" Rahkki asked.

"Yes, I trimmed that wild braya's wings so she can't fly away. The feathers will grow back in time for the auction, if she's still alive."

Rahkki tensed. "What do you mean, *if she's still alive?*"

"That's why I'm here. She won't eat or drink," Brauk grumbled. "You call her a warrior, but I say she's a mule. If you can't fix her, I'm going to put her down tomorrow."

"You can't kill her, Brauk! She's a Kihlara. She's too . . . valuable."

Brauk shook his head. "She's weak and untrained, worthless the way she is, and I won't let her starve to death in her stall. That's cruel."

Rahkki imagined the wild silver mare. She'd been

fierce and wiry when he'd seen her four days ago, and he couldn't imagine her giving up. Then he remembered her stillness, like a hunting serpent. *She's waiting for what she wants*, he thought. But what did a wild Kihlara want? Rahkki thought hard and then he smiled. "I think I can help her."

18

THE LANDWALKER CUB

QUIET FOOTSTEPS TAPPED ACROSS THE DIRT floor, approaching Echofrost's stall. She was still reeling from Hazelwind and Dewberry's visit earlier that evening. Shysong was back in her stall now, and she'd not taken the news well that Storm Herd was hiding in high nests they'd built in the jungle, plotting on how to help them escape. "We're all going to end up captured," she moaned.

"Not if we keep our heads," said Echofrost. It was late, and her exhaustion had returned. But Echofrost recognized the footfalls of Brauk coming toward her. She'd hoped he'd let her sleep, but he was back again, and he'd brought his small look-alike brother with him.

"There. Take a look at her," Brauk said.

The cub named Rahkki peered over her wall and gasped when he saw her. He opened her stall door and dropped to his knees, but out of her striking range. Tears filled his eyes, and Echofrost blinked at him, shocked. *Could Landwalkers cry?*

The boy spoke in a choked whisper. "Why'd you wait so long to get me, Brauk?"

"I didn't think she'd be this stubborn."

A voice interrupted them. "Ay, who goes?"

Rahkki looked up to see Koko facing them with a loaded bow, the arrow drawn back.

"It's us, calm down," said Brauk.

She lowered her arm. "Two a their wild friends came outta the sky. Tried ta free 'em."

"You saw them?" Rahkki asked. Echofrost watched the pulse quicken in his throat.

"Well, I didn' imagine 'em," she answered. "A buckskin and a pinto, standin' righ' there." She pointed to where Brauk was standing in front of Echofrost's stall. "I chased 'em off."

"Well done," said Brauk, and Koko ambled away, looking as smug as a monkey.

Rahkki turned back to Echofrost and lowered his voice. She pricked her ears, listening to the soothing sounds emitting from his throat.

Rahkki reached his hand toward her, and Echofrost shied away from him.

"She doesn't like to be touched," Brauk said.

"I know that," Rahkki whispered. "Just stop talking."

The cub inched closer to her, and Echofrost realized his arm was there to keep *her* away from *him*. She twitched her tail. Even weak and starving, she could slice his soft, hairless belly wide open with her sharpened hooves.

Rahkki exhaled, long and slow, pushing his warm breath toward Echofrost.

She startled. *This* she understood. She closed her eyes and drank in his odors—the scents of wet soil, burned wood, the jungle air, and Rahkki's essence: his spirit. It melded all the other scents together into a blend that was unique to him, and his scent was peaceful but tinged with caution. He inched closer.

She blinked her eyes and stared at him. Why did he come closer if he was afraid of her? Was he stupid or brave? Echofrost huffed, curious. The cub lowered his arm and turned his back on her.

She lifted her head higher, her ears flicking front to back. What was he thinking to show her his back? She couldn't see his eyes or smell his essence. She glanced at

Brauk. The big Landwalker watched, standing lightly on his feet, ready to intercede. But his little brother sat in front of her, not moving. She stretched her neck toward Rahkki, growing more curious by the moment. Her nose reached his neck. She opened her mouth, thinking to lip at his bare skin.

"Get away!" Brauk dived into the stall swinging his club and struck Echofrost across her jaw.

She reared back, and Brauk yanked Rahkki out and slammed the door.

"I thought you understood the Kihlari?" Brauk said, breathing fast. "She was about to bite you."

"Sula was just smelling me."

Brauk groaned. "No, she opened her mouth. I know her better than you do."

"But I wasn't threatening her; I was making her curious about me. Now look at her; she's spooked."

Echofrost quivered in her stall, furious.

"I'll have to start over with her; Sula doesn't trust me now," said Rahkki.

"Start over? You haven't *done* anything yet."

"She was studying me, and now she's blocking me out."

Brauk dropped his face into his hands and groaned. "Tuni said you'd know how to help her, but you're crazy, aren't you? You read things into these animals that aren't there."

"Just put a halter on her," Rahkki said. "Let's get her fed and watered, then I'll start again."

"She won't eat or drink. I've tried." Brauk entered Echofrost's stall with his club lifted high and strapped the halter onto her head. She trained her eyes on his weapon, tired of being struck by it. When he yanked on her lead rope, she walked forward.

When they were outside, Echofrost halted and stared at the stars, hunting for Hazelwind and longing to fly. She glanced back at the Kihlari den. Shysong was inside, munching her hay like a tame pegasus. She wondered if that meant the mare was losing her motivation to escape. Echofrost chewed her lip. Her hunger made it difficult to think straight.

Rahkki touched his brother's shoulder, making him pause to wait for Echofrost. Brauk rolled his eyes and fidgeted with his belt.

Echofrost took a long, slow breath, looking again at the stars, but she couldn't reach them, not yet. It had only been four days since Brauk cut her flight feathers and five days since her capture—her chopped plumage wasn't even close to being sky worthy.

Rahkki stood in front of her but with his back turned, making her curious about him again. He was leading her somewhere, and she didn't think he meant to hurt her, so what did he want? She stepped toward him, and he resumed walking. He and his brother led her toward the jungle. Echofrost remembered the black spit dragon and the killer ants, and she dug in her hooves.

Rahkki and Brauk stood patiently, not tugging on her. When she let out her breath they walked forward and she followed, feeling soothed.

Soon they reached the rain forest's edge. Brauk grabbed Rahkki's shoulder and forced him to stop. "What are you doing? We can't go in there."

The cub lifted his chin. "I'm taking Sula to Leshi Creek. She wants to drink from a running stream, and she needs to graze. You waited too long, and now we have no choice. We have to go into the jungle. Look at her."

Both males turned, staring at Echofrost, and she took a big, wavering step backward. They dropped their eyes and continued whispering.

Echofrost's mind filled with doubts. Why hadn't she just eaten their food? Then she would at least be healthy.

Finally, the brothers finished their argument and entered the woods. "Stay behind me," Brauk ordered. "It's dark enough for dragons." He took the lead, brandishing his sawa sword, a weapon that had a long, curved blade the color of the moon. Echofrost knew the name of the sword because while she'd been slowly starving to death in the barn, she'd also been listening to Kol. The stallion liked to talk, mostly about himself, but he'd also begun teaching her about the Kihlari army. He'd told her that all the Riders carried a sawa sword, a dagger, and their arrows. Some also wielded spears.

Echofrost followed the brothers, her ears pricked for danger. As much as she hated to admit it, she was counting on their weapons to protect her. Until she could fly, she knew she wasn't safe alone in the jungle. The mist was thick in the forest tonight, hanging low over her head and blocking her view of the sky. If Hazelwind was out flying, he wouldn't be able to see her or she him.

Foreign animals shrieked in the trees, and night insects chirped with irritating enthusiasm. But when Echofrost heard the sound of bubbling water ahead, her heart lifted. She nickered and surged forward, following Rahkki, who'd taken her rope and was leading her toward the creek. When they arrived, the cub walked into the water, clucking to encourage her.

Echofrost stepped closer, flaring her nostrils and

scenting the water for contamination or danger. But the brook seemed fresh, clean. Rahkki tapped the surface. "Come on, girl."

She stepped into the creek and then plunged her muzzle deep into the cool liquid, sucking it down her gullet and splashing Rahkki. He laughed, sounding like a nickering foal.

Brauk watched them from the bank where he was squatting. Leaning over, he selected a small stone and tossed it at a tree, striking it dead center. "This is the same creek I use to fill her water bucket," he said. "Why will she drink here and not in her stall?"

Rahkki shrugged. "She's wild, Brauk. That's why."

"But that's stupid. She'd let herself die of thirst next to a bucket of water?"

"She might," he answered. "But Sula's not stupid, just willful."

"I don't see the difference."

Rahkki chose a stone and threw it at the exact tree his brother had aimed at, missing the target completely. Brauk harrumphed. "You have perfect aim with your blowgun, but you can't hit a tree with a rock."

The cub shrugged and then sat next to his brother on the bank, holding Echofrost's lead rope in one hand. "Once

Sula's and Firo's feathers grow back, you should let them go, Brauk. Maybe they can catch up to their herd."

Echofrost waded to the creek's edge and grazed on the succulent plants that bordered it, too hungry to test for what was poisonous and what wasn't—she'd die anyway if she didn't eat *something*, so she munched on every plant that smelled good to her.

Brauk shook his long hair at Rahkki. "I can't let them go," he said. "I promised the Sky Guard I'd use their profits to buy hay and weapons for us all. Whoever buys Sula can deal with her attitude. I just need her tame enough to trot in a circle and fat enough to look good doing it. I only have twenty-four days left until the auction. Will you help me?"

Rahkki sighed. "I'll do what I can."

The brothers kept watch over her while Echofrost drank and grazed. Rahkki was distracted, flicking small black ants off his knees. Echofrost rotated her ears and flared her nostrils at every scent and sound. The fog rolled in thicker, if that was possible. She couldn't see but a winglength ahead of her. A spit dragon was too big to sneak up on them, but what else lurked in these strange woods? Where was the panther that had chased her? And what about the huge, stinging red ants? Did they swarm animals as large as she?

A loud cracking noise spooked Echofrost and sent her trotting in a wild circle. In her fright she knocked Brauk headfirst into the riverbank.

He leaped up and shouted at her, making a fist. She reared away from him.

"Brauk, no!" Rahkki sprang on his brother and shoved him off-balance. Brauk fell into the creek, and Rahkki landed on top of him. The brothers rolled like crocodiles while Echofrost swung her neck, searching for the source of the noise that had spooked her.

"Get off me," Brauk yelled, flinging Rahkki aside.

"Don't hit Sula," Rahkki said. "Please don't do that."

"Land to skies! I was just threatening her."

The brothers sat in the stream, panting. "I think you broke my nose," Brauk grumbled.

Rahkki scooted out of his brother's punching range. "I didn't break it; you fell on it."

"Nah, it was you." Brauk jerked his nose straight with a sickening crack. "Own the deed, own the consequences, Brother. Just be glad I'm not in the mood to thrash you."

Brauk stood up, squeezing water out of his boar-hide

trousers, and then he lent his hand, helping Rahkki to his feet.

Echofrost watched them, feeling curious. Were they playing or fighting? She was so distracted by the brothers that she didn't immediately notice the hot breath on her neck.

"Sula's quiet," Rahkki said. Then he turned and saw why. "Giant!" he screamed.

But the warning came too late for Echofrost. Huge fists wrapped around her neck and dragged her off her hooves. She kicked; she couldn't breathe.

"Let go!" Rahkki bounded toward her.

Echofrost twisted her head up and saw her attacker towering over her: his pale skin, red hair, small blue eyes, and thick dry lips. He was so wide she couldn't see around him. Muscles bulged down his arms, an animal hide draped across his shoulder, and he grunted like a buffalo. His long exhale blew back her mane, and her heart hammered. She guessed she was face-to-face with a Gorlan giant.

He tightened his grip around her neck. Her vision darkened and her body went limp.

19

LESHI CREEK

RAHKKI SNATCHED BRAUK'S DAGGER OUT OF HIS brother's sheath and leaped at the giant, climbing onto his back. "Let her go!" The words blasted from his mouth with such savagery that he didn't recognize his own voice.

"Rahkki, get off him!" Brauk shouted.

This Gorlan beast was at least twelve lengths tall and dressed in goatskin—he was from the Highland horde, Rahkki guessed by the cut of his clothes. The Gorlander held Sula by her throat with both hands, trying to suffocate her so he could drag her away. Her tongue lolled from her mouth, and her eyes popped wide.

The giant shrugged, trying to throw Rahkki off his back, and then Rahkki's thoughts caught up to his actions.

I'm attacking a giant!

Brauk drew his sawa blade, shifting through the moonlight like a shadow, his eyes glinting. "Rahkki, get off that giant," he said.

But Sula needed Rahkki's help, so he grasped Brauk's dagger in both fists and drove it toward the giant's brain. The Gorlander released one pale, meaty hand from the mare's neck, snatched Rahkki's arm, and tossed him into the creek before the blade could find its mark.

Rahkki landed in the water with a loud splash. His upper arm went immediately numb where the giant had squeezed it.

"Run!" Brauk ordered, keeping his eyes on the Gorlander. He twirled his curved sawa sword and trotted lightly forward, springing off his calves. Where size was the giant's friend, speed was Brauk's.

Rahkki swam out of the creek, clutched the dagger, and followed his brother. The beast watched them come, his eyes as fearless as Lutegar's, and for the same reason. What could hurt him out here? Even drooling dragons switched paths when giants walked the woods. This one lurched toward them with one fist twisted in Sula's white mane and the other poised to strike. The giant grunted with each footfall, and his great weight rattled the soil.

"Go," Brauk ordered again.

But Rahkki trotted closer. Sula twisted and kicked. Her hooves sliced through the Gorlander's goat-hide vest, raking red streaks across his moon-pale skin. He roared like a lion, his attention divided between the mare and Rahkki's brother. Brauk danced, light on his heels, transfixing the giant with his swaying movements. Rahkki clasped Brauk's short dagger in his left hand, since his right arm was throbbing.

The flame-haired warrior motioned at Brauk in Gorlish, speaking with his hands. Brauk, and all the Sandwen warriors, learned simple Gorlish as part of their training—and Brauk answered back quickly. The gestures were oddly familiar to Rahkki, which was strange, because he didn't speak Gorlish.

Brauk translated. "The giant is alone."

"He told you that?"

"Not exactly. He said his horde is sneaking up behind us."

Rahkki glanced fearfully at the trees.

Brauk grinned. "But giants are terrible liars." He gestured again in Gorlish, and the giant responded by shaking his head. "He won't let Sula go," Brauk said. "I'll have to fight him for her. You need to leave. If I have to tell you again . . ."

"I'll bring help back then," said Rahkki. He charged toward Fort Prowl to call out the army.

"No!" Brauk's harsh tone stopped him. "It's *one* Gorlander, Rahkki. Don't embarrass me. Just get."

Rahkki ripped his eyes from the seething giant to his brother, the last living member of his family, besides Darthan. If Rahkki wasn't getting help, then he wasn't leaving at all. He crossed his arms.

Brauk unleashed a stream of curses. "Sun and stars, Brother! If this giant doesn't kill you, I will. Just stay behind me then." Brauk shook his long, dark hair, jingling the bells tied within, and darted forward, slicing the giant's free arm.

The beast charged. His flat, naked feet thumped the soil, and he dragged Sula behind him. He backhanded Brauk, but his brother ducked as the big arm whooshed by his head and slammed into a tree, snapping it in half. Brauk dived in and stabbed the Gorlander through the calf. The giant groaned, and his fist squeezed Sula so tight that her legs curled.

The giant drew his bludgeon, a solid ivory club, and swung it at Brauk; but Rahkki's brother was too quick, and the spikes stuck in the soil, giving Brauk the second he needed to stab the giant's bicep muscle.

Snarling, the Gorlander's white face turned the color of his hair. He coiled his body for attack.

Brauk parried in and out, slicing at the giant in sections from head to foot until the beast was streaked in blood. But these wounds were not fatal, nor were they meant to be—Brauk was whipping the giant into a crazed frenzy and throwing him off his guard.

Rahkki leaped and dodged in the background, ready to help but staying out of the way. Sula was panting hard, but her eyes had cleared. The giant had loosened his grip, and she could breathe well enough now. He saw that she was watching the Gorlander too, waiting patiently for her moment to strike.

"Get him, Sula!" he called to her.

As if she understood, the winged mare whipped her head around and bit the giant, clamping her jaws around his forearm. He stifled a roar and shook her, but she held tight, sinking her teeth deep into his flesh. She pulled herself closer and then kicked him in the chest, stunning him. He released her, and she spilled onto the ground and rolled out of danger.

Rahkki rushed in, grabbed Sula's lead rope, and meant to pull her away; but she galloped past him, dragging him off his feet and through the tangle of undergrowth. By the time he thought to let go of the rope, she was with Brauk, battling side by side with him.

Rahkki lay on the jungle floor, stunned. Sula could have run away, but instead she stayed and attacked the giant with the skill of a warrior. Using her flightless wings to propel and balance herself, she reared and clubbed the giant with her front hooves. Meanwhile Brauk hacked at the Gorlander like he was chopping down a tree.

The giant finally toppled when Brauk sliced his ankles, severing the tendons. He leaped onto the beast's chest, gestured in Gorlish, and then slew the giant cleanly and quickly, like he would a wild buck. Brauk swept back his hair, inhaled a deep breath, and then edged toward the creek to wash his sword.

Rahkki stood up, his legs shaking, and he dusted the muddy soil off his trousers. He inched toward Sula. Her eyes were fixed on the felled giant, but her ears swiveled back, letting him know she heard him coming. He picked up the end of her lead rope, expecting her to bolt. She didn't. Her eyes turned toward the sky, gazing hopefully at it. Rahkki looked up and saw nothing there—the mist had cleared for a moment, but it was quickly rolling back in.

She dropped her head, seeming disappointed, and Rahkki wondered if it was because she couldn't fly, or because her friends weren't up there.

He reached out to touch her, to inspect her bruised neck and tangled mane. She shied away from him, so he tucked his free hand behind his back.

Brauk finished at the stream and faced Rahkki, eyeing him from head to toe, his gaze settling pointedly on the dagger.

Rahkki handed it over.

His brother slid the dagger into its sheath with well-practiced speed and then tore off his bloody shirt and crammed it into his pocket. "How old are you?" Brauk asked, his eyes hard. "Ten? Eleven?"

Rahkki's jaw dropped. "I'm twelve. Don't you remember? You gave me a . . ." Rahkki trailed off because it suddenly occurred to him he hadn't received a present or even a candied melon from Brauk this year. *When had they stopped celebrating birthdays?*

"Twelve already?" Brauk rasped. "And still playing at knives like a tot." His brother ran his hands across his scalp, cursing in the language of the empire. "Sa jin, Rahkki, you don't have the skills to fight off a mosquito. This dagger is more dangerous in your hands than in your ene-mies'. *Sa jin huruk!*"

Rahkki felt suddenly cold, and he was still shaking from facing the giant, but his right arm was hot with pain. "I'm sorry . . . ," he said, fumbling. What was the correct response for turning twelve while his brother wasn't pay-ing attention?

"Nah. This is my fault. I haven't taught you." Brauk turned and watched the winged horse. "But you were brave the way you attacked that giant," he said, his eyes softening. "I haven't seen you that spittin' mad since Mut Finn dunked you in pig slop."

Rahkki's throat tightened. "I wasn't . . . brave. I just wanted to save her."

Brauk frowned at Sula, his face a mask of smeared dirt and blood. "I don't know what you see in this stubborn cow. Come on, we'd better go before the animals come to feed on this giant."

Rahkki turned away, feeling sick about what they'd done, but also knowing that they'd saved Sula. That Gor-lander had grabbed the mare to take her back to Mount Crim, probably to throw her into his horde's soup pot. The giants hated the Kihlari as much as they hated the

Sandwens, and it was because the winged army had given the Fifth Clan the final advantage in their longstanding war over the farmland valleys.

Now, in retaliation, the giants made sport of harassing the Sandwen settlements—stealing children, killing livestock, stomping on crops, and capturing Kihlari. They raided several times a year, and with the Clan Gathering and auction coming up, the Sandwens were on the move and vulnerable. Each Sandwen clan had its own Sky Guard and Land Guard armies, but they left most of their forces at home to protect their settlements. A Gorlan horde could do a lot of damage to traveling clans.

As they walked back to Fort Prowl, Rahkki stared at his hands. "Brauk, how do I know Gorlish?"

His brother's eyes rounded. "You remember it?"

"A little. Some of the gestures looked familiar."

Brauk let out his breath. "Mother taught you when you were a baby, before you could talk. It was brilliant, really. You weren't so frustrated about everything once you could communicate." He laughed.

"What did I say in Gorlish?"

"Mostly just *no* and *more*. That's all I remember."

Rahkki pointed back toward the felled Gorlander.

"Was that giant hunting?" he asked. "He was awfully close to our village."

"No. Giants hunt with spears, not bludgeons," Brauk answered. "He was scouting for the horde. I suspect they'll raid us soon."

"Not during the Clan Gathering, they'll be too many of us."

"True," Brauk said with a sigh. "It'll be right before, or right after. The queen has increased our patrols, but we haven't noticed any giants this close. I'm not sure how this scout snuck past our sentries." Brauk tugged on his belt, looking concerned as they walked between the trees. Rahkki led Sula, and she followed quietly.

While they traveled, Rahkki studied his brother's strong hands—hands that had fed and cared for him since he was four years old—and a confession burst from his lips before he could stop it. "I wasn't just worried about Sula," Rahkki said. "I was more scared the giant would kill *you*."

Brauk halted, his face shadowed from the moon by the trees. "I'm a warrior, Rahkki, and I'll die someday; but when it happens, it won't be some stinking giant that does it. It'll be something much grander." He smiled widely and pulled Rahkki close. "Got it?"

Rahkki wiped his eyes. He couldn't imagine his life without Brauk.

His brother stiffened. "By Granak, Brother. If you cry, I'll break *your* nose."

Rahkki nodded.

Brauk led Rahkki and Sula to the stone fort where the gate crew rose and greeted them in the dark. "Ay, who goes?"

"Ay, it's Headwind Brauk Stormrunner of the Sky Guard," his brother said. "I killed a Gorlan scout in the woods, by Leshi Creek."

"Bloody rain," said a guard, and then all of them, including Rahkki, spit on the ground. The guards quickly dispatched messengers to the queen, to General Tsun, and to the other two Headwinds in the Sky Guard, Tuni and Harak. "Sound the alarm," said one guard to another. Soon the clanging of bells drifted out across the training yard, the horse arena, the village, and the farmlands. The fortress awakened as the land soldiers prepared to reinforce the perimeter of the Fifth Clan territory.

Brauk was off duty, so he walked Rahkki and the mare down to the Kihlari barn. "Put Sula away and get Kol. I'll fly you home."

Rahkki paused as he considered returning to Uncle's quiet hut at the rice farm.

His brother read his mind. "Let me guess, you've realized you hate farming?"

Rahkki exhaled and grinned.

Brauk smacked Rahkki's back, throwing the boy forward. "Accept your fate, Brother. We need the wages. And tell Uncle to teach you how to fight."

"But *he* can't fight!"

Brauk grinned. "Darthan might surprise you. Now go get Kol, and remember—you're twelve, so don't cry." Brauk's grin disappeared. "Don't ever cry."

They flew back to the farm on Kol, and Brauk dropped him off at Uncle's door. Rahkki entered the hut, which was cool now that the fire had gone out. Darthan was snoring on his mattress. Rahkki removed his wet boots, changed, and climbed to his loft, peering out the window. In the far distance he watched his brother fly away on Kol, heading back to Fort Prowl. Rahkki's uneaten dinner remained in the satchel, but he wasn't hungry.

He slid onto his pallet, pulled the covers over his head, and did not cry.

20

ACCEPTANCE

ECHOFROST WAITED UNTIL THE LANDWALKER brothers exited the barn, and then she collapsed in her stall, her muscles shaking. She hadn't thought of herself as *food* since she was a weanling. Sure, bears and pumas had stalked her when she was a young filly, but she'd had a herd to protect her. Since leaving Anok, she'd been hunted by sharks in the Dark Water, stalked by a panther, and nabbed by a hungry giant. She remembered how the Gorlander had snorted up her scent like a lion, and a hard shudder ran from her ears to her tail.

"Shysong?" she nickered.

"Yes, I'm here," said the blue roan.

"How are you feeling?"

Shysong hesitated before answering. "I'm eating their hay," she said, sounding guilty.

"I know, and it's okay. I was stupid to refuse it."

"Where did you go just now?" Shysong asked. "Why did the Landwalkers take you out at night?"

"They took me to a creek to drink and graze. It was to save me." Echofrost pricked her ears, realizing the truth of that statement. Brauk, for all his blustering abuse, had fetched his little brother to help her. And Rahkki had known what she needed—which was flowing water and grass that she cut with her own teeth. "But while we were at the creek, we were attacked," Echofrost added. "It was one of those Gorlan giants, a Landwalker the size of a hill. He grabbed me."

Shysong gasped. "Are you hurt?"

"I'm sore," Echofrost admitted.

Apparently eavesdropping, Rizah interrupted them. "You saw a giant?" she asked.

"Saw him? I smelled his breath."

Rizah stamped her hoof. "A giant in the woods—that explains the alarm. Maybe he was just hunting, but he's too close." Then she inhaled hard and nickered. "Tuni is coming."

Moments later the sound of footsteps filled Echofrost's

ears as dozens of Riders from the fortress flung open the barn doors and charged through the rows. Their long hair flashed with the bright bells and hard, colored beads they tied throughout the braided strands. They donned armor and shiny helmets, shouting to one another. A loud rumbling filled Echofrost's ears as huge tumblers turned, opening the ceiling above her head. Tuni spoke to Rizah, who was prancing with excitement. "Shh, my golden girl, hold steady."

Echofrost knocked over her water bucket and planted her front hooves on it so she could see farther over her walls. Tuni had retreated to the tack room and was now coming back, carrying Rizah's things. Echofrost had learned the names of these adornments from Kol. The leather seat that Tuni heaved onto Rizah's back was called a *saddle*. It was decorated with carved metal accents and tassels. Next Echofrost heard the soft clink of the *bit* as it settled between Rizah's teeth. This was how Tuni controlled the mare—by pulling on a piece of metal in the pinto's mouth.

Echofrost stood taller, peering through the netting that penned her. Shysong did the same, and Echofrost noticed that her friend's coat was glossy and that she'd gained back the weight she'd lost when they'd crossed the Dark Water.

"Did you see Storm Herd while you were out?" Shysong asked.

"No, it was too foggy."

Shysong tossed her long mane, which was brushed and shiny. "Hazelwind should go. He doesn't understand how powerful these Landwalkers are."

"He's staying hidden, which is what I should have done. If I'd stayed loose, I think I could have freed you by now."

"What do you mean, *if you'd stayed loose?*" whinnied Shysong. "Did you *choose* this? Did you let yourself get captured, for *me?*"

Echofrost had let Shysong assume she'd been captured against her will, but now the truth was out, so she didn't deny it. "Yes, I let them take me."

"Why?" Shysong whinnied. "Storm Herd needs *you*, not me! The Landwalkers caught me because I'm slow. I probably shouldn't have left Anok in the first place. I'm not as tough as I thought I was, but you!" Shysong stamped her hoof. "You're the heart of the herd. You're the one who led us out of the Flatlands. And now look what you've done! Hazelwind can't . . . no, he *won't* leave you. He's risking the entire mission by sticking around here."

"But do you remember what I'd said, Shysong? I promised I wouldn't let them take you. And you're *not* slow;

you're injured. That's different."

Shysong's voice quivered. "This is my fault, and now we're *both* trapped here, unable to fly. We're never getting out."

Around Echofrost, Kihlari steeds were being saddled and mounted. They walked into the aisles and flew out of the open ceiling because the barn doors were too narrow for them to exit in large groups.

"Dusk Patrol, flying out!" shouted Tuni aboard Rizah. Her dark-red hair danced on her shoulders.

The Dusk Patrol steeds snorted, excited, and their Riders hollered, their voices rising and falling in unison. Each Landwalker was armed with the sharpened sticks they called *arrows*, plus short daggers and sawa blades.

Echofrost watched them sail into the night sky and thought of Shysong's words, *We're never getting out.* She turned to her friend. "Have you lost hope? Are you giving up?"

Shysong turned up her eyes, thinking for a moment. More Kihlari flew out of the barn, and their bright feathers drifted down like plucked flower petals. One landed on Echofrost's nose, and she shook it off. Overhead, the Sky Guard glided in tight square formations. Tonight the steeds wore horned armor over their heads, shiny metal plates across their chests, and shields around their lower legs. Spiked beads had been braided into the Kihlari's tails, and the beads sliced the air as the winged steeds lifted off. Echofrost watched them pass over her, their feathers rattling, and she knew this wasn't a regular patrol—the winged army was hunting giants. The queen must have finally given the order.

Shysong answered Echofrost. "Look at them," she said, pointing at the Sky Guard with her wing. "I'm not giving up, but I've accepted my fate. There is *no way* to escape that army."

Echofrost flattened her ears. "Accepting this *is* giving up!"

"I don't agree, but I see no point in fighting them. I know Brauk hits you—I hear the blows—but Tuni is kind to me because I do what she says. I'm trying to survive. I'm sorry if you don't like it."

"Are you blaming *me* for what Brauk does?" Echofrost kicked her wall, splintering off a piece of wood. "Blasted Landwalkers, they've turned you into a horse."

Shysong gasped, and tears filled her eyes. "Don't judge me," she rasped.

"Then don't judge *me*," Echofrost whinnied. "This is *wrong*. We're meant to be free. Don't you want to escape?"

"I didn't say that," said Shysong. "Of course I want to escape, but I won't fight them. The Landwalkers are too powerful, just like you said. Look at them!" she repeated.

Echofrost glanced at the patrol gathered overhead. The Riders and the Kihlari were flexed for battle, their eyes gleaming bright even beneath the dim crescent moon. Then Tuni shouted an order and the Riders kicked their mounts, sending them forward. The Kihlari blasted across the sky, snorting, their Riders whooping.

"The Landwalkers are the over-stallions of this herd," Shysong continued, "and so they're easy to figure out. Just do what they want, eat their food, and they'll treat you right."

"Landwalkers aren't over-stallions, Shysong. And we can't trust them. None of this is natural." Echofrost exhaled, realizing it wasn't Shysong's fault she was overwhelmed. "Listen to me," she said. "You're as precious to Storm Herd as I am. I will free you."

But Echofrost didn't know how much more she could take from Brauk. He'd saved her from the giant, true, but it was because she was his *possession*, not because he cared about her. She owed him nothing.

As the last of the Sky Guard patrol flew out of the

retracted ceiling, Echofrost searched the heights for Hazelwind. He would find a way to help them out of this terrible place. Then Storm Herd would resume their journey to new lands, never to return here.

C∞ 21 ∞

THE KIHLARI
ANCESTORS

THE SKY GUARD RETURNED LATER THAT NIGHT, their energy deflated. Next to Echofrost, Kol whinnied. "What happened?" He'd been left behind because it was Dusk Patrol that flew out, and he was part of Dawn Patrol.

"The giants are spreading out. Soon they'll surround us," said the mare Rizah, swinging her armored neck as she landed in the aisleway.

Echofrost watched the Riders rub down their mounts, feed them grain, and remove the spiked beads from their tails and the battered armor from their bodies. The fitted metal shields were returned to the armory at the south end of the barn. Echofrost memorized each Flier, each Rider, and noted where the grain and hay were stored. She also

193

studied where the *tack*—the saddles and bridles—were kept, and she inspected the retractable ceiling, watching the tumblers turn as the Landwalkers outside tugged the attached ropes to close the roof.

Then the Riders left the barn, murmuring to one another, spitting and gesturing angrily, and soon after that, the dawn sun split the horizon and the clanging of the morning bells wafted down from the eight-sided fortress on the hill.

Kol shifted in his stall. "Greet the sun," he brayed to the Kihlari.

Around Echofrost, all the pegasi faced east, including Shysong. Echofrost turned her tail and faced west. Kol flashed his teeth. "Show respect."

"I'm not one of you," she grumbled.

Kol shook his fiery red mane, which was streaked in yellow. He had a gleaming coat, thick muscles, and silky mane and tail. In Anok he'd have tangled hair, cracked hooves, and flies on his face; and he'd be much leaner. He'd be a steed who was long familiar with hunger and thirst, but he'd be afraid of neither. He'd know where to dig for roots, which tree barks were edible, where to search for moisture, and how to gather nuts.

But here food was thrown at his hooves, water was

carried to him in a bucket, stable grooms raked up his droppings, and he was walled off from predators. The Landwalkers had robbed Kol of purpose and cursed him with dependency—but Kol didn't get it. He didn't understand that *he* was the one who'd lost everything.

After nickering toward the sun, the stallion took a long swallow from his water bucket and then turned back to her, still unsettled. "The Sandwen clans protect us," he said. "And they're willing to protect you too."

Echofrost had planned to ignore him but quickly changed her mind. "You don't owe them anything for locking you up. They use you for war; that's why they feed you."

Shysong pinned her ears. "Echofrost, don't . . ."

"No, we were wild once, like you," Kol whinnied, his voice rising. "We also flew here from another land, from a place that had become, how did you put it . . . *inhospitable*? The Sandwen clans found us in the jungle—sick and starving and hunted by dragons. The tales are old, mostly forgotten, but we would have died without their help."

Echofrost's mane prickled at his words and she exchanged a glance with Shysong. "Do you know *where* you came from?"

Kol shuffled his hooves. "There are elder steeds at the Ruk who might know."

"What's the Ruk?"

Rizah interrupted, nickering sleepily. "Oh, you don't want to go there. It's where the foals are born and where the old and sick steeds go to die."

"But won't you go there when *you* have a foal?"

Rizah sputtered. "I'm a Flier, a warrior. Warriors don't have foals."

"But—" It didn't make sense. In Anok, battle mares had foals all the time, and Echofrost didn't know what to say about that. She glanced at Kol. "Don't you want your own family?"

"Family?" he asked, mouthing the word. "Brauk is my family."

Echofrost tossed her mane, frustrated. "So you don't have any idea where your ancestors came from?"

"We flew here from lands in the north," Rizah said, yawning. "That's all I know."

Echofrost felt the air squeeze from her lungs, and Shysong gasped. *Anok was north.* She whispered over the wall to Shysong, "Do you think these Kihlari are from our homeland?"

"They could be," the mare answered. "You heard what Hazelwind told us right after we landed here, didn't you? Some of our elders believe that the lost Lake Herd steeds fled from Nightwing four hundred years ago, when he first took power. Maybe they crossed the Dark Water like we did. Maybe these Kihlari *are* the descendants of those steeds."

Echofrost ransacked her memories for the Lake Herd pegasi legends, again wishing Morningleaf were here. Her friend knew most of them by heart. She returned to her overturned bucket and stepped up to better see the entire barn.

There were hundreds of Kihlari in here, more at the Ruk, and hundreds, maybe thousands, living with the other Sandwen clans—and she bet they were *all* refugees from Anok, all descendants of pegasi who'd once lived free. And now they lived in pens and nickered for food. Now they carried Landwalkers on their backs and suffered cold metal in their mouths.

She dropped to her hooves, panting and scared—more scared than she'd ever been in her life. She was staring at her future, *and the future of all pegasi,* if Storm Herd didn't break free of this continent and these Landwalkers for good. But what about all these trapped steeds? She had to help them too!

"I think you hail from our land!" she blurted. "You fled across the Dark Water like we did, but you once lived in a herd."

"Not me," spit Kol. "I was born at the Ruk and then Paired to Brauk. I'm not *wild*."

He said *wild* like it was a dirty word, and Echofrost huffed. "You weren't *Paired* with Brauk," she said. "He bought you."

"What's the difference?" Kol asked. Other Kihlari listened, some offended like Kol, others intrigued.

"The difference is, you didn't have a choice," said Shysong.

Kol went silent, thinking.

Rizah leaped in. "You speak about us coming here and getting captured like it *just* happened to us," she said. "But it was long ago. It doesn't matter anymore how we used to live."

Echofrost tossed her mane. "But it does! Your ancestors, my ancestors, I think they're the same! Doesn't that mean anything to you? And your herd, Lake Herd, once controlled one of the largest territories in Anok—you made your own rules, slept when you wanted, flew when you wanted. You weren't locked up. And what about your foals? Do you want them sold to other clans?" Echofrost shivered.

"It's an honor when a foal fetches a high price," Ilan neighed.

"An *honor*?" Echofrost stamped her hoof. "To sell your offspring?"

The Kihlari exploded into angry whinnies, denials, and shed feathers. Echofrost and Shysong let the Kihlari argue and debate, waiting for them to settle down.

"Your words change nothing," Kol finally whinnied at her. "It's more important to be safe than free."

"I think you've got that backward," said Echofrost.

Kol kicked the wall between them. "You're a foreigner; you don't understand our ways."

Echofrost pricked her ears, stunned that they would fight so hard against their history. She'd expected them to feel relieved, empowered, maybe even angry with the Landwalkers—not angry with *her*!

But she wouldn't give up. "It's easy to turn your head from it," she said, breathing harder. "Since you're not allowed to choose a mate and have foals. You don't make any choices at all. You refuse to see the truth."

The Kihlari Fliers fell absolutely silent.

"We can leave, all of us together," Echofrost nickered. "My herd will help us, and we can all find a new territory. If I'm right about you, then when your ancestors left Anok, they weren't searching for *this*. They were fleeing from the immortal Destroyer, a pegasus named Nightwing—just like my herd, but yours was captured by the Sandwens. It's time you left this place and continued the journey your ancestors began. You should be angry about what happened to you."

Rizah exhaled. "But I love Tuni. I'll never leave her."

Echofrost sputtered. "How can you *love* a Landwalker?"

"We're Paired," Rizah explained, glancing at the scar on her shoulder that matched Tuni's. "I swore to protect her life and she mine. I think it's *you* who don't understand. The Fifth Clan needs us."

Echofrost shook her head, feeling frustrated. "How can I make them understand they're being used?" she asked Shysong.

The mare shrugged her wings but then asked Rizah a question. "What if you flew without permission? What would Tuni do?"

"She would come find me," said the golden mare.

"But would she let you go if you wanted to explore?"

Rizah huffed. "Of course not, but not because she's cruel. The jungle is full of predators, and I don't know what's safe to eat. She'd bring me back to protect me because she loves me."

"You're like weanlings then," Echofrost said, exasperated. "Mother pegasi don't let their foals wander because they can't survive on their own. And that's what's happened to you all. You don't know how to survive and so you're afraid."

Kol whipped his tail, interrupting. "Don't pretend you aren't also afraid. You two don't know how to survive in that jungle either."

Echofrost bit her lip. That was true, but not entirely. "That's only because we weren't raised here, and yes, I'm afraid to wander in it *alone*," she clarified. "But I'm not suggesting any of you travel alone. Together, you would learn to survive, and then you'd teach your foals. You'd look out for one another—that's what a herd does."

"But the Gorlan hordes are out there," a bay mare pointed out.

"I'm not going anywhere," said Rizah.

"I won't leave Brauk," Kol said.

Most of the Kihlari agreed, but a few considered leaving.

I didn't know my ancestors were wild.

It would be nice to graze on fresh grass every day.

I'm not afraid of the jungle.

Echofrost listened, memorizing who was interested and who was not.

When Hazelwind and the Storm Herd steeds came back for her and Shysong, she hoped to take some of these Kihlari steeds with her. Not all the Landwalkers were as kind to their mounts as Tuni was to Rizah, and those mistreated steeds were the most interested.

Echofrost also wanted to free the pegasi at the Ruk. Since they weren't bonded to Riders, they might be more willing to escape, but she had no way to talk to them.

"One day Shysong and I will escape this clan," Echofrost announced, interrupting the nickering Kihlari. "Whoever wants to join us will be welcomed by Storm Herd." Echofrost wasn't completely sure that was true, but she hoped she could convince her friends to accept any tame pegasi who chose to join them. Storm Herd was small. It would be good for them to increase their numbers. "Think about it, about living free," Echofrost finished.

More excited nickering erupted, followed by loud arguments and shuffling hooves.

Echofrost closed her mouth. She would give her words

time to sink into the minds of the Kihlari steeds. *No pegasus will endure captivity again, not while I'm alive.* That promise felt heavier now than ever, but if these were truly the lost pegasi of Anok, she owed it to their ancestors to try and help them.

22

THE QUEEN

IT WAS LATE MORNING AND ALREADY BLAZING hot. Insects swarmed over the dewy grass in the fallows, chirping and feeding furiously before the sun rose higher. Nine days had passed since the giant attack at Leshi Creek, and since then Rahkki had come twice a day from the farm to tend to Sula. Brauk offered to pay him for the work after he sold the mare, but Rahkki had refused. "You need to get her fat and teach her to trot and canter in pretty circles," Brauk had instructed him.

"Are you going to sell her as a Flier or as a pet?" Rahkki had asked.

"Don't know yet," said Brauk. "All I know is that I can't

sell her like this." And then he'd poked her in the ribs.

Now the silver mare chomped at the grass, her appetite hearty. Rahkki listened to General Tsun's land troops chatting in the jungle nearby as they guarded the perimeter of their settlement. The sky patrols had increased, and escorts had been sent to help the traveling clans arrive safely at the summer Gathering. It was the Fifth Clan's turn to host this year and the Kihlari auction was in fifteen days.

Brauk and Rahkki stood side by side, grazing with Kol and Sula. "I should do this more often," Brauk said. "Grazing is free. Hay is expensive." Then he kicked at the trampled scrub. "This forage isn't the best quality though."

When the Kihlari had eaten their fill, Rahkki and Brauk led their steeds back to the training yard. All Riders were on call in case the giants attacked, and so they sat at tables in the shade, passing time by fighting their bright horned beetles against one another. The insects battled on pedestals inside intricate cages. The Riders bet on the outcome of each contest. A loud cheer went up when Mut Finn's insect beat Harak's. "Pay up," said the teen, grinning. Harak scowled, and Rahkki heard the jingling of coins as they passed hands.

Brauk returned Kol to his stall and then stood with

Rahkki and Sula beside a large eucalyptus tree to discuss her training. They had to teach her to walk, trot, canter, and gallop in circles and on command. It was an exercise Rahkki knew from day one she'd despise, and she had. Even Brauk's club couldn't get Sula's hooves moving, and his brother cursed her to the skies and back.

Suddenly Brauk straightened. "The queen's coming," he said.

Rahkki's excitement chilled, and the entire yard silenced as the Riders and grooms stopped what they were doing, wiped their hands on their trousers, and pushed their hair into place. Tension wound through the yard like a snake.

From the iron gates of the fortress, the queen had emerged, riding her blood-bay stallion, Mahrsan. Lilliam kept his reins short, cranking his neck into a tight arch. The stallion walked with his mouth open, straining against the bit. His long black mane swung against his knees, and he carried his white-trimmed blue wings folded at his sides, covering the queen's bare legs. She wore matching white and blue wildflowers in her curled hair, and her white fur cape was edged in black mink. Patterns of the Fifth Clan marked her face and hands, drawn in ochre. Her eyes, which were as dark blue as her stallion's feathers, glittered in the hot sun. Bright gloss shined her lips.

Behind her walked her bloodborn princesses—the three living threats to her throne. I'Lenna was the eldest, and Rahkki studied her face, remembering how they'd laughed together in the barn some days ago. There was no evidence of her bright smile now. I'Lenna walked with her back stretched tall and her features fixed into a bland expression, but when she noticed Rahkki, her eyes brightened. Queen Lilliam glanced from her daughter to Rahkki and frowned. I'Lenna looked away quickly, and the boy's face flamed.

Her mother's sharp reaction reminded Rahkki that I'Lenna was on the cusp of her twelfth birthday. It was an age that threatened many queens, for it was around this age when exceptionally ambitious crown princesses began plotting to usurp their mothers. And since Lilliam already feared retaliation from Rahkki and Brauk—the children of her predecessor—she'd never condone a friendship between either of them and her eldest princess. It was the brutal irony of being queen—that producing heirs also produced rivals.

Clucking softly to her stallion, Lilliam leaned back in Mahrsan's saddle, and her huge belly swelled in front of her like a monsoon river, full to overflowing with her fourth child. She didn't smile, nor grimace, nor strain her eyes to look at her subjects. Serenity dripped from her like the cold rain that precedes a storm. Her Royal Guard surrounded her, but aimed their spears at her people.

The queen's gaze shifted from Rahkki to Sula. "What's wrong with that new mare?" she asked, sweeping her dark eyes across Sula's body, which had not yet begun to plump. Her lips tightened, and she turned to Brauk. "Is she ill?"

"She'll recover in time for the auction, my queen," Brauk said.

Lilliam's nostrils flared gently, absorbing his words like a foul odor. "You have fifteen days to make that happen," she said. Then her gaze found Tuni, who had just flown in on Rizah and was hovering overhead. "Where is the other mare?" she asked. "The one with the blue eyes?"

"Firo is resting inside the barn, my queen," Tuni answered.

"Bring her to me."

Tuni nodded and shouted an order to Koko, who was cleaning buckets. The head groom loped inside the barn and soon returned with the roan mare. She'd had the good sense to quickly pull the straw from Firo's mane and to smooth her coat before presenting her to the queen. The roan glistened in the sunshine, and her light-blue eyes were striking against her long black lashes.

Brauk used the moment that the queen was looking away to tuck Rahkki behind his back, but his quick movement drew her attention back to them. Rahkki's heart skittered as her cold eyes regarded them with open disdain. He knew that the only thing protecting him and his brother from her was the bargain that Uncle Darthan had struck—feeding the Land Guard for free in exchange for their lives—but sometimes, like now, it seemed a fragile covering.

Sula's hot breath on his neck drew Rahkki from his thoughts, and he looked over his shoulder at her. She was standing closer to him than she ever had, her eyes trained on the queen.

Lilliam nodded toward the other mare, Firo, and then spoke to her daughter I'Lenna. "What do you think of the roan?"

I'Lenna grinned. "She's pretty."

"She's also rare," said Lilliam. "A wildling. Take a closer look." Her dark-blue eyes softened toward I'Lenna, and Rahkki wondered what it was like—raising a crown princess who could not rule until you were dead. He imagined it drove a wedge between them.

I'Lenna approached Firo slowly, studying her. She lifted the roan's hooves one by one, ran her sure hands down her legs, and stroked her feathers. After her inspection, she nodded. "This braya will fetch heavy coin, Mother, but not as a Flier. She's a pet."

Rahkki's eyes widened. I'Lenna saw what he saw— that Firo was not powerful enough for war. The princess glanced at Rahkki and he smiled at her, but she looked quickly away.

Queen Lilliam returned her attention to Sula. "I agree with my daughter about the roan. Sell her as a pet. But this silver mare is a Flier." She glared at Brauk. "Put some fat on her first, because I will not be embarrassed. If she's not trained and shining like a star by the day of the auction, I will tie her up and feed her to Granak myself. You are running out of time."

Rahkki's blood drained at her words.

Brauk bowed his head and balled his hands into tight fists. "Yes, my queen."

Lilliam clucked at Mahrsan, and the big stallion flew forward, whipping his adorned tail at Brauk as he passed. The sharpened beads she'd tied into his hair sliced Brauk's face, drawing red stripes across his cheek.

Rahkki's brother mouthed silent curses at Mahrsan as the winged steed glided away. The guards ecorted the princesses across the yard, but I'Lenna stayed behind to admire Firo.

When the queen and her younger daughters were out of sight, Rahkki slumped over like a half-empty sack of grain, and Brauk spit in the dirt. Tuni flew lower, still aboard Rizah, her expression anxious. "You two want to go for a ride? Get out of here for a while?" She glanced at Rahkki. "You can sit behind me."

Brauk exhaled. "I do, but you heard the queen. The auction is in fifteen days. Rahkki and I have to train this mare."

Tuni nodded, and Rahkki noticed she'd tied the roan's black-edged feathers onto her wrists along with Rizah's.

"You've done well with Firo," Brauk said to her.

Tuni shrugged, tugging on Rizah's reins to keep the excited mare close to the ground. "I chose the less-stubborn wildling," she said. "But your Kihlara is coming around." She smiled at Rahkki, addressing him. "I knew you'd understand her."

"How did you know?" he asked, hoping she wouldn't call him a Meld in front of everyone. No one liked animal speakers since most turned out to be charlatans.

"You always understood Drael," she answered.

Rahkki's chest tightened at the mention of his mother's winged stallion.

Brauk scowled. "Rahkki was four years old. He doesn't remember anything about Drael."

"Wait," Rahkki said. "I do remember. He was a bay stallion. He was small."

"Yes," said Tuni. "You used to sleep in his stall, and you flew him by yourself. Scared your mother to death." Tuni stopped short at the word *death*. "I'm sorry."

Memories of soaring over the village slammed Rahkki. These were things he rarely thought about—the things before his mother died. But he used to enjoy flying. It was difficult to believe now.

"We've got work to do," Brauk interrupted. He loathed talking about the past. After Reyella died, he'd spent years trying to forget what had happened. He'd gambled and stayed out late and fought anyone who looked at him sideways. Those were the awful years for both brothers. Rahkki was left to fend for himself, often taking to the jungle to find food. That's where he'd learned to run fast. Spider armies, giant ants, panthers, and the smaller dragons had all hunted Rahkki. He'd been scratched, stung, bitten, and even sucked into a carnivorous plant. He'd survived it all while living in terror that one night his brother would not come home.

Darthan had tried to help them, but Brauk had stolen from him, and their uncle had cut ties with Brauk for years. Not for stealing, lying, and destroying his property, but because he said that Brauk had to run himself out. He insisted that the less he helped Brauk, the quicker this would happen.

And Darthan had been correct about that. One day Brauk just quit it all. But by then their inheritance was almost gone. They had just enough money left to purchase Kol. And the way Brauk had thrown himself into that stallion—Rahkki believed with all his heart that his love for the chestnut Flier had saved Brauk's life.

Tuni loosened her reins and urged Rizah into the sky. "All right then, I'll see you at dinner." She and Rizah surged toward the clouds.

"Take Sula to the round pen and work on her gaits," Brauk said to Rahkki. "I have drills to run on Kol, but if Sula's not ready in fifteen days, there'll be nothing we can do to save her."

Except to set her free, thought Rahkki, and his heart tumbled. How he'd love to see her loose and flying, but how he'd mourn to lose her. Since he'd begun training her, he'd become attached. Yes, she was sour and stubborn, but he didn't blame her for that. She wanted to be wild again—he was sure of it—and she had friends waiting for her. The Sky Guard had spotted Sula's herd several times, circling overhead, higher than the Riders could fly. They were watching and waiting.

If he were still a prince, he could command her release, or buy her and set her free. But as an orphan he had no coin, no power. Rahkki imagined collecting his wages from Uncle, ten dramals for a full season of labor, a fair wage for an apprentice; but even if Sula sold for a tenth of her value, ten dramals would not be enough to bid on her.

He kicked the ground, frustrated. Sula would sell to a Rider from another clan, and Firo would be purchased by an ignorant gem trader or given to a spoiled child. Or worse, Sula wouldn't cooperate, and the queen would feed her to Granak, the dragon.

As Rahkki led her toward the round pen, Sula inspected her surroundings. She was already plotting her escape, he was sure of it. And since Rahkki couldn't buy her, maybe he could help free her. He blanched at the thought. The punishment for destroying or losing clan property was *tyran*—stinging of the ants—and repayment to the clan at full value. Rahkki would never earn enough wages to repay the value of a missing Kihlara. But there was a solution to that—not getting caught. Rahkki sighed. He had fifteen days to figure out how to train this wild mare or free her.

23

SHAME

ECHOFROST HAD LOST TRACK OF THE DAYS AS they passed, each the same as the last. She had not seen Hazelwind again, and that disturbed her. But the little cub, Rahkki, visited her twice a day. She'd begun to look forward to his arrival because the rest of the time she was left completely alone. Shysong spent all day outside because she was obedient and everyone had come to trust her. Even the youngest groom could be seen leading her across the yard or bathing her. But those same grooms weren't allowed anywhere near Echofrost.

One morning when Rahkki had arrived late, a nicker rose in her throat—a greeting. She'd suppressed it, of course, but she was beginning to understand how the

Landwalkers had tamed the pegasi four hundred years ago by locking them in stalls and forcing dependency on them. Without Rahkki, Echofrost would starve to death, and that bound her to him.

Now the cub was leading her toward the stupid round sandpit again, a place he led her every day after she drank and grazed. She knew he wanted her to run in a circle along the edge of it, but she saw no reason to do that, so she didn't. His brother, Brauk, had given up on her, it seemed, because he rarely showed up anymore; she was mighty pleased about that.

They halted just outside the gate. Shysong was in the pit now, and Echofrost rested one leg and watched her friend gallop in an elegant circle with her neck arched and her wings tucked high on her back. Koko stood in the center, directing her. Rahkki's friend Princess I'Lenna leaned on the rail, but when she noticed him, she skipped closer.

"Rahkki," she said. "Look at Firo's gait! She trots like she's floating. I bet she's a wonder in the sky."

Rahkki glanced around the yard, looking nervous. "I'm not sure I'm allowed to talk to you."

I'Lenna frowned. "Who told you that?"

"Harak Nightseer."

She considered his words and then brushed them off. "Then let's not tell him."

"What about your mother?"

"She's meeting with General Tsun," I'Lenna said. "Want some spearmint?" She handed Rahkki a sprig of the herb wrapped in a flat leaf.

As Rahkki chewed the plant, he relaxed, and Echofrost turned her attention to Shysong cantering in the pen. Her friend's hide glistened with sweat, her muscles had hardened from the work, and her mane and tail flowed behind her, free of tangles and burrs. All the baths had erased her natural scent, leaving her smelling like them—the Kihlari.

Shysong slowed her pace to whisk off an aggressive fly, and Tuni tapped her rear with a whip. Her friend reared, surprised. Tuni tapped Shysong again, not hard enough to hurt her but hard enough to get her attention. "Canter," Tuni commanded.

Echofrost watched Shysong tamp down her rage and canter forward, but deep fury lurked behind the roan's flat expression. Echofrost sucked in her breath, suddenly realizing that Shysong was using *all* her strength to remain obedient. She'd thought that Shysong had grown to trust the Landwalkers, but that wasn't it. Shysong was coping by *cooperating*. It was perhaps less silly than *not* cooperating, which was how Echofrost was coping. Her ears burned with shame for judging Shysong earlier.

When they were finished, Tuni and Shysong exited the sandpit.

"We're next," Rahkki said.

"Can I watch you train her?" I'Lenna asked.

"Sure," he said, smiling. "If you tell me how you sneak out of the fortress."

"What?" I'Lenna's jaw dropped, and she turned on her heel to leave. "I will not."

Rahkki spoke quickly. "I'm sorry! Please stay. Look, you can watch me make a fool of myself while Sula ignores me."

I'Lenna crossed her arms. "Promise?"

"Promise what?"

"That you'll make a fool of yourself?"

Rahkki chuckled and led Echofrost into the round pen. "Trot," he commanded, but Echofrost paid no attention to him.

"See," Rahkki said. "She ignores me. Much like you."

I'Lenna climbed onto the rail and leaned over it. "I think I'm doing the opposite of ignoring you, Rahkki."

"Then why won't you tell me how you get out of Fort

Prowl? Unless you're scaling the walls, it's impossible."

"Come here," she said.

Rahkki strode across the sand toward her, and Echofrost sensed the tension building inside the princess, but the girl hid it well. I'Lenna lowered her mouth to Rahkki's ear. "It's too dangerous for you to know," she whispered. "Don't ask again."

Rahkki blinked at her and then I'Lenna jumped back, her eyes on someone behind him. Echofrost followed her gaze and spied Harak emerging from the Kihlari den. He spotted I'Lenna and clenched his fists.

"I have to go," she said. She whipped around so fast that her hair fanned around her like petals around a flower stem. Then she was gone, her sandals kicking up hunks of mud.

Rahkki stared after the princess, looking confused. Echofrost shoved his arm with her muzzle, drawing him out of his thoughts. "Sorry," he said absently. Rahkki closed the gate and unhooked her lead rope. The first few times they'd entered this pen, he'd held a whip in his hands, not to hit her, but to direct her. Still, she didn't like the sight of it, so she'd snatched it out of his fingers and broken it. From that day forward he just stood in the center of the pit and waved his arms at her.

"Trot," he said again, clucking at her this time.

Echofrost stared at him like she usually did, with her hooves rooted in the sand, but her shame about Shysong returned. *Could* Echofrost obey Rahkki? Did she have that kind of strength? She shrugged her wings; there was only one way to find out. Echofrost trotted forward.

Rahkki's eyes popped wide. "Good girl," he whispered.

Echofrost proceeded to do everything he asked of her. She trotted and cantered in both directions. She did it with her wings high and her wings low, folded and open. She galloped. She stopped and turned when he asked. She sped up and slowed. It wasn't so terrible if she shut off her feelings.

Finally he signaled her to stop. She was wet with sweat, but strangely, she felt better for the exercise. Her muscles were getting soft in the stall, and it struck Echofrost that cooperating could be good for *her*. Eating their grain and exercising would make her more powerful, more ready for escape. She lowered her head—she'd been a fool. She'd let her body become weak, all because of pride.

Wingbeats drew her attention. Kol flew overhead, with Brauk on his back. "Look at the mighty Sula," the chestnut stallion brayed to the Kihlari steeds present in the yard. "Tamed by a boy."

"He didn't *tame* me," she snorted. "I chose to obey him."

The Kihlari in the yard burst into amused nickering.

"What do you think taming is?" Kol asked.

She stared at him, her confidence melting.

Rahkki grinned at Echofrost, flashing his little white teeth, which she knew meant that he was happy. He approached her and snapped on her lead rope with less caution than was usual for him. Echofrost resented his joy, but noticed that he believed in her obedience. She tucked that information away for later—the Landwalkers were easy to fool.

She flexed her wings, studying her flight feathers. In ten days, maybe less, she'd be able to fly again. She gazed at the clear sky overhead. Nothing would keep her on land once her feathers grew back.

"Let's bathe you," Rahkki said, leading her toward the water-filled buckets.

But then a sudden cold feeling, like ice in her blood, made Echofrost pause and listen. *Something was wrong.* Around her, every single pegasus lifted its head. Kol swiveled his ears. *They feel it too*, she thought. A young mare spooked and brayed an alarm that erupted like a flame, blazing through the Kihlari steeds. Everyone sensed danger, but what was it?

Then the land shook beneath Echofrost's hooves.

The birds, monkeys, insects—all went silent.

"Giants!" Kol brayed.

"Giants!" Brauk shouted.

Echofrost whipped her head around. The trees in the forest that bordered the yard crashed against each other, and her ears filled with a ferocious, trumpeting roar—a sound she'd never heard in her life. It vibrated her ribs and pierced her ears. She flapped her useless wings and turned to Rahkki. Fright rounded his golden eyes.

"What do we do?" Echofrost whinnied to the Kihlari, but they were in motion, gliding toward the armory with their Riders. She faced the forest with her heart slamming her chest and her ears pinned. Whatever was coming, she and Rahkki would face it together.

24

RAID

RAHKKI SIDLED CLOSER TO SULA, TOUCHING HIS shoulder to hers. The ground shook beneath his boots as the giants crashed through the jungle toward them. Every single Sandwen grabbed a weapon. Warning bells clanged from the fortress, calling all the Fifth Clan's armed patrols in from the jungle and the sky. Fierce shouts and the distant cries of children reached his ears. This wasn't one Gorlander. This was an attacking horde.

He glanced at Sula. Her eyes were as black as pitch and trained on the trees. She faced the coming enemy with her wings flared, her head low, ready for battle. Rahkki's legs wanted to run, but he was twelve now, no longer a child. He would help his people. Brauk flew overhead on

Kol, and Rahkki shouted to him, "Brauk! What do I do?"

"Get out of here. Get to Uncle!" Brauk ripped at Kol's reins, flying toward Fort Prowl to call out Tuni and the rest of the Sky Guard. The giants must have busted through the tight perimeter patrolled by the Land Guard. But how?

The Gorlan horde stomped closer, leaving a wake of swaying trees. Rahkki couldn't see them yet, but he smelled them on the wind.

As the alarms blared down from the fortress, the village folk on the hillside screamed for their children. Dozens of kids raced home from the fallows. Mut Finn and his gang trotted past, carrying slingshots and clubs. Mut's eyes drifted toward Rahkki, and he nodded in truce.

Rahkki's blowgun was tucked in his satchel, but the darts weren't poisoned. He doubted the small tips that killed fish in the river could kill a giant. He had no way to protect Sula, and she couldn't fly yet. If the giants caught her, they'd steal her and eat her. He had to get her out of the yard. "Come," he said, urging her forward. Sula's ears swiveled, and her eyes hunted for danger. She didn't budge.

The Sky Guard Riders burst through the iron gates of the fortress and scrambled down the hill, whooping and hollering. The strongest grooms gripped the ropes and cranked open the barn ceiling. Rahkki leaped sideways as Riders stormed past him. One smashed into him, knocking him flat. He lost hold of Sula's rope. She flapped her wings and lifted an inch off the ground but could rise no higher. Landing, she stomped her hooves, snorting and whirling in a circle, and just missed trampling Rahkki.

"Easy, Sula," he called to her, and she jerked her head toward him as if just remembering he was there. Rahkki pushed himself up, spitting dirt and coughing. He grabbed the end of her rope just as she bolted toward the barn and was yanked off his feet. Not thinking to let go of the rope, he bounced across the yard, yowling as his bones scraped the soil. No one paid him or his runaway mare any attention.

Sula halted when a trumpeting roar pierced the chaos. Rahkki staggered upright and shook the dirt out of his ears. "Elephants!" he shouted, but the elephants themselves drowned out his warning. He hadn't heard any mention of them in Brauk's reports. He'd assumed the giants had left their massive leviathans at home. *I need a weapon!*

He touched Sula to get her attention. They needed to get to the armory.

She coiled back her neck and met his gaze, her eyes glittering.

"Please," he said to her. "Follow me." He tugged gently on her lead and she followed him, seeming to understand.

They jogged into the barn and past the tack room. The Riders had already raided it of saddles and bridles, and had moved to the stalls to tack up their mounts. All around him, Rahkki heard loud buckling and the clang of metal. One by one, the Riders flew out of the stalls and out of the barn. Overhead, Tuni sailed by on Rizah. The woman's dark eyes blazed, and her expression was fierce. She had three sisters and two brothers living in the village with her parents, and so this Gorlan raid was personal to her, and to the entire clan.

Tuni caught sight of Rahkki. "Get safe!" she hollered.

How, he wondered.

Tuni kicked Rizah, loaded her bow, and swooped toward the Gorlan horde.

Rahkki trotted Sula past the tack room to the armory, wincing at the bruises blooming across his body. He pushed open the wooden door and was disappointed. The armory had also been plundered by the Riders and left a mess. Rahkki led Sula into the cluttered room with him and searched through the leftover weapons, hunting for anything small enough to wield.

Outside, the roar of elephants and giants grew closer. This was the fault of the queen. Her incompetent Borla had a bad dream, a bad omen, and so she hadn't sent her full militia out to take care of the Gorlan hordes when they'd first descended from Mount Crim. Born tenth in line to her birth clan's throne, Lilliam had not been educated to rule. She was superstitious and inexperienced. His mother would not have let the giants get so close!

Sweat dripped from Rahkki's forehead, and Sula pranced next to him, spooking at every noise. "Shh," he said, trying to soothe her. "We're okay." But they weren't okay. He could feel the thudding of the elephants through his frayed boots. He spotted Brauk's weapon box, remembering that his brother kept his first sawa blade inside as a spare. It was the one he'd learned on when *he* was twelve. Rahkki threw open the lid of the trunk and shifted through Brauk's pieces of cracked leather, doeskin gloves, sealed rations of jerky, wide selection of shields, and items that were more difficult to decipher.

Ah, there it was—the blade. He slid it from its sheath, checked the edge for sharpness, and sliced open his finger. Perfect. He attached the sword to his belt and was about to leave when he spotted Brauk's old helmet tucked beneath a pair of crocodile-skin riding boots. Rahkki donned the helmet and strapped on an oversize chest shield. Then he led Sula out of the tack room.

The silver mare whinnied to her roan friend, and Firo whinnied back. Rahkki realized that Firo was trapped in her stall—and this was probably why Sula had dragged him into the barn—to save her friend. Rahkki raced toward the penned mare with Sula in tow. He found Firo's stall, grabbed the halter hanging on the door, and slipped it over her head. She was the only winged horse left in the barn—the rest had been taken out to fight the giants, even the few that were sick or injured. Rahkki led Firo and Sula out of the stable, and the mares calmed instantly at the sight of each other.

Outside the barn, Riders charged in formation toward the giants; their steeds flew fast with their ears pinned and tails lashing.

The Land Guard soldiers trooped across the yard, rows and rows of them—some mounted on land horses, the rest marching on foot. They'd coated their spears in boar's blood for luck.

Rahkki glanced at the stone fortress that protected the queen and her daughters. I'Lenna was inside; he'd seen her return after she left him at the round pen. The queen's archers lined the tops of the walls, their arrows drawn, waiting.

Rahkki could head to the village, or to his uncle's farm as Brauk had instructed; but Uncle was alone.

He paused—*Uncle was alone!*

Now he knew what to do. Rahkki would help his uncle defend the farm.

"Come, Sula. Come, Firo," he said, whistling softly to the wild Kihlari. They pricked their ears and followed him with a light prance in their steps.

Behind Rahkki, the jungle groaned, and a fifty-length banyan tree cracked and toppled toward the fortress with a hard shudder. Startled, the archers loosed their arrows. They struck the tree, piercing it in a hundred places. From the ground, Rahkki heard Lilliam screaming in rage. The harmless banyan crashed down like a murdered corpse.

Then an elephant trumpeted and the giants appeared. Hundreds of them poured out of the trees, roaring and draped in buffalo hides that were stained red and as bright as their hair. At least fifty giants sat astride tusked elephants. The rest walked on land, swinging bludgeons and spears. They gestured in Gorlish, sending commands so fast their fingers blurred.

Sula brayed, loud and ferocious, and Firo copied

her. The two mares lowered their necks like wolves and clenched their jaws. Rahkki's heart raced, but his feet seemed rooted to the grass as he watched the giants emerge.

The Sandwen Land Guard galloped toward them astride their chargers, hefting spears. General Tsun barked orders from the rear. The giants lifted heavy shields and mowed down the front line of Sandwen soldiers, crushing them under their elephants' feet and stabbing them with their spears. The horde roared in unison and advanced over the bones of the dead. Rahkki's people swarmed, quick and organized, like ants.

Rahkki drew the sawa blade, his hand shaking. The tallest Gorlanders towered to fourteen lengths, but most stood around eleven or twelve lengths. All of them were as thick as they were tall, and they dwarfed the lean Sandwens. The elephants loomed sixteen lengths at the shoulder, some taller. Their tiny eyes flashed in their gray heads, and Rahkki thought they looked terrified, but that made them no less deadly. One had a Sandwen warrior hanging off his tusk. The elephant tossed him off, and a giant speared the man straight through.

Rahkki bent over and threw up.

Sula nickered for his attention. Rahkki wiped his

mouth. The mares wanted to fight or run, and he'd lose control of them if he didn't act soon.

He glimpsed Brauk soaring into the battle flanked by Tuni and Harak, and his heart tightened. The Sky Guard shot another round of arrows, slowing the giants' speed as they paused to lift their wooden shields. The Land Guard rallied, and soon the clanging of metal and the thud of blows filled the yard. Brauk guided Kol lower and slayed giants from the chestnut's back. Kol kicked them with his hooves, twisting as he flew to avoid being grabbed.

But the giants kept coming. From the eight turrets of Fort Prowl, more archers appeared, prepared to shoot if the elephants came close enough to batter down the front gates. Rahkki glimpsed the Queen of the Fifth watching the battle from her perch on the highest tower, I'Lenna at her side. The crown princess wrung her hands, her eyes fixed on the fighting below.

Mut and his friends leaped from one wounded giant to the next, quickly ending their lives. Koko had joined them, her weapon a four-pronged pitchfork.

Without thinking any more about it, Rahkki leaped onto Firo's back, slipped his legs beneath her wings, and kicked her toward Uncle's farm. She surged forward, almost toppling him off her back. He curled his hands into her black mane while keeping hold of Sula's lead. Firo galloped, quick and sure, and Sula kept pace with them.

Rahkki guided Firo as best he could without a bit or reins. Kihlari were smarter than horses, so within minutes she understood to move opposite his leg pressure. When his heel pushed on her right side, Firo turned left, and when it pushed on her left side, Firo turned right. If he squeezed with both heels, she ran faster. As soon as she did as he asked, he released the pressure to reward her.

In this manner they galloped past the village and across the lowland plains, heading north. And each time Firo jumped a bush or a ditch, she flapped her wings and this buoyed them over the obstacles and caused Rahkki's belly to float. On the way he passed the soldiers who had been sent to guard the outlying farms like Uncle's. They were galloping back toward the fortress on their war horses, called by the bells. "How goes it?" one shouted to Rahkki.

He shook his head. "They brought elephants."

"Stinkin' giants!" All the soldiers spit on the ground and kept going.

Soon Rahkki reached the rice farm and Firo halted, sliding through the mud in front of Uncle's hut.

Darthan stepped out his door in full armor and with a

long-handled Daakuran sword at the ready.

Rahkki gaped at him. "Where did you get that?" He stared at the weapon, which was etched with a fiery sun. The sun was the symbol of Daakur, the eastern empire on the other side of Cinder Bay.

"That story is for a hot fire and a peaceful day," said Darthan. His eyes flicked over the mares. "Did you steal them?"

"No. I'm *saving* them. They can't fly."

The corners of his uncle's lips twitched. "Put them in Lutegar's stall."

"But where's Lutegar?" Rahkki asked, feeling panicked. His head swam with images: the redheaded giants, the trumpeting elephants, the army, the storming Kihlari Riders, the blur of the land under Firo's hooves, his uncle's armor, and the foreign sword—he didn't even know his uncle *had* a sword, or armor.

"Put your winged friends in there *with* Lutegar," Darthan clarified. "It's the biggest stall, and the rest are full. I put all the animals away when I heard the bells. Hurry, Rahkki, then meet me at the mill. We have to move the seeds in case the giants come."

Rahkki led the mares into the barn. They balked at the darkness of it, but he coaxed them inside with soft urgings. Lutegar sniffed the air when he opened her stall door. The two wildlings spooked at the sight of the big buffalo. Rahkki threw fresh hay on the floor, and Lutegar moved aside, making room for the winged mares.

Sula and Firo glanced at each other and then entered the stall. Rahkki closed the door. "I'll be back for you," he said. "I'll protect you; I'll protect this barn. Don't worry." He licked his hand and wiped it across the wood, making his words an oath.

Then he walked out, locked the barn, turned around . . . and froze. Three hulking Gorlanders stood in the distant rice field, facing him. They licked their overstuffed lips, and their eyes, which gleamed beneath their crinkled foreheads, stared at him hungrily.

"Bloody rain," Rahkki whispered. He drew Brauk's sawa blade and faced his enemies.

25

DEFENSE

THE LARGEST OF THE THREE GORLANDERS stomped toward Rahkki, huffing from traveling so far so fast. By the cut of the giant's tunic, he guessed it was a male—but it was tough to be certain with giants. Rahkki lifted his sword to chest height and then sputtered into hysterical laughter. The small blade might be good for trimming the giant's nails, or cutting his unruly hair— but for killing him, useless.

The giant roared, beating his chest like a lowland gorilla, and Rahkki's blood drained to his toes.

Leaning forward, the Gorlander increased his pace, charging headfirst. The swampland rippled out from his heavy steps, rolling like a landquake.

Rahkki turned and ran away from the barn, leading the giant away from Sula, Firo, and Lutegar, heading toward the River Tsallan. The giant picked up speed, and the pounding of his footfalls vibrated Rahkki's chest.

The other two Gorlanders got busy digging up the rice plants and ripping the stalks in half. The attacking horde had tricked his clan! They assaulted the fortress with such force and numbers that the queen had to call in all her armed forces, and that left the farms vulnerable to smaller groups of raiding giants. These three were sent to ruin the Sandwen army's food supply, and now Rahkki was extra glad he'd come to check on Uncle.

"Grrrahar!" growled the giant.

Rahkki glanced behind him.

The Gorlander swung his arms, rocketing across the mud now. His bare feet slapped the soil, leaving footprints like craters. His fist was wrapped around the large handle of an ivory bludgeon, his blue eyes promised death.

Rahkki hadn't known giants were so fast! He sprinted toward the river, leaping over woody vines and brush. Brauk had told him once that Gorlanders didn't swim well—perhaps he could lose him in the water. Rahkki's blood roared in his ears as the giant raced toward him and lifted his weapon. He'd never reach the river first, so Rahkki turned to face him. The giant smiled, showing rotting teeth and his short tongue. He signed in Gorlish, but his hand moved too fast for Rahkki to translate.

The boy crouched, flashing his blade.

The giant rushed forward, swinging his club, and Rahkki knew that the male was too big to stop his charge quickly—his momentum was too great. So Rahkki galloped toward the nearest tree and at the last second leaped behind it. The giant followed him, but as Rahkki predicted, he was too large to change course. His eyes widened, and then he slammed into the trunk. The tree cracked and splintered.

Rahkki raced away from it, but the tree broke toward him. It was at least thirty lengths tall and heavy enough to squash him flat. Rahkki bounded like a deer, hopping and dodging boulders as the tree crashed toward him. He dropped and rolled out of its way just as it struck the ground.

The boy sat up, covered in leaves, in time to see the bludgeon coming down. He rolled again. The ivory smashed into the mud, and the sound shocked his eardrums. He stood, staggering, and the giant's breath blew at him like a hot wind.

Having given up on reaching the river, Rahkki raced

into the jungle. The Gorlander followed, enraged by the tightness of the trees that slowed his pace. The sawa blade slipped out of Rahkki's sweaty palm. He turned, grabbed it, and spotted the two other giants approaching the barn with their weapons raised.

The mares!

Rahkki whipped around faster than the giant could switch directions and sprinted back to the barn. His heart fluttered and his feet blurred beneath him—he had to defend Sula.

"Uncle!" he screamed.

"Here," cried Darthan. He'd returned from the mill and was now running to help Rahkki, drawn by the crashing sound of the tree no doubt. Darthan had his Daakuran sword drawn and a shield attached to his left arm. At the sound of his voice, the giants turned toward him.

Rahkki took that moment to leap at the nearest Gorlander, a female, he guessed. He stabbed her straight through her naked foot. She threw back her head and howled. *No one likes to be stabbed in the foot*, thought Rahkki. *Not even a giant.* He yanked his blade out of her.

She snatched his arm.

Oh no.

The female lifted Rahkki off the ground until they

were eye to eye. She shook him so hard his teeth rattled.

He stabbed at her, but she swung him like a doll. Then she dropped her ivory club and grabbed his other arm, stretching him and studying his face as he yelped.

Uncle Darthan fought the giant next to her, leaping and slicing like a trained Guard (*when had Uncle learned to fight?*), and the third giant was on them both. Inside the barn, Rahkki heard hooves shuffling madly, and then violent kicks against the barn door. The wildlings wanted out.

The female giant tugged Rahkki's arms hard enough to make him scream, and then she reached into the pocket of her tunic and pulled out a dirty piece of sinew. She wrapped it around Rahkki several times, balling him into it, and then she lifted him over her head and dropped him into her back sack.

Rahkki gasped. *She was stealing him!* He squirmed, but his arms were bound tight. It was dark inside her pack, but Rahkki felt creatures crawling on his exposed skin. Terror tore through him. In the dim light filtering through the seams, he spied hunks of rotting fruit swarming with black ants. The ants had begun to climb up his legs, scurrying toward his head. He shrieked and kicked. Rahkki hated ants almost as much as he hated giants!

The barn door shook with the pounding of Sula's and Firo's hooves, his uncle was now fighting three giants by himself, and Rahkki was wound up like a toy yo-yo. *We need help*, he thought.

And then help arrived.

26

HELP

ECHOFROST STRUCK THE OLD, WEATHERED BARN door with a final mighty kick that broke it. Bursting outside, she saw three giants engaged in battle against Rahkki's uncle. The cub was near; she could smell him, but she couldn't see him. Shysong galloped to her side. "What now?"

Echofrost glanced at the jungle, thinking to flee, but she knew she wouldn't get far without her ability to fly. A sprout of dark hair caught her eye and she turned in time to see Rahkki's head poke through a sack tied to the female giant's back. His expression was twisted, desperate, and his golden eyes were as round as twin suns. Black ants swarmed his face and neck. The sorry sight

242

of him shot unexpected rage through her. "Charge the giants!" she whinnied to Shysong.

The mares surged forward, each attacking a giant so that the man Rahkki had called Uncle could focus on the third. Echofrost struck the female Gorlander as Redfire had instructed her in Anok when she was training for Star's United Army. She imagined kicking straight *through* the giant, and soon she felled her like a tree. Rahkki spilled out of her pack.

Echofrost turned on the second giant, and Shysong galloped to help Uncle with the third. The red-haired beast swung a weapon at Echofrost that was spiked at one end. She dodged it, barely. He swung at her again and knocked her into the side of the barn. With her head ringing, the giant stomped toward her—his bludgeon lifted.

All of a sudden, jade feathers shot across her vision. *Hazelwind?* Echofrost peered skyward. Hazelwind and Graystone, Dewberry and Redfire and fifteen pegasi from Storm Herd swooped down from the clouds and attacked the giants from above.

Shysong whinnied a rally cry. Dewberry's voice joined hers, and Echofrost felt a sob of joy rise in her chest. With fresh energy, the pegasi fought side by side. Rahkki rolled out of the melee, struggling with the fibrous cord that bound him.

Echofrost pinned her ears and joined them, slamming the large male Gorlander with both hooves and kicking the breath from him. Seconds later the giants gave in and fled, snatching up their clubs as they left. The creature that Rahkki called Lutegar charged out of the barn and bellowed as though she'd chased them off herself.

"I've never seen her move so fast," Rahkki said, staring at Lutegar.

Uncle chuckled and sat down, wiping his sword.

Echofrost felt the tension leave the Landwalkers, and herself. Her friends landed, and she trotted to Hazelwind's side and pressed her muzzle into his neck, inhaling his warm scent.

"I'm back," he said, wrapping his neck around hers.

Dewberry folded her wings. "What should we do with these two?" she asked, eyeing Rahkki and his uncle, who were each gaping at the wild herd.

"Nothing," Echofrost answered. "They haven't hurt us."

Hazelwind drew back to speak. "We've been watching you as best we can since that Landwalker shot at me," he said. Echofrost noticed the long scabs across his chest where Koko's arrows had cut Hazelwind. "But we haven't been able to get close."

"Those Kihlari warriors patrol the sky night and day," Graystone added.

"It's because of the giants," said Shysong. "They increased all their patrols."

"Little good it did them," Dewberry huffed, clutching her sides with her wings.

"Are you sick?" Echofrost asked. Dewberry appeared thinner than ever but her belly had swelled as if filled with gas. Perhaps she'd eaten a toxic plant.

Dewberry lifted her chin, her eyes glittering. "I've never felt better."

Echofrost knew the mare would never admit to weakness, so she turned to Hazelwind, thinking of all the dangers that lurked in the jungle. "Have you lost anyone?" Echofrost asked.

"No. We're safe in the nests, but we've eaten all the leaves and figs. We have to fly down twice a day to graze."

Echofrost, still catching her breath, drank in the sight of Hazelwind, standing right in front of her—his lean muscles, battle-scarred hide, tangled tail, and suspicious eyes all looked beautiful to her. He was wild and free, relying on himself and his herd to survive. And now, with no barrier between them, there was nothing ahead but their future.

Rahkki rose off the ground and limped toward Darthan. Echofrost's friends shied away from the boy. "He's so small," Redfire commented.

"His name's Rahkki," Echofrost told him.

"The Landwalkers have names?"

"Yes, and they also name their Kihlari. I'm called Sula. They call Shysong Firo."

Hazelwind examined Echofrost's feathers. "You still can't fly," he said, frustrated. "That's going to make this difficult."

"What difficult?"

"Leaving this place."

Echofrost glanced at her snipped flight feathers and then at Hazelwind's ruffled expression and Dewberry's impatient posture. It was time to go.

Just then Rahkki approached, speaking his soothing words. She smelled his essence: the burned wood, wet soil, and jungle air, all of it tinged with sorrow. He'd fought for her today, battling giants three times his size. He had the heart of a stallion.

Was it possible that some Landwalkers were good?

She and Shysong allowed Rahkki to approach, and the others watched wide-eyed. "What's he doing?" Dewberry asked.

Graystone and Redfire tensed, ready to attack. "Hold," Hazelwind cautioned. He knew Echofrost best and seemed to understand that she wasn't concerned about the cub.

Rahkki reached Shysong first, untied her halter, and slipped it off her head. Next he turned to Echofrost and stared into her eyes. "Sula," he whispered. He untied her halter and let it fall from her face. "You're free. Go with your friends." Tears sprang to his golden eyes, turning them bright yellow. He stepped away from her. "Go," he said, "before the Land Guard arrives to check on the farm. I'll tell everyone you and Firo broke free during the attack."

Echofrost understood what he was doing, if not his words; he was letting her go. But Kol had told her that she and Shysong were valuable to the queen of Rahkki's clan. He'd also explained to her that these Landwalkers would never turn her loose. She imagined that Rahkki would be punished for what he was trying to do. She exhaled. Beneath his fear and uncertainty, the little cub was brave.

Rahkki lifted his hand toward her and then snatched it back.

"He knows I don't like to be touched," Echofrost explained to her friends.

Rahkki turned away, wiping his eyes. "Good-bye," he said. And then he motioned for the man called Uncle to follow and they disappeared inside the nearby Land-walker hut.

"That was easy," Hazelwind said. "Now let's go."

They turned and walked away on hoof since the mares couldn't fly, and Echofrost felt a tug of sadness. Not for herself, but for Rahkki. The cub would miss her; she'd seen that in his golden eyes. But she doubted the Kihlari would miss her.

"There's something you all should know," she said to her friends. They slowed, listening. "The pegasi that live here—they say their ancestors came from the north. That they flew here from across the sea about four hundred years ago. I believe they're *all* descendants of the missing Lake Herd pegasi." She let her words sink in and then continued. "They carry our blood, our history, and they're trapped here. I feel like we should help them."

Her rescuers halted, stunned.

But Hazelwind didn't lose a moment considering her words. "No," he snapped. "If we don't leave now, then *we* could end up like *them*. This is what I'm trying to prevent. This is why I didn't want to come back for you—at first—because I don't want to tell Star and Morningleaf, if I ever see them again, that I *failed*, that I led Storm

Herd straight into a trap. We have to leave these foreigners behind."

"But they're from Anok, and they're *slaves*, just like we were to Nightwing."

"Do they want help?" Redfire asked, curious.

Echofrost didn't answer that because she wasn't sure—but how could the Kihlari understand freedom when they'd never experienced it?

"Look," Hazelwind said. "I understand why this is important to you, but it's too dangerous for us. Their captivity is proof of that."

She nodded. "I understand."

He nudged her, and his long black forelock fell across his eye. "Are you ready to leave this place behind? Are you ready to find a new home . . . with me?"

She met his gaze, wondering how deep his question flowed. "Yes, I'm ready."

"Seize them!" shouted a Landwalker.

Echofrost spun around, expecting to see more giants, but instead there were soldiers, fifty of them on horseback. They burst from the tree line, swinging ropes at the Storm Herd steeds. Hazelwind and the others lifted off and glided forward to fight.

"No," Echofrost bellowed. "Fly away!"

Hazelwind swooped down on the soldiers, kicking them.

Since Echofrost and Shysong couldn't fly to safety, they galloped into the empty rice fields, but the swampy turf swallowed their hooves, slowing them. They flapped their wings to help pull up their legs. Twenty horses followed. They were faster and more powerful than pegasi on land, and they leaped through the mud, splattering it across their chests. The soldiers swung ropes and tossed them around Echofrost's and Shysong's necks, pulling the nooses tight.

Echofrost trumpeted in outrage. Graystone landed in the midst of the land horses and barreled through a group of soldiers, tossing them in every direction.

A heavy shield struck Echofrost in the head, followed by a wave of dizziness. Then a dark hood was pulled over her eyes.

Rahkki's screaming reached her ears. "*Let them go!*"

She heard feathers fluttering and grunts of pain, from both pegasi and Landwalkers.

"What's happening?" Echofrost whinnied.

Hazelwind's voice drifted down to her. "Graystone's been hit. We're carrying him back to the nests!"

"Is he alive?"

"For now," Dewberry grunted.

Echofrost panted beneath the dark hood, her heart breaking.

"Don't give up," Hazelwind whinnied. "We'll get you out as soon as we can."

Echofrost wanted to scream his name, to call him back, to say *Please don't leave me here.* But Hazelwind had to protect Graystone and the others.

Shysong moaned.

"Are you hurt?" Echofrost asked her.

"No, I'm mad!"

Strong hands dragged Echofrost back into the barn and locked her in a stall. Shysong was dragged in next. The soldiers grumbled, and the barn animals oinked and bleated.

Later that evening, Rahkki entered the barn escorted by soldiers. He removed Echofrost's and Shysong's hoods and wept. "I'm sorry," he said to the mares. Then to the soldiers, "Can I stable them together? Please."

"Yeah, but don't get smart," said a blond soldier. "I saw you trying to free them. You're bloody lucky we caught them before they ran off." The other nine soldiers stood with batons in hands, ready to smack Rahkki and the mares if they tried to escape again.

Rahkki led Echofrost and Firo to Lutegar's stall. They

entered and stood next to the swamp buffalo. Lutegar rolled her eyes over their feathers and hooves and then mooed with pleasure, as if deciding she fit right in with them.

The mares nickered back to her and Echofrost noticed that Lutegar's heart rate was slow, her breaths far apart. She was calm from her flat ears down to her heavy cloven hooves. She doubted that anything could spook this beast, not a spit dragon, not a Landwalker, and not a giant. But the buffalo's quietness soothed Echofrost's nerves much like a medicine mare's mashed concoctions had once calmed her after she was freed from Mountain Herd.

Rahkki pitched hay at their hooves and took their bucket to the river behind the barn and filled it. When he returned, he reached out his fingers to Echofrost, speaking softly. She flinched, and he snapped his hand back. "Sorry," he whispered.

"Be nice," Shysong scolded. "He set you free, and now look, he's in trouble."

The mare had a point. The way the guards glowered at Rahkki, she knew he'd displeased them.

Echofrost sighed, regretting her blunt show of revulsion. "I'm trying to trust him."

Rahkki exited the barn and latched the damaged door

as best he could. Outside, Echofrost heard the soldiers sur-round the barn and the hut, protecting the farm from the Gorlanders, she assumed, and guarding her and Shysong. Echofrost considered the fact that the Landwalkers were like a herd, working together, which made them stronger.

As usual, she'd underestimated them.

27

STOPPING TIME

AFTER RAHKKI LOCKED THE MARES IN FOR THE
night, he hurried to the River Tsallan. Rotten fruit and
dead ants still flecked his skin from the Gorlander's filthy
sack. He made a quick scan for alligators, undressed, and
then dived into the clear water, swimming to the deep-
est part. The cool liquid soothed his aching muscles and
bruised skin. He kicked against the current and then
turned onto his back and floated downriver, his eyes on
the clouds. High, high above, he spotted the small specks
that were the wild herd. They zoomed southeast, carrying
their injured friend.

"That's enough swimming!" shouted a guard, startling

Rahkki. A small unit of soldiers had followed him to the river. "Get inside where it's safe."

Rahkki paddled to shore, climbed out, and shook his wet hair. He retrieved his filthy outer clothing and carried it back with him to the hut. The soldiers watched, their eyes wary.

When Rahkki entered his uncle's small home, he saw that Darthan had built a fire and fried two small fish. Pulling on a clean shirt and soft pants from his loft, Rahkki straddled the chair next to Uncle's.

Darthan slid a charred fish onto a plate and handed it to Rahkki. He'd already poured him a cup of goat's milk.

Rahkki tapped his feet, staring at Darthan.

His uncle smiled. "Go on, ask me."

Rahkki's questions exploded. "Where did you learn to fight like that, Uncle? And where did you get a Daakuran sword? Did you travel there?" Everyone knew that the Daakuran smelters forged the best blades on either shore of Cinder Bay. "I've never seen one up close!" Rahkki ripped off a bite of the hot fish, suddenly starving, then jumped back in. "And where did you learn to swing it? You were like two people at once. Does Brauk know about this sword?"

His uncle sat on the chair where he meditated into

the fire each evening, waiting for his dinner to cool and cleaning his sword. He stroked the grooves with a polishing cloth, working with slow precision. "You squawk like a bird," he said, stuffing his smile.

Rahkki lowered his voice. "I thought you were a farmer, Uncle."

Darthan guided the clean sword into its sheath. "I *am* a farmer," he replied.

"But—"

"I'm *also* a fighter and a traveler," said his uncle, picking up his fork. "I'm not one thing, Rahkki, and neither are you."

"Did you learn to fight in the Land Guard?" It made sense—all Sandwen youths spent three years in the Land Guard, unless they purchased a Flier and joined the Sky Guard. But Uncle shook his head and lifted his sleeve, showing Rahkki the brand burned onto his shoulder, a Kihlari brand. Rahkki gaped at it. Was this why his uncle always wore long sleeves? "You were a Rider?"

Uncle nodded.

"Where is your Flier?" Rahkki blurted this, and then he slapped his hand over his mouth. Riders and Kihlari Paired for life, so there was only one answer to Rahkki's question—Uncle's Kihlara was dead. "I'm sorry," he said.

His uncle sheathed his sword and lit his pipe. "Don't be sorry; it has nothing to do with you." Uncle leaned back and cleared his throat.

Rahkki held still, sensing that one of Darthan's stories would soon pour from his lips as smooth as the smoke from his pipe. Outside, the soldiers spoke quietly and cooked their dinner, which was sadly Uncle's smallest pig.

Darthan drew on the pipe, and the clove leaves flamed red. "I was twenty-five when I first saw him," said Uncle. "He was a small bay stallion with sparkling feathers— dark amber, they were, and tipped in black. His tail waved behind him like a banner when he flew, thick and arched." Darthan used one hand to demonstrate the waving tail. "The stallion was faster than lightning and as comfortable to ride as a cloud." Darthan lipped his pipe, an expression of pure pleasure on his face. "The stallion's name was Drael."

Rahkki started. "Wait, Drael was my mother's stallion."

"Hmm," said Uncle, sighing. "Not yet he wasn't. I had my eye on that bay steed, but so did my sister." A slow curve touched Darthan's lips. "Reyella was younger than I, but she was ferocious. You know the clan called her the Pantheress?"

"I know."

"She was also my queen, but that stallion—he was perfection. I had to have him." Darthan tapped his chest over his heart.

"I know what that's like," Rahkki whispered.

Darthan nodded. "Reyella felt the same way about Drael as I did, but your mother, she wouldn't use her position to take him from me. She wasn't that way. No, she said she'd fight me for him."

"She wanted to fight you?" Rahkki couldn't believe it. He remembered Darthan and Reyella as being close.

"Yes, she did, and I couldn't offend her by backing down. She challenged me in front of the clan." Darthan pulled on his pipe and looked at Rahkki with a crooked smile. "Besides, I wanted that winged horse. I wanted him bad."

Rahkki was stunned. Uncle had always seemed content with so little. It was difficult to imagine him wanting anything so much that he'd fight his own sister for it. Rahkki studied his uncle's face, seeing past his sun-wrinkled skin to his younger self.

Darthan exhaled a long stream of smoke. "The next morning, when the sun cast its light into my room in the fortress, I knew that I would lose the stallion to her. I don't know how I knew it, but I was as certain of it as the rising sun."

Uncle paused, and spent several minutes shifting in his seat, fussing with his pipe, and clearing his throat until Rahkki felt about to explode. Finally, he continued. "We fought in the courtyard of Fort Prowl. She chose the staff as our weapon. Drael was there. He belonged to the First Clan, and his owner held his lead rope, waiting for one of us to win the fight and buy the stallion."

"How much did he cost?" Rahkki asked. His uncle stared into the fire, not answering, and Rahkki shut his mouth.

After a moment Uncle resumed the story. "Your mother faced me in the courtyard, fearless. When I charged her, she crouched, waiting for me. I was angry now because I didn't want to hurt her." He chuckled. "I needn't have worried. She sidestepped and threw me into the air. I charged again and she knocked me to the ground, then she flipped me over her head—but she didn't hit me, not once. Reyella used my force, my anger, against me. I'd never experienced anything like it. I was like Brauk then—a scrapper. I relied on my strength and speed, but in that fight those forces betrayed me."

"How could she do that?" Rahkki blurted, unable to

stop himself. "Was she magical?"

"If only she had been magical," Darthan said, his expression wistful. "But no, she was not."

"Then how—"

"Our mother sent Reyella to Daakur for training. She learned many things there—letters and science and number figuring—but she also learned the Daakuran fighting art called *Sehvan*. *Sehvan* means "flow" in Talu."

Rahkki mouthed the word. "Sehvan."

"She controlled the flow of my energy, all the while remaining calm and serene. It was powerful, and she won Drael. She paid four full rounds for him."

"That's four hundred dramals!" Rahkki whistled.

Darthan puffed on his clove leaves, allowing Rahkki to ponder a moment.

"So if my mom won Drael, then how did you become a Rider in the Sky Guard?"

His uncle's eyes sparkled with tears, and it was a few moments before he spoke again. "Your mother knew something I didn't."

"What?" Rahkki asked, his heart speeding as he leaned forward. "Tell me!"

His uncle inhaled slowly, then let out his next words in a puff of clove-scented smoke. "Drael had an identical twin."

Rahkki leaped out of his chair. "No way!"

"He did. A stallion chipped from the same stone, so to speak. Her personal guard led the bay steed out of the stable and trotted him into the sunlight." Darthan wiped his eyes. "His name was Tor, and he was just as exquisite, just as fast, and just as smooth to ride."

Rahkki's thoughts swirled. "But then, why did she fight you if she knew Drael had a twin?"

Darthan laughed in a short, hard burst. "That was for fun." He sighed. "Though I can't say I enjoyed it. But she also did it to teach me."

"To teach you how to fight?"

"No, to teach me not to fight *her*. After she beat me she paid the First Clan for my stallion too, the same sum she'd paid for Drael, and she gave him to me as a gift. When she handed me Tor's reins, she said, 'We're family, Darthan.'" Now Uncle's tears flowed silently down his cheeks. "And I understood. She was telling me that we were stronger standing together than fighting against each other."

He tapped his pipe into the fireplace. "You see, her Borla had a vision that she'd bear only sons while she was queen, and she knew that having an unsecured throne would cause trouble for her. She wanted me by her side in all things."

Darthan set down his pipe. "I never challenged your mother again. She taught me Sehvan, and I joined the Sky Guard with Tor. But three years later Tor died."

Rahkki dropped his fork. "So soon?"

Uncle nodded. "We were flying on patrol, and his . . . his heart failed. He died instantly, and we crashed. The trees saved me, cradled me like a babe, but Tor—his body broke on the ground."

His uncle paused. "Poke the fire, will you?"

Rahkki clasped the poker and shoved on the wood, pushing it back toward the center of the fireplace.

"I became a Half," Darthan said. "The Sky Guard Riders avoided me after that. It's bad luck, you know, to be friends with a Half. I moved out of the fortress, bought this farm, and didn't look back. Reyella didn't ask me to stay, but I knew she wished I had. And now, so do I." His eyes met Rahkki's. "I wasn't there the night she died. I didn't really understand her lesson until it was too late: we're stronger standing together."

Rahkki stared down at his hands, remembering that awful night. Brauk had spent years training him not to cry, but Brauk wasn't here. He bent over and watched his tears splat onto the dusty wood floor.

Darthan smoked while the energetic firelight danced

across his face. When Rahkki finished crying, his uncle warmed up another cup of goat's milk and sent him to bed.

"Uncle?" Rahkki asked. "What happened to Drael? I mean, I know he died too, but how? Why can't I remember?"

Darthan's expression tightened. "It happened the same night Reyella was assassinated. He died saving you and your brother."

"Yes, but all I remember is riding him down the hall in the fortress and jumping out the window." Rahkki hugged his warm cup to his chest. "How come Brauk doesn't talk about it? How come I can't remember anything else?"

"I suspect that Brauk doesn't talk and you don't remember for the same reason. You aren't ready."

"But I want to know."

Uncle inhaled deeply, sitting taller. "Your mind will lift the veil when you're strong enough to know the truth. Until then, that veil is a gift. Let it protect you."

Rahkki wasn't so sure, but he trudged up the ladder to his loft and lay in bed. He doubted he would sleep, but by the time he pulled the blankets to his chin, the world went black and he drifted into dreamlessness.

* * *

Two long days passed at Uncle's farm. The Land Guard had banned all civilian ground travel and ordered Rahkki, Darthan, and the wildlings to stay put. The Sky Guard had finally driven the Gorlan horde back to their temporary camp at the base of Mount Crim, but no farther.

Messengers had been sent on winged broodmares to the traveling Sandwen clans to warn them again about the giants and to hurry them along the travelways to the annual Gathering. The approaching clans had weapons and Riders and land soldiers that would reinforce the armaments of the Fifth Clan if the giants attacked again.

Meanwhile, under the watchful eyes of the soldiers, Rahkki helped Darthan repair the damage to the fields. Many rice plants had been destroyed, and the harvest would be light this season, but the seeds were safe in Darthan's mill. Rahkki also tended the animals and exercised the brayas.

It was evening now, and Rahkki was standing on the bank of River Tsallan watching Sula and Firo graze on water reeds. He skipped stones as the sun set in the west. Four soldiers stood near, guarding the valuable mares. They'd insisted Rahkki tie nooses around their necks so they could control the wildlings if they tried to run away.

As Rahkki studied Sula, she stopped grazing and watched the river. He had the eerie feeling she was thinking. "I wish we could talk," he whispered to her.

She pricked her ears toward him.

He glanced at her flight feathers, noticing how much they'd grown. She'd fly soon. "I would buy you if I could," he said, dreaming out loud. "I'd keep you as a pet, and we could live here together. I wouldn't cut your feathers or tie you up. I'm not a Rider; I wouldn't ask anything of you, just that you trust me."

Although Sula had accepted his touch with less bitterness since they fought the giants, Rahkki knew she hadn't truly changed. When he tried to stroke her soft hide or scratch behind her ears, she jerked away from him. Firo didn't mind being petted, but he didn't feel the same connection to the blue roan that he felt for Sula. It was something Rahkki couldn't explain, but the longer he was around the wild mare, the louder he heard her heartbeat, the more familiar became her scent, and the more the sight of her filled his heart with happiness.

But soon he would lose her.

"You know I would help you if I could, right?"

Sula huffed and pawed the grass, snuffling for the sweetest blades. The sun dropped lower, setting her silver hide aglow. The breeze cooled, and dozens of fireflies flew out of the jungle. They massed over Sula's ears like a shining crown. She flared her nostrils and arched her neck, watching them swirl above her. Her white mane fluttered against her darker coat. Rahkki gazed into her eyes, and they were as deep and mysterious as the river. His heart swelled, and he exhaled with wonder.

"That's enough grazing for tonight," said a very bored-looking soldier. He and the others stood.

Rahkki skipped the rock he'd been holding, counting four strikes before it sank into the river. Time had passed too quickly. Between his days of training Sula in the yard and his time stuck here on the farm, there were now only five days left until the auction. Sula would be sold to a Rider, unless no one bid on her. In that case she'd be delivered to the Ruk to birth foals. Or maybe her friends would come back and free her. Maybe they too were just waiting for her feathers to grow back—but no matter what happened, she'd soon be gone. And although they hadn't officially Paired, and never would or could, Rahkki knew he'd feel like a Half without her.

If only the future could stay in the future, he thought. *Did Uncle or anyone know how to do that—to stop time?* Rahkki doubted it. He and Sula would have to face it.

28

DESTRUCTION

ONE MORE DAY PASSED AND THEN BRAUK SENT a messenger. Rahkki and the soldiers could return the mares to the Kihlari barn.

"I'll be back after they're settled," Rahkki said to Uncle.

Darthan leaned forward, his old chair creaking. "You can stay with them until the auction," he said. "Don't rush saying good-bye." He winked, and Rahkki's throat tightened. The auction was in four days and then Sula would be sold. He clenched his jaw, remembering his brother's words, *Don't cry, don't ever cry.*

A few hours later Rahkki, the mares, and their armed escorts were marching down the packed road that led from

Uncle's farm to the Fifth Clan village. The messenger had brought an ill-tempered pony for Rahkki to ride home, a glistening steed who'd once belonged to Princess I'Lenna. The pony jerked her head up and down and pranced sideways, sometimes hopping like a crow or bucking. Rahkki knew he looked ridiculous sitting astride a small white pony that he could barely control, especially since they were flanked by ten magnificent and well-trained warhorses. Sula and Firo trotted behind him, attached to long lead ropes that were held by the soldiers. But as they crested a hill that overlooked the fallows, the Kihlari barn and training yard, and Fort Prowl, Rahkki paused, forgetting himself completely.

The yard had been destroyed, like a hurricane had blasted through it. Tree-sized spears were stuck into the sides of the barn; bloody armor, weapons, and saddles had been cut off the land horses right where they'd fallen; and long tracks showed where the bodies had been dragged away. The buckets, fences, tables, and wash racks had been splintered into kindling; and gray smoke drifted into the sky—something had caught fire.

"There's still a lot of cleaning up to do," said one soldier to the others.

"Bloody giants," said another, and they all leaned over their horses' necks and spit.

Kihlari Riders flew above the yard, some returning from patrol, some just heading out. They shouted instructions, warnings, and coordinates to one another. The clan Borla had set up extra tents to help the injured. The Kihlari Fliers and their Riders were treated side by side inside the tents—each refusing to leave the other. Several Riders sat in the shade, looking dead but breathing. Rahkki understood instantly that they had lost their winged steeds in battle and that they were now Halves, like Uncle.

A blond soldier kicked his horse closer to Rahkki, his face grim. "We should have been here helping our clan, not guarding you and those wildlings."

Rahkki gaped at him. "I thought you were guarding the farm."

The soldier narrowed his eyes. "It was both," he admitted, slightly less angry.

Rahkki squinted at the mournful and furious faces around him as the soldiers watched their clansfolk scurry about, repairing the damage.

Glancing up from the yard to the fortress, Rahkki noticed that the gates had been bent and possibly breeched.

"The queen?" he asked aloud, his tone hopeful and sad. He wanted Lilliam gone, but he didn't wish her dead.

"The flag is at full mast. She's alive," said the blond soldier. "But look, the giants burned down the hay barn."

"What will we do?" Rahkki asked, thinking of all the Fifth Clan horses, the Kihlari steeds, the breeders at the Ruk, and the livestock.

"We'll have to order from the trading post on the bay," he answered."

"Daakuran hay is too expensive," mumbled another soldier.

The blond grunted. "What choice do we have? We need hay now and the Fourth Clan is here. We can't buy from them until after the Gathering."

Rahkki glanced toward the fallows. The Second through Fourth Sandwen clans had arrived and settled. Their traveling tents were staked, and their flags waved their colors. Makeshift corrals held their horses, and their well-trained Kihlari grazed free. The youngest Sandwen children played with abandon, ignoring the mess around them.

Traveling was hard on the clans, but now they were here and getting to visit with friends they hadn't seen since last season's Gathering. The elders collected in small groups and spoke heatedly—about the giants, Rahkki guessed—while the younger men and women sharpened their weapons. Cooking fires burned low, and delicious aromas scented the wind. Each encampment had one brightly colored tent, which belonged to its queen. The rest were gray or sun-bleached yellow.

The slapping sound of hoofbeats on mud echoed across the valley, and Rahkki turned toward the noise. He spotted the queen cantering Mahrsan across the fields. Her personal guards followed on their winged steeds. When Lilliam noticed Rahkki, the wild mares, and the soldiers standing on the hill, she dug her spiked heels deep into Mahrsan's sides. He lifted off and sailed toward them.

Sula spotted them coming. She blew hard out her nostrils and stamped her hoof.

The queen landed her stallion near Rahkki, and her royal entourage halted. "Give your report of the farm," she ordered the lead soldier.

"Secure, my queen. The seeds are safe, but many plants were lost." He hesitated and glanced at Rahkki.

"What is it?" Lilliam pressed.

"The wild Kihlari herd showed up at the farm. They

271

helped drive off the giants, and then this boy tried to set these two mares free. We trapped them before they could run away."

Rahkki stared down at his toes, but he felt Lilliam's gaze boring into his skin like a tic.

"The wildlings belong to the clan. Not to you," she said to him, her voice lighter than the wind.

"Yes, my queen," he mumbled. His body began to tremble.

Lilliam drove Mahrsan forward, threatening Rahkki. "Speak louder."

Sula drew back her neck and whinnied a piercing warning.

"Easy, girl," Rahkki said to her, touching her neck. For the first time his mare did not pull away from him. Rahkki dragged his eyes toward Lilliam's face. "Yes, my queen." He said it louder this time. Sula flattened her ears and edged closer to him, and he was stunned. The mare wanted to protect him—from Lilliam!

Mahrsan huffed, eyeing Sula warily.

Queen Lilliam's jaw twitched as she spoke. "The punishment for losing or destroying clan property is tyran."

"I know," he said, gulping. *But he hadn't lost or destroyed property; the mares were right next to him.*

"The auction is in four days, and the other clans have arrived. There is much excitement about these mares. Had you succeeded, Rahkki Stormrunner, you would have robbed our clan of their worth."

He began to sweat through his cotton shirt.

Lilliam nodded to the soldiers. "Put the mares in the stable and assign a watch. They aren't to leave their stalls for any reason until the auction." The soldiers tugged on the wildlings.

Sula reared. Firo whinnied and tried to bolt.

"Please don't hurt them," Rahkki begged.

The soldiers tightened the nooses, subduing the mares quickly. Rahkki clenched his legs around his pony, causing her to buck and spin. Sula flew up a winglength but immediately fell back to land. Firo spun in a circle, kicking wildly. The soldiers used the strength of their horses to drag the wild mares toward the yard and the Kihlari barn.

When they were out of sight, Lilliam turned to Rahkki, looking as serene as a well-fed dragon. "Teach this runt a lesson," she said to her personal guards.

"Please," Rahkki gasped.

The queen's guards tugged him off the pony, and he fell headfirst onto the ground. He flipped onto his back, looking up at the stern faces of full-grown men. A guard lifted his club, his blue eyes flashing, and Rahkki threw his arms up to protect his face and head.

He didn't see the blow, but he felt it. Once. Twice.

An earsplitting scream. That was him.

Then a command. "Leave him for the snakes." That was the queen.

Then one more blow. And darkness.

29

CRUMBLING

ECHOFROST FOUGHT AGAINST THE ROPES THAT had closed around her neck. As the Landwalker soldiers guided her back to the barn, she tripped on rocks and slipped in muddy ditches. She swiveled her ears, listening for Rahkki, who was far behind her now. When she reached the yard, Tuni approached and touched her shoulder. For the second time today, the touch of a Landwalker didn't anger Echofrost, because she was learning that some could be trusted and some could not. "What happened?" Tuni asked, sounding anxious.

A soldier answered. "Rahkki Stormrunner tried to set these mares free at his uncle's farm. We're bringing them back."

"Where's Rahkki?"

The soldiers glanced at each other, shifting nervously.

"Where is the boy?" Tuni asked again. Her voice was calm but full of static, like the clouds before a storm.

"With the queen," one answered.

Echofrost watched Tuni's white face turn whiter and her brown eyes burn brighter. She knew they were talking about Rahkki because they kept saying his name. She wondered if something had happened to him after she was dragged away.

"Where are they?" Tuni asked.

The lead soldier pointed north. "Yonder," he said. "Past the fallows." He grabbed Tuni's arm. "But I wouldn't interfere if I were you."

She ripped her arm free. "You *aren't* me, are you?" She turned on her heel and rushed out of the barn.

The soldiers locked Echofrost and Shysong in their stalls. Two stayed behind to watch them. Koko came out of the tack room. "Ay, what's this?" she asked.

"We've been ordered to guard them. That runt prince tried to set them free."

Koko glowered at the men. "Rahkki's nah a runt."

"He's no prince either," said the other soldier. "Not anymore."

"But e's still a bloodborn," said Koko. "The mum dyin' didn' change nuthin'. Nah in 'is veins."

"Semantics," said the blond soldier.

Koko tilted her head. "What?"

The soldiers laughed at her, and she turned her back on them, peering at the mares. Echofrost stepped away from the girl who'd shot at Hazelwind. "There's no food for yuh," Koko said as if Echofrost could understand her. "Later this day maybe, but nah now. Yuh all rest, right? Right." Koko shuffled away, tending to injured steeds.

Echofrost leaned against the wooden wall, her ears flicking back and forth. Her neck ached, scraped raw by the ropes. She was burning mad.

"How will we escape now?" Shysong whinnied. "They're guarding us!"

"Don't worry," said Echofrost, "*nothing* will stop us from breaking free of this place." But right now it was Rahkki she was worried about. The queen was furious with him, that much was obvious. And Echofrost guessed it was because he'd tried to free them. Had the queen punished him for it? Was Rahkki in danger? She threw back her head and whinnied for him.

But there was no answer. Just silence.

In the darkness that surrounded her, Echofrost confronted the truth. She wasn't in control of anything.

C ∽ 30 ∽ ○

NOT A DOG

RAHKKI OPENED HIS EYES TO A BLURRY BLUE SKY
and a mud-filled mouth. His left ear rang like an echoing
bell, and he was sprawled on his side. He lurched up to
his hands and knees, feeling dizzy. Bright wings fanned
his face, cooling him. Then he heard snuffling and felt hot
breath on his cheeks. He blinked hard, clearing his vision.

Free-grazing Kihlari from the visiting clans had gathered around him in a circle, and some hovered overhead.
They watched him with interest and sniffed at his body,
nudging him to stand. He smiled at them then groaned
when his head throbbed in angry response. He tried to
rise up and fell back on the mud with a splat.

A little pinto braya knelt beside him, and he realized

she was offering him a ride on her back.

"No thanks," he whispered. The ground already felt like it was spinning, and the last thing he needed was a ride on a flying steed. "Just help me up, please." He knew she couldn't understand his words but hoped she would understand his intentions. He gripped her mane and she stood, pulling him up with her. Another Kihlara approached, and Rahkki wrapped his arm around him too. They supported his weight and walked with him slowly back to the yard. The other steeds went back to grazing.

Rahkki's head pounded where the Royal Guard had struck him, and his right side hurt too. Hot, angry tears stung his eyes. The guards had dragged Sula away and locked her up, just as he'd begun to gain her trust. Besides that, the auction was in four days, and Sula would never be able to escape now—not with the soldiers keeping watch over her and Firo.

As Rahkki stumbled into the yard, he spotted Tuni rushing toward him. When she came closer, her eyes popped wide. She picked up her pace and everyone paused to watch the Headwind run.

Tuni reached him just as his legs buckled, and she swept him up into her arms. The two Kihlari steeds took off to rejoin their friends in the fallows. Rahkki felt as light as a feather in Tuni's embrace, and his cheeks burned at being carried in front of the Riders and grooms. "Put me down," he said, his eyes pleading.

She ignored his request. "Did the queen do this to you?"

"Do what?"

"Your ear is smashed, and your head is bleeding."

"I fell."

Tuni swore and spit on the ground. "Tell me the truth. Was it the queen or did that wild mare kick you?"

"Sula? Never."

"Then who did this? Was Mut behind it?"

Rahkki tightened his lips. "No, it wasn't Mut."

Tuni squeezed him, probably harder than she realized. "You're as stubborn as Brauk."

"It's so bright," he said, blocking his eyes from the sun.

Tuni trotted into the Borla's emergency medical tent and laid Rahkki on an open cot. "This boy needs help."

The Borla turned from his smoking candles and glanced at Rahkki, his eyes dull and drooping. He shook his head. "No. Too busy."

"What?" Tuni sputtered.

"I'm fine," Rahkki whispered, tugging on the sleeve of her tunic. "Just take me to my brother."

Tuni folded her arms and glared at the Fifth Clan's healer. "I know you have your priorities, and this boy's not a Rider or a warrior, but he's a *child*."

The Borla's expression pinched into something unrecognizable, something between pity and fear. "He's *not* a child. He's twelve. Take him away." He waved his hand as if blessing Rahkki. "I have wounded warriors to see."

Tuni swore again, so low only Rahkki heard her.

"Please, Tuni. Let's go." Rahkki understood the lay of things. The clan Borla took orders from the queen, and the queen had no interest in keeping Rahkki alive. She couldn't kill him outright because of the deal she'd made with Uncle Darthan, but that didn't mean she couldn't make Rahkki's life miserable, or deny him medical care. "Take me to the animal healer," he whispered.

Tuni whipped her gaze from the Borla to Rahkki, and understanding dawned. She scooped him back into her arms and carried him to the animal healer's shed, north of the Kihlari barn. Here the medicine woman named Brim Carver treated pets and working animals. Tuni didn't knock; she burst inside Brim's work space and laid

Rahkki down on a flat wooden table.

The animal healer turned around. "Oh," she said, blinking at Rahkki lying on the gurney. Her voice was high-pitched and sweet. "That's not a dog."

Tuni frowned at her. "Can you fix him?"

Brim leaned over Rahkki's head and examined him with sure fingers. The skin on her face was deeply lined but looked soft, like melted wax. Crinkling lines reached out from her eyes like wings, and they made her appear to be smiling even when she wasn't.

"Your eyes are as bright as coins," she said to Rahkki. "Do you remember what happened to you?"

"It's better if you don't ask questions," Tuni interrupted.

Rahkki realized then that Tuni had guessed the truth—that it was the queen's guard who'd done this to him. And if Brim knew that, she might refuse to treat him. But looking at her kind face, Rahkki doubted it. Still, he kept his answer brief. "I got hit in the head, that's all I remember."

"Please lift your shirt," Brim said.

Rahkki lifted it and winced.

"Hmm," said Brim. "Whoever did this didn't stop at

your head." She looked at Tuni. "See the marks, here and here." She pointed at Rahkki's ribs.

Tuni sucked in her breath. "By Granak," she whispered, clenching her fists.

"I need to feel your belly and your bones and listen to your lungs," said Brim. "It might hurt, so no barking."

Rahkki glanced at Tuni. She nodded, assuring him.

Brim's cold hands touched Rahkki's bruised flesh, and he clamped shut his mouth to keep from groaning. With each hard push into his belly and ribs, Brim yelped, "Ouch, ouch," making Rahkki smile. Next she brought out a wooden cone and listened to his lungs as he took deep breaths. "I hear the ocean," she exclaimed, making even Tuni laugh.

Then Brim soaked a cloth in water and washed out his bleeding head wound. She continued her yelping. "Oh, that stings. Oh, I can't stand it."

And it did sting, and it did hurt; but Rahkki was transfixed by the animal doctor's reactions, watching her say everything he felt. *She's crazy*, he thought.

When she finished cleaning the wound, she frowned. "Well, I have good news and bad news." She sat heavily on an old teakwood chair. "The good news is that you'll live to fight another day—or maybe that's the bad news, because you're clearly not good at it, although I haven't seen the other guy—but still, you'll live, and that is ultimately good."

Rahkki glanced at Tuni, and she raised her eyebrows.

"What's the bad news?" Rahkki asked, wondering if it had to do with the ringing in his ear.

"After a thorough examination, I've concluded you're definitely *not* a dog. I'm sorry." She patted Rahkki's shoulder.

"That is unfortunate," Tuni said, her mouth twitching.

Rahkki sat up, but Brim discouraged him. "Not yet, young warrior. Let me bandage you and make you a packet of medicine. Then you can go and rest, but no sleeping. Not right away. Can you watch him until evening?" she asked Tuni.

"I'm off patrol, so yes, I can watch him."

Brim nodded and went to work, bandaging Rahkki with sure hands. She treated the cuts on his head with salve and then wrapped him in a snug, clean narrow cloth. "Is this ear singing to you?" she asked, pointing to the smashed left ear.

Rahkki nodded.

"Sing with it," she suggested, and her sweet, high voice broke into a lullaby.

Rahkki listened, letting her song float around him like the gentle arms of a mother. Tuni lowered herself onto a bench and listened too. Brim made three packets of powdered medicine for his swelling and pain, and then put her supplies away. When she was finished cleaning up, she was also finished with her song.

Tuni reached into her purse and pulled out two coins. "Here."

But Brim covered Tuni's hand with gnarled knuckles. "Nope, I don't take payment for humans."

"But you treated him," Tuni protested. "Here's two dramals. I'll bring more if it's not enough."

Brim clucked and shooed her hand away.

Tuni looked helplessly at Rahkki, who sat up. "Thank you," he said to Brim.

The animal doctor nodded and fluttered off to the back of her shed where she had a patient—a real dog—recuperating in a cage. Ten warhorses, two baby goats, and a sow pig stood in stalls, also recuperating from various ailments and injuries from the recent giant attack.

Understanding that they'd been dismissed, Rahkki and Tuni turned to exit the shed. Before they left, the Headwind slid her two dramals onto Brim's chair. She gave Rahkki a sly wink, and they slipped out into the sunshine.

31

THE BLANKET

AS RAHKKI MADE HIS WAY BACK TOWARD THE training yard, leaning lightly on Tuni, the Headwind reopened the subject Rahkki didn't want to discuss. "It was the queen who hurt you, wasn't it? I knew it the second her Borla refused to treat you. Why? What happened?"

"I tried to free Sula," Rahkki confessed. "I know she's too valuable to lose. I just wanted to help her."

Tuni swallowed this quietly.

Rahkki stared at the ground. Tuni was his friend, but she was also a Headwind in the Sky Guard—the flying army that would hunt down Sula if she escaped. He didn't know what to say. "I made a mistake," he offered, but really it was the opposite; he was trying to *correct* a mistake. The Kihlari were the sacred Children of the Wind; the clan should have left the wild ones alone.

Tuni dropped low and faced him, her brown eyes sparkling and her dark-red hair loose around her face. "I wish we hadn't captured them," she whispered.

Rahkki's eyes widened.

Tuni glanced up at the clouds that drifted overhead. "There was something so beautiful about those wild Kihlari," she said. "Seeing them free and fighting for each other, living in a herd like horses, it was . . . incredible. Our Kihlari are used to us, but Sula and Firo, they don't belong here."

Rahkki nodded. "But the auction is in four days, and Sula doesn't understand what's going to happen to her." He dropped his face into his palms. "I would buy her if I could."

Tuni took his chin in her hand and lifted his face. "I would buy her *for* you if I could," she said. "You'd make an excellent Rider."

Rahkki laughed so hard he choked. "I wouldn't," he protested. "Why does everyone think that?"

"Because you used to love to fly, remember? By the age of three you were riding Drael to the lowest clouds and back. The clan knew you were destined to become a Rider."

Rahkki remembered very little about that. What he knew now was that he was afraid of heights—it was a secret he kept close.

Tuni chuckled. "I remember your mother's frequent and frantic searches through the fortress, shouting for you. But you were always with her stallion, Drael, sleeping in his stall or sneaking him out of the barn to fly."

Rahkki's emotions swirled like a cyclone, making him dizzier and dizzier. He staggered sideways. "I need to sit down."

"Of course." She paused and brightened. "I'll take you to the shade."

They'd reached the training yard where Harak and his friends had gathered at the tables beneath the palm trees, avoiding the afternoon heat. They were all playing stones with furious concentration. Rahkki guessed they were trying to distract themselves from the chaos and destruction around them, if just for a moment.

Tuni led him to the table and lowered Rahkki onto a bench. She handed him her water skin. "Drink," she said.

Harak moved closer to them. "Ay there, little farmer,"

he drawled. "Want to play stones with us? Yeah?"

Rahkki shook his head.

"I'll front you ten jints," said Harak's friend. "A small bet for a small boy?"

Rahkki enjoyed a game of stones as much as any Sandwen, but he had no energy or inclination to play.

"Let him rest," Tuni said.

Harak pointed at Rahkki's bandages. "What happened? Fall off your pony?" He chuckled, referring to the stubborn white steed Rahkki had ridden back from the farm.

So fast Harak didn't see it coming, Tuni coiled back her fist and punched him square across the jaw, knocking him off the bench. Rubbing her knuckles, she turned to Rahkki. "I'll be over there washing Rizah if you need me." She strode away, followed by the laughter of Harak's friends.

The tall, green-eyed Rider pulled himself back up to the table. "I think she likes me," he said, causing more laughter. "Let's play then, yeah?"

Harak went first, taking a handful of stones and dropping them strategically into the cups on the playing board.

Rahkki listened to the Riders, the clanging of the stones, and the exchanges of coin; but he was thinking about the night he'd escaped Lilliam. Uncle had reminded him that Drael had saved his life. Rahkki closed his eyes, thinking of his mother. He exhaled, remembering her soft skin and her long, fragrant hair. Then he forced his mind back to the night she'd died, trying to rip the veil that shrouded that evening.

A vision of Drael appeared, and the bay stallion's image stung his heart like a hornet. How he'd loved that Kihlara! Then, in his mind's eye, Rahkki was riding Drael, hurtling across the night sky with his arms wrapped around his brother's waist. Next he saw blood dripping, and he heard the amber-winged horse scream in anger or pain, he couldn't be sure. Rahkki's belly looped, and he threw his hands out like he was falling and opened his eyes. "I can't," he said out loud.

"What'd you say?" Harak asked.

Rahkki shook his head, making it throb worse.

"He said he can't play. The little farmer has no money to bet," said the Rider sitting next to Harak.

His words struck Rahkki square in the gut; they were so painfully true! He had no money. No way to help the wild mares. Rahkki stared at the Kihlari barn, thinking of the upcoming auction. *Oh Sula,* he thought. *What's going to happen to you?*

Then Rahkki spotted Koko leading Kol toward the stable. The stallion's leg was dressed in herbs and wrapped in cotton bandages. Long scratches marked his flanks, but the wounds had been cleaned and treated. Kol nickered softly, and Rahkki's belly lightened. He leaped up—too fast, and after swaying a moment, he caught up to Koko and entered the barn with her. "What happened?" he asked her. "Where's my brother?"

"Here." Brauk limped out of the tack room.

"You're hurt," Rahkki said, panic bubbling up from his gut.

"Steady, little brother," said Brauk. "It's a few bruises. I'm not gonna die. Not today." He frowned. "What happened to you? And why are there land soldiers in the barn?"

"We're guarding the wildlings," explained the younger, brown-haired soldier. "Queen's orders. Until they're sold."

Brauk grimaced at the mention of Lilliam. "And you?" he said, turning to Rahkki and inspecting his bandaged head. "What happened?"

Rahkki glanced at the two soldiers, willing them not to challenge the lie he was about to tell. "I fell off that stupid pony I'Lenna used to ride," he said, snatching the idea from Harak's assumption.

His brother laughed. "It's always the ponies, isn't it? Stinkin' ponies."

The older soldier glanced up at them and then back down, deciding not to intervene. No one in the clan wanted to set off Brauk's anger at Lilliam again. Not after Brauk had finally pulled himself out of the deep hole of hatred in which he'd rooted like a pig for years.

Meanwhile, Rahkki gazed at his brother's wounds—a cut leg, bruises up and down his shield arm, a deep gash along the side of his head, just below the helmet-line—and he blinked hard. Brauk could *never* die, not any day.

His brother's eyes turned cold. "Come on, Rahkki, don't do this."

Rahkki nodded. "I just—"

Brauk's hands tightened like the bite of a crocodile. "We're at war with the giants, do you understand that?"

"Aren't we always?" Rahkki shrugged away from his brother.

"This wasn't the usual raid," Brauk answered. "The Gorlanders almost breeched the fortress, until our archers drove them back. They brought elephants, and they're working together. They've dug into the forest at the base of Mount Crim, and they're preparing another attack, I'm sure of it. We were able to turn the Sixth and Seventh clans back home. The Second through Fourth clans are stuck here, for now, and there's no sign of the First."

Rahkki brightened as a hopeful thought struck him. "Has the auction been canceled?"

Brauk glared east. "No bleedin' chance of that. We won't let the giants change our plans." Then he marched back to the tack room and Rahkki followed. Brauk shut the door and lowered his voice. "There's more, Rahkki. The clan is fed up with the queen."

"Fed up? What do you mean?"

"There's talk of an uprising," Brauk whispered. "Some are meeting in secret."

Rahkki's first thought was for Princess I'Lenna. If unhappy clansmen were meeting to overthrow her mother, she was in danger! "How serious are they?" he asked.

"I don't know; I'm staying out of it."

"You are?" Given Brauk's feelings about Lilliam, this surprised Rahkki. "Why?"

His brother squatted to Rahkki's height, his golden eyes meeting his. "Plots and secrets aren't for me. If I wanted to usurp the queen, I'd shoot her straight through her wicked heart." Brauk drew back his arm and pretended to loose an arrow. He grinned. "Talking is for tots, Rahkki. When the time is ripe—*thwack!* She's gone."

"You wouldn't!" he rasped.

Brauk shrugged and limped back to Sula's stall. Rahkki trailed after him, stunned. His brother inspected Sula. "She looks good, really good. She'll fetch a pretty price."

Rahkki's upset stomach churned harder at the thought of someone purchasing the silver mare. He'd come to think of her as *his* mare.

Brauk turned and leaned on the stall door. "So I was looking through my trunk, and guess what? My little sawa blade is missing."

A small smile crept across Rahkki's face.

Brauk grinned and dipped his head gallantly. "Rumor has it you battled three giants, saved Uncle's farm, *and* protected the wildling mares."

Rahkki's smile faded. "Actually, a giant tied me up and stuffed me in her lunch sack. It was full of ants—"

"Shush." Brauk laughed, and his big, gleaming smile was the sun. "Never dispute your own legend, Brother. Let it bloom." He opened his fist slowly, his fingers unfurling like flower petals.

Rahkki exhaled. "Okay."

Then the clouds returned, crossing his brother's face.

"Follow me; I have something to show you."

Rahkki followed Brauk out of the Kihlari barn, glancing at Sula as he left. She returned his gaze with eyes full of anguish. He smiled at her, hoping to soothe her. Then he shuffled to catch up to Brauk. His brother limped, but his back was straight, his shoulders square. He led Rahkki to Fort Prowl, spoke his credentials, and the guards admitted them through the dented gates.

Inside the compound, soldiers, messengers, and clansfolk scurried about, their faces full of purpose. A line of villagers and soldiers waited to see the queen. Rahkki glimpsed her as they passed her chamber. She sat back on her tall throne, her skinny limbs poking away from her round belly like sticks, and she appeared crushed by the weight of her unborn baby.

Brightly woven reed mats decorated the floor, and dyed tapestries hung on the walls. A table laden with steaming boar's meat, salted fish, cut melons, fresh goat's milk, and rice wine stretched for fifteen lengths behind her. Her two youngest children played at her feet. Rahkki looked closer, trying to remember the days when his mother had sat on that throne.

He faltered when he spied I'Lenna. She was sitting straight-backed on a miniature throne, listening intently to the concerns of her mother's subjects. The queen's blue eyes darted to the passing brothers, and Rahkki turned his gaze to the floor. Once they'd moved farther along, Rahkki spoke. "Where are we going?"

"To my room," Brauk said.

My room, Rahkki thought. He wished it were *their* room again.

They trotted up the steps of the northwest tower. Rows and rows of small doors circled off the central spiral floor. Brauk halted at the twelfth door and shoved it open. They entered the small chamber, and when Rahkki saw what was lying on Brauk's cot, he gasped.

"It's for Sula," Brauk explained. "To wear at the auction."

Rahkki stared at the Kihlara ceremonial blanket that was draped across the old mattress, though the word *blanket* was a flat word for such majestic fabric. The bulk of it was dusky blue, like the sky after a storm. The seams were trimmed in white rabbit fur, and tiny bells lined the hem. Jewels—mostly garnets, sapphires, and precious crystals—were beaded in intricate patterns across the hind end of the blanket. Red and blue tassels hung from the front end. A matching blue headdress, like a bride's veil, completed the costume.

"Where did you get this?"

"It was our mother's," Brauk said, his voice drifting. "She bought it for her winged stallion, Drael."

"What happened to him, Brauk, after we escaped Lilliam? Do you remember?"

Brauk fingered the delicate cloth, breathing hard through his nose. "He's gone. That's all that matters."

The two brothers stared at the beautiful cloth in silence. They had very few pieces of their mother left—Rahkki knew of a pearl-handled comb and a plain ring—and Brauk kept these items in his dresser. But Rahkki had not known about Drael's blanket, and it was a wonder his brother hadn't gambled it away years ago. He imagined it was quite valuable. Rahkki tried to picture Drael wearing the blanket, but all he remembered about that bay stallion was that he was small and fast and gentle. His mother had loved to fly him, and Brauk had inherited his love of the clouds from her.

"If Sula wears this blanket at the auction, she'll fetch more coin," Brauk said, shrugging off his gloom. "And we need her profits to buy hay from the Fourth Clan. I don't know if you heard, but the giants burned down the supply barn."

"I heard," Rahkki said, feeling sad.

"For now we're buying hay from Daakur, but that won't last long."

"Sure, okay."

"Hey, we'll get the blanket back," Brauk said, misreading Rahkki's glum expression. "The handler will bring her out in it, and that alone will impress the buyers. Then he'll slip it off her, and the bidding will start. Her new owner gets her and her halter—that's it, not the blanket."

"All right."

"She's gained plenty of weight," Brauk added. "How are her gaits and circles?"

Rahkki had continued her training at Darthan's farm, and once Sula had started obeying his commands, she'd learned fast. "They're good," he said. "She'll do well."

Brauk slapped his brother's shoulder. "That's dramals in our pocket, Rahkki." He folded the blanket.

The brothers left the room, Brauk in front, Rahkki jogging behind; and they spent the rest of the day cleaning blood and broken things, and not talking much. Tuni joined them, her brow stuck in a worried crease. She didn't speak either, except to greet Rahkki.

But for all the quiet, Rahkki's brain was loud with questions—about Uncle, about the giants, about his mother, about the auction, and about Sula. Who would buy her? Where would she go? And what about her wild friends?

His heart lurched. In four days' time, Sula and Firo would be sold, and he had no idea how to help them.

32

THE VISIT

IT WAS THE DAY BEFORE THE AUCTION NOW, AND Echofrost flinched at every loud noise. She and Shysong had been trapped in their stalls for three days. They'd passed the time sharing stories and legends from their homeland of Anok with the Fliers. About forty Kihlari had confessed a desire to live wild—a miserable number, but it was preferable to *no* Kihlari.

But none of that mattered if she and Shysong couldn't break free themselves. The Landwalkers had held them in captivity for twenty-nine days. The only good news was that their flight feathers had finished growing back. If they found a chance to escape, they would take it. They could jet to the altitudes high above the clouds where the

Landwalkers couldn't breathe. They would be free.

Shysong nickered, her voice trembling. "I hate this place," she admitted. "I hate this stall, the halter they strap to my face, trotting in the round pen, the hay . . . it's too dry." She snorted. "I want to go home."

"Home?" Echofrost whinnied.

"Not back to Anok, but to Storm Herd. They're home. Wherever we settle, I don't care, as long as we're together."

Echofrost shut her eyes, willing away the tears that formed suddenly at the mention of Storm Herd, and she saw Hazelwind's handsome face. She imagined him in contrast to the Kihlari steeds she'd been living with— Hazelwind's wind-blown mane, his tail that would be adorned with burrs instead of bells, his cracked hooves, and his whisker-sharp muzzle. He would smell of soil and moist clouds, and he would enter the barn with all the majesty of his deceased sire, the past over-stallion Thundersky. And he would have no idea that he was striking or handsome, because he was not vain. He was wild. Untamable. Free.

"What's wrong?" Shysong asked.

"It's nothing," she said to her friend, deciding to keep her thoughts about Hazelwind private. "I'm just worrying about Graystone. I hope he heals."

"I'm worried too," Shysong whispered. "But the auction is tomorrow, and they'll have to take us out of our stalls. Maybe we'll find a chance to escape then."

"True," said Echofrost. And the mares fell silent, waiting.

Later that evening, Echofrost heard Rahkki's familiar footfalls as her cub jogged through the barn door to be with her. She'd not forgotten how hard he'd fought to protect her at the farm. The cub was neither large nor strong nor trained to fight, but she had to admit, he was devoted.

"Sula," he greeted her, grinning wide. She snorted, remembering her first day with the Landwalkers. She'd vowed to kill this foolish cub, but that seemed like a long time ago now.

He leaned over her stall door and stared at her, his eyes glowing. He did this a lot, and she didn't know why. A new pair of guards had replaced the first two. They gave Rahkki a cursory glance and then went back to their conversation.

A voice interrupted all of them. "Rahkki! I should have known you'd be here."

Echofrost flipped her ears forward and glanced down

the row to see a Landwalker female walking toward them. She recognized her instantly. It was the queen's offspring, Princess I'Lenna.

Kol had explained to her how I'Lenna's mother had killed Rahkki's and taken her position as ruler of the clan. It made perfect sense to Echofrost, because it was similar with over-stallions. They often battled to the death to take command of a herd. But Lilliam reminded Echofrost of Petalcloud, the mare who'd joined with Nightwing the Destroyer against the pegasi of Anok. Echofrost sensed that this queen, like Petalcloud, was bad for her people.

I'Lenna sidled up to Rahkki, looking pleased until she noticed his bandaged head. "When did that happen?"

"A few days ago," he said quickly, then dropped his eyes toward the long green stalks in her hands. "What're those?" he asked. "Sugarcanes?"

"That's right." I'Lenna's eyes flicked to the mares. "I bought them to cheer up the brayas." The princess stepped closer to Rahkki, her arm brushing his.

Echofrost inhaled, drawing in the delicious scents of the plant stalks and wondering at Rahkki's sudden burst of perspiration.

"Do you want to give one to Sula?" I'Lenna asked.

"Sure." He took a stalk and held it out to Echofrost.

I'Lenna leaned over Shysong's stall door with a long sigh. "She's beautiful."

"She is," Rahkki agreed. He turned to Echofrost. "Don't swallow it. Just chew on it."

Echofrost had come to enjoy the sound of Rahkki's voice even though she understood little beyond her own name. She lipped at the plant stalk since it smelled good, and then she bit into it. It was woody and dry. She shook her head, and Rahkki laughed. "Keep chewing."

Next to her Shysong bit into her stalk and held it in her mouth. Soon she was nodding her head. "It's sweet," she nickered to Echofrost.

I'Lenna giggled and watched Shysong play with her stalk. "All the Kihlari like sugarcane once they get the hang of it. Your mare is too suspicious."

"Come on, girl, try it again," said Rahkki.

I'Lenna reached her hand out to pet Shysong. "My mother told me to come look at her to see if I still like her." I'Lenna's voice vibrated with excitement. "Tomorrow's the auction and my twelfth birthday. I think she might buy Firo for me!"

"Firo? Not Sula?" he asked.

"That's right. She's hoping Sula goes to another clan, says she's too wild."

Rahkki's fists tightened, and his lips turned down. "Firo will make a fine pet."

The princess touched Shysong gently, scratching behind her ears and stroking her face, slowly tracing her fine bones. "Just look at her eyes," she said. "They're the color of the sky, the ocean, and the rivers all at once. I wish I were this pretty."

Before Rahkki could respond, the princess continued. "I want to fly, don't you?" She smoothed Shysong's feathers, and her dark eyes filled with longing. "I want to see the world."

"You will," he said.

The princess turned abruptly, startling Echofrost and Shysong. "I should get back, but I'm glad I ran into you."

"Wait," he said.

But I'Lenna left as quickly as she'd come, galloping like a skinny-legged foal.

Rahkki watched her go, and he stared after her for a long time. Echofrost dropped the plant stalk once all the sweetness was gone, and Rahkki turned to her, attracted by the noise of the falling plant. He had three pieces of twine in his hands, and he was braiding and unbraiding them with breathtaking ease. Echofrost cocked her head, studying his agile fingers and again wondering from where the Landwalkers derived their power. They controlled fire, tamed animals, and grew food. They were intelligent and could communicate, but so could pegasi. It puzzled her.

"Can I go inside her stall?" Rahkki asked the soldiers.

"No," they answered in unison.

"But it's our last night together," Rahkki said. "Please."

They glanced at each other, and the older one rolled his eyes. "All right, but if she tramples you . . ."

Rahkki grinned. "She won't." He unlatched Echofrost's stall door and entered slowly, shutting it behind him. He pressed himself against the wall, as far from her as he could get, and he didn't try to touch her.

After a while the cub pulled a red blanket out of his satchel and spread it on the straw. Echofrost watched his dark lashes droop over his golden eyes. He was injured and tired. He should be with his people, in his own nest, not here with her. What did he want?

But Rahkki wanted nothing. He slumped down and curled up on top of the blanket. "Good night," he said to her, closing his eyes.

"He's going to sleep in my stall," Echofrost nickered to Shysong, her nerves jingling. "Why would he do that?"

"It means he likes you," the mare named Rizah interjected. "It doesn't always take a ceremony to bind a Rider and a Flier. Sometimes a Pair forms by itself."

"We're not *bound*," Echofrost sputtered. "I don't . . . I don't like him, not at all. He smells. He can't fight. I . . . I can't understand a thing he says. Besides that—*he's* a Landwalker and I'm a pegasus—we're enemies. How do I make him go away?"

Rizah nickered. "It's funny you're afraid of *Rahkki*, of all the Landwalkers." Several Kihlari nickered with her.

"Afraid?" Echofrost snapped. "I'm *annoyed*." She and Rizah drifted into silence, but Echofrost was careful not to step on Rahkki, who was asleep at her hooves. She cast her gaze toward the ceiling, willing it to open, to see Hazelwind's broad buckskin face, his wide blaze, his deep-brown eyes, and to fly into the night sky, never to return. There was more at stake than just her freedom; there was the mission. Storm Herd hadn't crossed the Dark Water to end up enslaved. She owed it to each steed in Anok to break out and settle the herd in a safe land, and so far, she'd failed miserably.

❧ 33 ❧

THE LONGEST DAY
OF THE YEAR

DAWN BROKE, AND THE MORNING BELLS RANG
from the fortress. Echofrost stretched her wings. Rahkki
was gone; he'd slipped out of her stall a few hours earlier.
Today was the Kihlari auction, and dread oozed through
her veins.

"Today is the longest day of the year," Kol nickered, as
if Echofrost cared. "The clans will celebrate the sun that
grows our hay."

She startled at his words. "I thought the Landwalkers
grew the hay."

"They plant the seeds, but the sun grows them," he
explained.

Echofrost swiveled her ears. Perhaps the Landwalkers

didn't wield supernatural power like Star and Nightwing did; perhaps they simply possessed a deeper understanding of the land. This realization chipped away at their mystery, and Echofrost added it to her growing bank of knowledge about the Landwalkers.

"Wait until you see us fly the Tugare," Kol whinnied.

"What's a *Tugare*?" Echofrost asked. The more she learned about the day's events, the better.

"It's the big show before the auction," he said, and he was practically drooling with anticipation. "You think we're soft and tame, but today you'll see! We'll fly cartwheels, loops, and nosedives—things you can't imagine."

Echofrost snorted. The Kihlari thought they knew how to fly. *They knew nothing.*

"The Land Guard will play their drums while we perform," Kol added. "It's spectacular. The crowd will be on fire to own a Kihlara steed when we're finished." He glared at her over the wall between them. "You'll sell fast."

Echofrost listened to Kol's excited speeches and to the annoying sound of his feather preening. Rizah was equally excited and prancing in her stall. They reminded Echofrost of foals playing in their birth meadow. The Kihlari enjoyed their captivity with the innocent, careless abandon of creatures who knew nothing else.

Brauk and Tuni had gone to the tack room to retrieve their mounts' saddles and armor. Now they entered the rows with the rest of the Sky Guard, and the Kihlari steeds burst into nickers of greeting. Echofrost lifted her head, wishing she could see the entire barn. As good as her hearing was, she trusted her eyes more. The Riders walked with quick steps, and she heard lots of buckling and tightening of straps as they dressed their Fliers. She peeked into Kol's stall, curious.

He stood in its center while Brauk brushed out his yellow-streaked red mane and tail and glossed his chestnut hide with a soft brush. Next he cleaned Kol's hooves and polished them with oil. He rubbed the same oil around the stallion's eyes and muzzle, darkening the areas and setting off his chiseled face. Last, he misted Kol's feathers with water, removing the straw dust, and then he dabbed them lightly with more oil. Kol lifted his neck into a high arch and twisted his wings so that his shiny yellow feathers reflected the light. He caught Echofrost watching him. "Impressive, yes?" he asked.

"You outshine the sun," she said.

He startled at the compliment and then nickered with pleasure.

Vanity was a rare trait in a wild pegasus, but Echofrost added it to the Kihlari's long list of weaknesses.

Outside the stall stood Brauk's tack trunk, which he'd dragged over from the tack room. He moved back and forth between it and Kol, carefully lifting out piece after piece of polished leather and metal and then buckling it onto his mount. Brauk's arms were bare, and she noticed again the scar burned into his flesh. It matched the scar on Kol's shoulder. It was the symbol that meant the two were Paired. She shuddered, wondering if receiving the brands had been painful. She stamped her hoof. Of course it had been painful!

"How long have you been with Brauk?" she asked Kol.

"Three glorious years," he answered.

"What if something happens to him?"

Kol twisted his ears back. "We Kihlari don't talk about that. To become a Half is to die."

"Not really. It just means you don't have an . . . owner. It means you're free."

"Free? No. I would be lost."

She tossed her head. "You could leave."

Kol pawed his straw floor, and Brauk mumbled soothing words to him. "I belong with the clan," Kol whinnied.

"I was born to the clan."

"But your ancestors were born in Anok," Echofrost neighed, loud enough for the entire barn to hear her. "You're all Lake Herd steeds; you just don't remember."

Kol turned his attention back to his Rider, tuning her out.

She watched them together. Kol didn't fuss or flinch when Brauk tightened his cinches and straps, placed a helmet over his head—a helmet that had cutouts for Kol's eyes and ears—and strapped shields onto his neck and chest. Then he braided bells, spiked beads, and feathers into the stallion's tail. Panic rose from deep within Echofrost as she imagined how all that tack and armor would weigh her down, but Kol was proud. "It's *full* battle armor today," he announced, preening a loose feather. "And Brauk shined it for me. His armor too."

"It's magnificent," she said, noticing Kol was talkative when he felt flattered.

Around the barn, Echofrost heard bells jingling and smelled the plant dyes the Landwalkers used to draw colorful patterns on their mounts' flanks, and she heard the clanging of swords being checked and then sheathed. The Riders spoke to one another quickly and fluidly, their conversations like a flowing river. Excited whoops spiced the flat roar of it.

Outside the barn, hundreds of footsteps marched toward the large riding ring that the Fifth clan used for horse training. The day she'd returned from the farm, Echofrost had noticed that the sand arena had been smoothed with tools they called *rakes*. The area around the ring had been cleared of shrubs and debris so that the visiting clans could gather close around it. The auction would take place inside the arena, and she assumed the Tugare would occur above it.

One by one, the Kihlari left the barn with their Riders, leaving Echofrost and Shysong alone. "What if we're sold to different clans?" Shysong asked.

Echofrost's heart thumped hard, fast. "We'll be gone before that happens. Just keep their trust, wait for them to let down their guard, and then go—take *any* chance you get to escape. I'll do the same. Fly east. Look for the Storm Herd nests."

"All right," Shysong agreed, but Echofrost heard the uncertainty in her voice.

Then the drumming began, a steady rhythmic beat. Hoots and hollers rose above the deep percussion as the

Landwalkers cheered for the Tugare. Echofrost imagined the steeds of Anok—the blistering speeds of their nosedives and the stunning arcs of color when the pegasi turned circles in the air, their bright feathers flashing. No matter how impressive the Kihlari show was, Echofrost doubted it could match the flying skills of free, unadorned pegasi.

After a while the drumming ended to roaring cheers from the crowd. Music played and time passed. Then more time passed. Echofrost grew impatient and anxious. Finally, the barn door opened.

"I got Sula," said a voice that Echofrost recognized. It was the green-eyed, yellow-haired Landwalker named Harak.

Where was Rahkki? Brauk? Someone familiar!

"Come, Firo," said the other voice; it was Tuni come for Shysong.

Harak strode into Echofrost's stall, grabbed her muzzle in one hand, and yanked a halter over her head with the other. She reared back, and he jerked down on her lead rope. "Quit it," he snapped.

Be patient, she told herself, *don't attack him*. But her back legs twitched with the desire to do just that.

Harak also slipped a rope around her neck and then

he jerked her forward and she walked behind, listening to the clopping beat of Shysong's hoof steps as she followed them. They halted in the yard. Echofrost pranced as grooms swarmed her. Rahkki had bathed her yesterday, but these grooms went over her again—brushing her mane and tail, braiding bells and her own purple feathers into her white hair, smoothing her plumage, and dressing her hooves in oil to make them shine.

Then Harak slid a grayish-blue blanket across her neck and back. It was decorated with shiny stones and colorful tassels. Next he covered her head with a sheer veil of the same gray-blue color. Echofrost reared again, confused by the transparent cloth and the ringing of the bells in her tail, the noise seeming to chase her as she moved.

"No," Harak snapped, and he yanked on the rope around her neck, briefly choking her.

Echofrost planted all four hooves into the soil and took a deep, steadying breath, but inside, her pulse raced. She glanced at Shysong and saw the ropes tethering her, and the bells and beads braided into her mane and tail. They looked identical except for the blanket that Echofrost wore. It rippled across her body, soft as a foal's muzzle, and the colorful stones glittered in the sunshine. She guessed that Kol would enjoy wearing such a blanket, but she hated it and had already begun to sweat. "Stay strong," she whinnied to Shysong, shoving the fear out of her voice.

"You too," her friend neighed.

Harak jerked on Echofrost's lead rope again, for no good reason, and then said to Tuni, "We're ready."

The two Landwalkers faced the arena and walked Echofrost and Shysong toward the auction.

∾34∾

AUCTION

RAHKKI FOUND UNCLE DARTHAN ON THE northern side of the arena with the spectators from the Fifth Clan. Around him, men and women chatted on blankets they'd spread on the trampled grass. The visiting clans had lent their forces to the Fifth Clan army. Land soldiers and Riders guarded the Gathering in such great numbers that the Sandwens could relax and enjoy their annual celebration. The stable grooms, directed by Koko, trotted through the crowd with baskets full of shed Kihlari feathers. The bright plumage had been woven into bracelets and anklets complete with beads and bells, and were sold as charms.

"Ten jints for one, fifteen jints for two," they shouted.

The younger children tied the vibrant bracelets around their limbs and flapped their arms as if they were flying. Rahkki watched a young girl swooping in large circles, imitating the antics of a winged steed, and he smiled. He used to pretend he was a Kihlara too, but he was too old now to wear a charm and flap his arms.

"I'll buy you one," said Uncle, following Rahkki's gaze.

"It's okay, I don't need one."

Uncle grunted and took a long draw off his pipe. As he exhaled, the sweet smell of cloves filled Rahkki's nostrils.

Now the Tugare, which meant "aerial performance" in Talu, was about to begin. The Land Guard drummers entered the ring, and everyone hushed. They began playing, warming up the crowd with a slow beat, preparing them for the show. Clansfolk found their blankets and half tents and settled their children. The sun blazed overhead, and the heat was heavy, moist. The distant trees swayed in the hot breeze, and insects hummed softly. Rahkki flicked a grasshopper off his blanket.

When the crowd was ready, one hundred Pairs of Sky Guard Riders and Fliers emerged from behind the Ruk and galloped toward the spectators. The Kihlari hooves pounded out a beat matched by the drummers. Dust flew from their hooves, and their adorned tails jingled. The

Riders leaned forward, kicking their mounts ever faster. They charged toward the seated clansfolk with swords lifted, hollering their battle calls.

The Sandwen people hollered right back. Some tots burst into tears and the elders smiled. Mut Finn and his friends stood and raised their arms, wielding weapons made of wood. Mut would soon age into the Land Guard, a fate Rahkki knew the boy dreaded. Not because he was afraid, but because he'd rather be a Rider. Most kids felt the same, but most kids, like Mut, couldn't afford a Flier.

Rahkki watched Brauk, Tuni, and Harak—the three Headwinds—lead the charge with their jaws clenched and eyes narrowed, pinning the crowd with ferocious stares. Their bright armor flashed in the sun, their mounts' polished hooves thrummed the soil, and Rahkki's gut twirled. How did the Gorlan giants face these warriors with such little fear?

The Sky Guard whooped louder and galloped faster toward the spectators, aiming their sawa blades at the children. The front row screamed and covered their heads, and Rahkki felt the familiar tug of panic—*were they going to lift off in time?*

Then Tuni slapped Rizah's rump, and the Sky Guard leaped into the sky. Their flapping wings blew back the half tents. Their polished hooves just missed the front row of families. The Headwinds opened sacks of white flower petals and dumped them on the crowd. The petals streamed out and fluttered gently down.

The crowd cheered and laughed; some cried. The teens groaned, feigning disappointment. Rahkki let out his breath, and Uncle chuckled. It was always this way, but each summer there were those who feared the Riders would not stop, that they would accidentally trample the first few rows.

Now the beat changed as the drummers' rhythms followed the Kihlari into the sky. Rahkki lay back and watched the Tugare. The steeds flew precise patterns; performed mock aerial attacks; nose-dived at the crowd, causing more screams; and they flew dizzying circles and loops.

Across the arena, Queen Lilliam watched from the shade of her tent while her children sat outside. Princess I'Lenna held the hands of her younger sisters. Their eyes were trained on the Fliers, their expressions delighted. Rahkki wanted to warn I'Lenna about the secret meetings to usurp her mother, but she'd run off too quickly the night before when they'd fed the brayas the sugarcanes. Perhaps today he would find a chance to speak to her. I'Lenna glanced at Rahkki, caught him staring, and grinned.

Darthan noticed the exchange. "Be careful where you look, Rahkki. Your eyes forge your path." It was a Rider's phrase—meaning that your mount will fly the path your eyes take. It was advice on how to avoid crashing.

Heat rushed to Rahkki's cheeks as he tore his eyes away from the princess. "I know that," he said quietly. He focused on the Tugare overhead, watching Brauk fly. His gut lifted and twirled with Kol's acrobatics, making him feel queasy.

Soon his thoughts turned to Sula and the auction. Rahkki imagined buying her, and he became lost in a fantasy. She would live at the farm with him, and he would leave her stall door open. She could come and go as she pleased, but in his mind, she'd never leave him. He'd sleep in her stall and feed her treats. She wouldn't shy away when he touched her.

He'd work two jobs so that he could purchase the highest-quality grains and stall bedding. He'd clean and oil her halter each evening so that it would be as soft as doeskin on her face. He'd trim her hooves, and he'd take her to Brim Carver, the animal doctor, when she was sick.

His uncle exhaled a long stream of smoke, shattering Rahkki's daydream. "The queen thinks she can sell that silver braya you call Sula, but she's wrong. That wild Kihlara cannot be owned."

Rahkki glanced quickly at Darthan. Had his uncle read his mind? But no, Uncle was gazing up at the clouds with great interest, as if reading tea leaves.

"I gave her the chance to be free," Rahkki said. "But I failed."

Uncle Darthan tapped his forehead. "Her freedom is here. It has nothing to do with you."

Rahkki nodded. "But she'll be sold today, and there's nothing I can do to stop it." He looked again across the arena. The visiting queens had set up their tents alongside the Queen of the Fifth, displaying their colors. Their Kihlari mounts grazed behind them, and the tallest was Mahrsan. The Second Clan's queen was Tavara Whitehall, Lilliam's mother. Tavara hailed from the poorest clan, and it showed in her faded robes and snide expression. She leaned toward her daughter, speaking forcibly and angrily. Tavara had left Lilliam's nine princess sisters at home.

Soon the sound of a swamp buffalo horn carried over the gathered clans, followed by a sudden hush. The drumming stopped, and the Sky Guard retreated back to the barn. Queen Lilliam's musicians picked up their reed flutes. There was always a brief intermission between the Tugare and the auction.

Around Rahkki, the clansfolk stood to stretch their legs and talk. Children played stones or fought their scarlet beetles, betting on the strongest-looking scarabs. Folks purchased sugar-fried caterpillars and trinkets, and mothers nursed their babies. After a few songs the auction would begin.

Besides Sula and Firo, the Second Clan had brought a Kihlara broodmare to sell and three pet stallions; the Third Clan had brought two yearling colts that looked promising plus a young Flier; and the Fourth Clan had two Fliers, a yearling filly, and three pets. Only the merchants and Landowners who relaxed in the large tents were wealthy enough to purchase a Kihlara, but the folks watching from the open grassland were excited to see who would pay the exorbitant price required to own a winged horse.

Darthan handed Rahkki two jints. "They're selling honeyed peanuts over there," he said, nudging his nephew and smiling. "Why don't you buy some for after lunch?"

Rahkki didn't feel much like eating, but he nodded and jogged obediently to the vendor and traded the small coins for a bag of sweet peanuts and a skin of juice. He returned, handing Uncle the change.

The buffalo horn sounded again, cueing the first steed to enter the arena for the auction. It was the broodmare from the Second Clan, a light chestnut with violet wings and two hind socks. Her hide gleamed, and she was the perfect representation of a healthy Kihlara mare, bringing a round of cheers from the spectators.

Her handler trotted and cantered her in circles, showing off her even cadence and flawless form. When he was finished, he removed her tethers and commanded her to fly a circle over his head. There was a stunned gasp as she lifted off and flew a perfect arc around him. And then, for some excitement, he commanded her to swoop over the area of tents, where the wealthiest bidders watched her with open mouths.

She was not only well proportioned, she was also well trained for a broodmare; she flew without a Rider to guide her and without tethers to force her to return. She was controlled only by her handler's voice, and after she buzzed the tents, she returned to him and dropped her muzzle into his hands.

But then something unexpected happened: the handler slipped the broodmare a treat, but no training incentives were allowed during auction exhibitions. Rahkki examined the mare again, more keenly this time, and he noticed her large pupils and vacant expression. Rahkki gulped. "She's drugged," he whispered to his uncle.

Darthan peered at Rahkki. "And what does that mean?" he asked.

"It means she's not trained at all, not really. It means her clan can't control her, and they're trying to get rid of her."

Uncle squeezed Rahkki's shoulder gently. "You have good vision, Rahkki. You see past the show to the truth."

But the tented folk did not see the truth. They were spellbound. The bidding for the mare began high and raced quickly higher. Rahkki watched her sell for three times her worth to a Borla in the Fourth Clan. His groom collected the mare and led her away.

Rahkki's heart quickened as the crowd cheered. Soon it would be Sula's turn. She'd be shown off like a prize cow and sold; he felt sick. His head hurt. He stared at his uncle. "I can't do this," he said.

Darthan's lips tightened. "Go home then."

Rahkki folded his arms. He would do no such thing.

The two yearling colts sold next for fifty dramals apiece, a quarter of the price of the broodmare. One reared and one spooked, but Rahkki liked the colts. They were young and had never traveled. The cheering bothered them, and at least they weren't drugged. The one who reared was particularly well built, and the curve of his wings spoke of great agility. He was aggressive, but that was needed to become a Sky Guard Flier. Rahkki pointed him out. "That colt is worth more than that broodmare," he said.

Darthan drew on his pipe and nodded his agreement.

After the rearing colt left the arena, two pets and the yearling filly sold. Then there was a break in the auction for another performance. Queen Lilliam's dancers entered the arena barefoot. They were dressed in flowing robes dyed in shades of blue, violet, and gold. They paused until everyone was silent, and then the musicians lifted their reed pipes, drums, and lutes and played a soul-lifting harmony.

The dancers seemed to float on the wind. They twirled and leaped in ways that made their robes flash their colors, as if they *were* the music. Uncle Darthan opened his satchel and laid out spiced rice balls, smoked fish, fried hen eggs, and a large flask of coconut milk. Rahkki stared at the food without appetite. "Eat," Uncle commanded.

Rahkki ate and watched the dancing, shaded by Uncle's goat-hide half tent. Around them, children played and adults gossiped. The tented folk smoked pipes and drank rice wine. Uncle Darthan opened the bag of honey-coated peanuts, which he shared with Rahkki.

Then the blaring of the buffalo horn ended the dance. Rahkki wiped his mouth and faced the arena. The second half of the auction was about to begin.

35

HARAK

ECHOFROST TOSSED HER HEAD, TRYING TO DIS-
lodge the transparent fabric that covered her eyes. Harak
yanked so hard on her halter that the noseband cut into
her sensitive muzzle. "Quit that," he said, and his voice
sounded to her like the growl of a wolf. She rattled her
feathers, and Harak turned on her, his green eyes flat and
mean. He stung her legs with his riding crop until she
stood still.

Unable to move without risking a beating, Echofrost
stood beside Harak with her heart racing and her nerves
jingling like the bells tied to her tail. They waited in a
small holding pen that was attached to the ring. Echofrost

couldn't see outside the walls, but she knew that pegasi were being sold and taken away.

Then there was a long break; a few more pegasi sold, and now it was just her and Shysong left, and it was Shysong's turn to enter. Echofrost watched her friend's body sway back and forth. Tuni tried to soothe her with treats and a soft voice, but Shysong was shedding feathers all over the dirt floor.

The loud bray of the buffalo horn reached them. "Time to go," Tuni said to the roan. She opened her stall door and coaxed Shysong forward, but Shysong reared back. Tuni waited, and then once all four hooves touched ground, she urged her forward again.

Shysong glanced at Echofrost. "I'm scared," she whinnied.

"The Ancestors are with us," Echofrost said, her voice wavering but determined. "Just play along for now."

Shysong halted and stuck her nose over Echofrost's door so they could exchange breath a final time. "If I'm sold to someone like him"—she jerked her head toward Harak—"I won't last."

"You'll have to," said Echofrost, "but not for long. Keep their trust until you can fly away. It's that easy. Don't worry."

Tuni clucked and urged Shysong out of the small, dark barn and into the blinding light of day. The door closed behind the mare, and Echofrost moaned her grief softly, so Harak wouldn't hear.

When Echofrost heard the cheering, she knew Shysong was in the ring trotting and cantering her circles. Soon there was heated arguing. Kol had explained to her that the Landwalkers would try to outbid one another for the chance to own a wild pegasus. He said that she and Shysong were *exotic*, which meant "foreign."

A sudden swell of hollering noise filled her ears, and Shysong reentered the barn, looking stunned.

"What happened?" Echofrost nickered. "Was there no chance to escape?"

"There wasn't. I'm sold," she whispered, sounding shocked. "But I won't be leaving. Rizah's out there, and she told me that the queen bought me for I'Lenna. I'm a birthday present. A *pet*." Shysong's gaze was hollow, and her feathers drooped. "What does that mean?"

"I don't know," said Echofrost.

"I'Lenna seems kind, at least," Shysong nickered.

"But her mother . . ."

"I know."

"Be very careful," Echofrost warned. "If any harm comes to I'Lenna while you're near her, I imagine you'll be blamed."

Shysong nodded, but overall began to relax.

The buffalo horn sounded again. Harak yanked on Echofrost, pulling her from her thoughts. "You're up," he said.

Tuni's hand darted to Harak's. "Don't jerk on Sula like that," she said, her eyes darkening.

Harak broke free of Tuni's grasp. "I know how to handle a Kihlara."

"She's not fighting you," Tuni said. "I'll issue a violation if you abuse her without cause."

Harak spit on the ground. "You take her then. Or get Brauk."

Tuni sighed. "I'm on crowd patrol, and the queen doesn't want Brauk in that arena. Just lead the mare in and don't be a bully about it."

Harak grunted and pulled Echofrost forward, but with less force this time. He pushed open the gate and led her into the light.

When Echofrost emerged with the intricate blanket rippling around her, a hush fell over the crowd of

Landwalkers. Harak led her into the arena and then walked her once around so everyone could see her up close. She pranced, and he allowed it. The bells in her tail jingled merrily, the glittering blanket ruffled around her legs, and she was suddenly grateful for the soft veil covering her eyes, allowing her a measure of privacy.

She picked up a springing trot, almost floating across the sand, and the spectators made appreciative noises. An announcer spoke loud words, and Echofrost heard her Sandwen name often: Sula.

She passed a group of Landwalkers sitting on blankets and she glimpsed Rahkki. He sat with the man he called Uncle. He was upright and wide-eyed, and as awed as the rest of his kind. He mouthed something to her, and of course she didn't know what he was trying to say; but her heart slowed, and she realized suddenly, and quite unexpectedly, that she liked him.

But then in a flash he was gone. She pranced past him and toward a group of heavily robed Landwalkers who lounged inside large tents that were loaded with tables of steaming meats and padded with soft rugs. Then she passed Queen Lilliam's pagoda. Echofrost spotted I'Lenna first, and the little female's eyes were bright with joy. Behind I'Lenna, the queen reclined on a fur-softened platform, seeming flattened by her round belly, and she eyed Echofrost with the cold stare of a serpent.

Echofrost turned her head away and followed Harak to the center of the horse-training ring. A Landwalker dressed in black spoke to the crowd with dramatic flourishes of his hands, saying her name in a long rolling drawl. Echofrost understood that she was on display. She tossed her head and rattled her feathers in annoyance, but stayed near Harak, obeying him as best she could. Cooperating would benefit her, not hurt her; she'd learned that the hard way.

Ring attendants attached a tether to her halter and slid off her showy blanket and veil, handing them to Koko, who had appeared from across the arena to whisk them away. Now that the spectators had their first solid look at her, they whooped with approval and drummed the ground with their feet.

Harak grinned, enjoying the attention, and then cracked his whip, sending Echofrost trotting in a circle around him. As she moved, the crowd hollered louder. She turned her head toward the sky, scanning the clouds for Hazelwind, but the horizon was empty. Where was he? He'd said he'd come back for her, or was Graystone still recovering from his injury? Despair struck her. She felt like a weanling again, stuck in enemy territory.

Harak yanked on the tether and Echofrost slowed, confused as to what he wanted. "Git up," he said, and he stung her flank with the whip. Startled, she kicked out, and he struck her again. Echofrost whirled around, backing away from him. Harak's face turned red when a few Landwalkers laughed.

Echofrost stiffened and snorted.

Harak cracked the whip behind her, sending her forward again—*Ah*, she thought, *he wants more speed.* She broke into a gallop, but then he yanked on her nose and yelled at her. She stopped and threw back her head in frustration. Harak stumbled and fell in the sand, and more laughter erupted.

The Queen of the Fifth narrowed her eyes, and Echofrost's muscles quivered. She was trying to obey Harak, but she didn't know what he wanted. The whip meant go faster, didn't it?

Harak stood and ran at her. He slapped her chest twice with the slack in the rope, snarling and yelling, and then he cracked her again with his whip.

Her fury ignited, and Echofrost screamed a challenge at him. He wanted to fight; she'd fight! Maybe this was even part of the show; she didn't know, and suddenly she didn't care.

Harak bellowed back, swelling his chest and raising the whip over his head.

Echofrost pinned her ears even as her sensible side told her to calm down.

From somewhere behind her, a Landwalker shouted. "Stop! She'll kill you." It was Brauk, racing across the arena.

Echofrost shut down her thoughts and trained her eyes on her attacker. All the stress of her captivity erupted, and the world blurred. She saw nothing but Harak. Felt nothing but anger.

He advanced, murder in his eyes, and the crowd hushed.

Rahkki leaped over the fence and ran toward her, pumping his arms. "Sula, no!"

Harak snarled and snapped the whip across her neck.

Echofrost whirled around and kicked out with both hind legs. She heard a sharp crack when her hooves connected with flesh. A body flew across the sand and struck the fence.

Absolute silence dropped on the arena.

And then Rahkki screamed. "Brauk!"

Echofrost turned slowly around. There was Harak, standing off to the side, unharmed. Fifty winglengths away was Brauk, lying motionless in the dirt.

Echofrost dropped her head, her fury spent. The heat of her anger was replaced by cold dread.

She'd kicked the wrong Landwalker.

36

CONTEST

FEAR SQUEEZED RAHKKI'S HEART AS HE SPRINTED toward his fallen brother. "Brauk," he cried, his voice strangled. As Rahkki passed Sula, he noticed her panicked eyes and the big vein pulsing in her neck.

He reached Brauk and fell beside him, sobbing shamelessly while everyone watched, and he didn't care. Brauk's face was slack and his eyes closed. "Somebody help him!" Rahkki screamed.

Uncle Darthan and Brim Carver rushed to Brauk's side. The Fifth Clan Borla emerged from his tent, nodded to the queen, and entered the arena with his apprentices. Brauk was a member of the Sky Guard. The Borla could refuse to treat Rahkki but not Brauk, and not in front of the other clans. To let a Rider suffer would bring shame on the Fifth, but when the Borla arrived at Brauk's side, Uncle Darthan shooed him away. "We'll take care of him," he said.

The Borla glanced at the queen, and she turned her back, leaving the decision to him. He appraised Brauk, and then glared at Uncle and Brim. "You'll need more than this goat healer to save him," he said.

"Brim can handle it," Darthan insisted.

The Borla stood and motioned for his apprentices to follow him back to his tent.

Rahkki watched him go and was glad. His mother's Borla had been kind and helpful, but this one was in the pocket of Queen Lilliam. Rahkki held his brother's hand while Brim examined him.

"Don't move him," Brim said. Her face was creased with worry, and she made no jokes, sang no songs.

Brauk was unconscious but breathing, and that gave Rahkki hope.

He looked to the center of the arena where Sula stood by herself, trembling violently, with no one holding her. It occurred to Rahkki that she could fly away, but the second that thought hit him, Tuni and four Riders grabbed the ends of Sula's tethers and began leading her back to the holding pen.

"Halt," Queen Lilliam ordered. "This braya has yet to be sold."

Tuni stared at her, speechless. "What?"

"Keep her here. Resume the auction."

Tuni handed Sula's rope to the Riders with her. "You heard her," she said under her breath, and she rushed away to check on Brauk.

Rahkki squeezed his brother's fingers, and Brauk's eyelids fluttered. "What happened?" he groaned.

"Sula kicked you."

"That viper," Brauk rasped. "I knew one day she'd strike."

Rahkki brushed back Brauk's long hair and leaned over him, touching foreheads with him. He glanced at Sula. She watched them, her eyes ancient and sad. "She didn't mean it," he said.

Brauk's lips twitched. "Oh, yes she did." Then he opened his eyes when Rahkki's tears splashed on his face. "Are those tears for me? Or for her?" Brauk laughed, and blood sprayed from his mouth.

"For you," Rahkki said, wiping his eyes. "But she meant to kick Harak."

Brauk grimaced. "Don't fool yourself. She hates us all."

"Shh," said Brim. "Don't talk." She edged Rahkki

away from his brother and unbuckled Brauk's armor and cut open his undershirt, exposing his tan, muscled chest. Purple bruises bloomed there. Her gnarled fingers prodded his ribs gently but expertly, and Brauk growled like an animal. She felt his pulse and placed her ear over his heart. Rahkki watched in sickening silence, waiting to hear if his brother would die.

Brim sat up and gave orders to bring an animal-hide stretcher so Brauk could be removed to her shed. Brauk's eyelids fluttered shut, and he slipped back into unconsciousness.

"Well?" Rahkki asked.

Brim touched his shoulder. "His injuries are severe. If he survives the night, I think he'll live. That's all I can tell you right now."

Rahkki nodded, gulping air. He looked again at Sula. Amid much muttering, the auction had resumed, but the energy had left the arena. Sula stood like an elder Kihlara, hollow backed and lackluster. Tuni urged her to move, but she refused, not with defiance, but with dejection. Tuni tapped her rear lightly with the whip, but when Sula didn't flinch, Tuni gave up, not wanting to beat her with it.

The auctioneer, a small Sandwen man in a black tunic,

cajoled the spectators, but no highborn Sandwen wanted to bid on a man-killer, because that's how they viewed Sula now, even though Brauk was currently still alive.

The stretcher arrived, and Brauk was loaded carefully onto it. Uncle and a few Riders took the stretcher's handles and walked toward the arena gate. "Coming?" Brim asked.

Rahkki stood between his brother and Sula, looking from one to the other. He knew she hadn't meant to hurt Brauk. He knew Harak had pushed her past her limits. Sula stared back at him, her spirit appearing crushed. She took no pleasure in having kicked the wrong man. "I'm coming," he said to Brim.

But then the spectators burst into loud murmuring. Rahkki turned, wondering what was happening. Mut Finn was standing on the rail, waving his purse over his head. "Two dramals for her," he shouted.

Rahkki's heart sped a notch. Sula was worth a full round at least. Two dramals was nothing!

Lilliam rose up, her face inflamed by the low bid.

The grass folk surged to their feet, inspired by Mut. If the wealthy would not bid on the wild mare, then they would. It was the opportunity of a lifetime—a chance to own a winged steed for a song. Several young men and women rushed the fence, throwing out bids—two dramals and twenty jints, three dramals even, three dramals and ten jints—upping each other by the tiniest increments.

"No!" roared the queen. "The minimum bid is one round."

The young bidders spit on the ground and yelled at the queen. Dissatisfaction with Lilliam had begun long before it ripened, and now it ramped higher. She'd failed to protect them from the giants. She collected exorbitant tithes. And now the lowborn Sandwens saw their chance to strike a blow, however symbolic. Tuni and her Dusk Patrol rode in to threaten the crowd.

The bidding stopped, and the tented folk sat back, chomping on honeycombs and watching the crowd, looking bemused.

The auctioneer approached the queen and they had quick words, then Lilliam smiled widely. "This braya is no longer for sale," she announced.

The grass folk booed her, but the queen remained smiling.

"Instead, I'm going to *give* her away tomorrow . . . in a contest." She let her words settle on the gathered clans, and then she lifted her chin. "Whoever can fly her to the clouds and back can keep her."

The grass folk broke into wild murmuring. The tented folk leaned forward, interested in the new turn of events.

"But my queen, she's not saddle broke," said Tuni, loud enough for all to hear. "She's never worn a bit or bridle. No one can control her in the sky."

The queen smirked. "That's what makes it a contest, Headwind Hightower." Then she glanced toward the tented folk. "And to keep it interesting, my auctioneer will place odds on the contestants and organize the betting."

The tented folk slapped their legs in excitement, and Rahkki understood the queen's plan right away. She would make more profit on the betting than she would have made on the sale.

Lilliam motioned toward the young men and women who were eager to become Riders. "Come forward if you think you can ride this wild winged steed."

A flurry of young Sandwens, five females and seven males, including Mut and Koko, hopped the arena fence and gathered in front of Sula. The mare backed away, flaring her nostrils.

"And what if no one can ride her?" asked a young man from the Fourth Clan.

The queen's smile was ferocious. "Then tomorrow I'll feed her to our guardian mascot, Granak."

Rahkki gasped. Sula was a Child of the Wind. She was precious.

The silver mare fidgeted, uncomfortable with the throng of people staring at her; and Rahkki, who was still in the arena, stepped toward her, thinking to calm her.

The queen spotted him and frowned. "You have to be twelve or older to enter the contest," she said, making up the rule on the spot.

"I am twelve," Rahkki answered automatically.

There was some laughter from the other clans.

"So you're entering?" the queen asked, smirking now, her eyes daring him.

She hopes I'll fall off Sula and die, Rhakki thought, but his heart thudded with the possibilities. If he entered the contest and stayed on Sula for one ride, he could have her—and then he could set her free. *It's just one ride.* But then he glanced at her and saw the fear and desperation sloshing behind her gaze—and he doubted she'd ever been more dangerous. *No*, he thought. *No way can I ride her. And Sula would never forgive me if I tried.*

"No," he said. "I'm not entering."

Queen Lilliam nodded dismissively and then made her last announcement. "Entries close at morning bells tomorrow. All contestants have until then to put in their names"—she smiled and paused dramatically—"or to withdraw them."

Rahkki turned away, but deep inside him a voice flickered—*If you can't ride her, then who can?*

⟨⟨37⟩⟩

GRIEF

TUNI SLID A DARK HOOD OVER ECHOFROST'S HEAD
and then led her out of the arena with her mare, Rizah,
following. Echofrost swished her tail, hating the rattling
of the bells and the weight of the hard beads. Her legs
trembled and her thoughts tumbled—what was going to
happen to her? She'd kicked Brauk—a Rider who was not
threatening her. Harak must have anticipated her kick
and dived out of the way just as Brauk was running up
behind her. It was a mistake, an accident.

Tuni stroked Echofrost's neck. "It's not your fault," she
said.

Sadness caused Tuni's voice to warble, and Echofrost
heard it. Tuni and Brauk were friends, but Tuni wasn't

angry with her. No, but she sounded worried.

The pinto mare Rizah walked beside Echofrost, nickering to her. "Listen, Sula, tomorrow those young ones are going to compete for you. Sometimes this is done when a Kihlara doesn't sell."

"What does that mean?"

"It means you better pay attention, because whoever can ride you to the clouds and back gets to keep you. You'll be bound in a ceremony and sent to the Sky Guard of the Rider's clan."

I will never let that happen, thought Echofrost.

The familiar creaking of the barn door told Echofrost she was back in the Kihlari den. This was confirmed when Tuni led her into her stall and removed her hood. Tuni pitched her some hay, then she left without another word, leaving Echofrost alone.

"Shysong?" Echofrost nickered.

"She's gone," said Kol.

"Gone?"

"She lives in Fort Prowl now, with the princess. Probably in her bedroom, though she'll have a stall in the royal stable too. Your friend has done well, Sula. She'll have the best of everything."

"But she's alone! She has no herd. A . . . a person alone

is not good company for a pegasus." Echofrost's anger cleared away her muddled thoughts.

"What happened out there?" Kol asked, changing the subject. "Were you sold?"

Echofrost inhaled sharply. Kol didn't know what she'd done, that she'd injured his Rider. How could she tell him?

"If you'd been sold, your new owner would have marked your shoulder. Did that happen?" Kol pressed.

"No."

He huffed. "Well, it's the Ruk for you then. That's too bad."

"I don't think so," Echofrost replied. "Rizah said there will be a competition for me." Then she exhaled slowly. "But I need to tell you something. I—I made a mistake."

"Well, that doesn't surprise me," he said with a playful toss of his glistening mane.

Echofrost didn't want to draw it out, so she blurted it fast. "I kicked Brauk. He's hurt."

Kol went as still as death. "How hurt?"

"He's alive."

"I said, how hurt?"

Echofrost backed away from Kol's head, which was draped over her wall. "I'm not sure. It's bad though."

He blew hot air out his nostrils. "If Brauk doesn't recover, *I will kill you.*"

"It was a mistake," Echofrost whispered, knowing her words sounded weak.

Kol withdrew and spun a circle in his stall. Then he brayed so loud she had to cover her ears with her wings. It was the same cry of alarm the pegasi of Anok used to call for help. It was used only in times of extreme distress. Echofrost felt the pull in her heart to answer him, but she couldn't since she was the cause of his pain.

Rizah the palomino pinto lifted her head and joined Kol's cry with her own, and then the rest of the Kihlari in the barn joined them. Their trumpeting wails filled Echofrost's ears. She closed her eyes, thinking: *Stop, stop.* Images tumbled: Rahkki racing across the arena, shouting his brother's name; Harak's startled face, Tuni's rush of tears; the queen's sly smile.

The images merged and whirled in her head, forming and re-forming, and then reshaping into something else: her brother, Bumblewind. He appeared in her mind's eye as if he were standing right in front of her: his friendly face, his warm brown eyes, his brown-edged golden feathers. The anger and grief she'd been battling since his death reared up in her gut, strangling her and shattering her heart. It was time to stop running from it, blaming others for it, so she faced it—her brother's death in Anok.

She remembered the story as she'd heard it from Hazelwind. The dire wolves had attacked them. Their leader, a white she-wolf, had snatched Bumblewind and thrown him into a tree, cracking his head against it. He'd lived through the night, but the following day, still suffering from memory loss and confusion, he'd died with Hazelwind by his side.

She faced her memories while grief tore into her like a hungry lion. "I wasn't there when you needed me most!" She said the words in a gasp, and then she knelt down in her straw, racked with sobs. She was his sister, his *twin sister*. They'd shared the same womb and the same friends, but she hadn't been there when he'd taken his final breath. She'd lived an entire day and night in absolute ignorance that his cold body had been buried in stones. She'd blamed Hazelwind, but he'd told her as soon as he could. No, Dewberry was right: Echofrost wasn't mad at him—never had been; no, the creature she despised was herself!

Echofrost sobbed into her feathers, off and on, for the rest of the day. Bumblewind was gone, and she'd never cried for him, or let him go. Instead she'd coddled her anger, nursed it like a starving foal, but it was time to say good-bye.

When she'd cried herself out, she wiped her eyes. Lying in her stall, she'd never felt so alone. Rahkki would hate her now. The cub admired his brother, like she'd admired hers. Brauk was still alive; but she'd heard the snapping of his bones, the wheezing of his breath, and she'd seen his face turn white. His injuries were severe. She'd have to live with what she'd done, and so would Rahkki and Kol, and worst of all, Brauk.

"I'm sorry," she whispered to them all—and to herself; but no one was listening.

38

VIPER

THE FOLLOWING MORNING RAHKKI WOKE AND stretched, noticing his hair was full of straw. *Where am I?* He rolled to his feet, suddenly remembering. He was in Brim Carver's shed. He'd slept in one of her clean stalls with Uncle, but now he was alone. Rahkki opened the stall door and spied Brauk asleep on a cot.

The animal healer sat by his side, singing a clan lullaby, different from the one she'd sung to Rahkki. Darthan was outside smoking his pipe. The sky was warming from silver to gold, and the insects chirped with raucous abandon. It was almost time for morning bells.

"How is he?" Rahkki asked Brim. His brother's suntanned skin was pale. His wave of dark hair lay flat.

"He's not going to die," Brim murmured, but by her eyes Rahkki knew something was terribly wrong.

"What?" he asked as his throat tightened.

"He can't feel his legs, Rahkki."

"What does that mean?"

Brim met his gaze and told him straight. "When Sula kicked your brother, her hooves broke several ribs. But those aren't the injuries I'm concerned about. When she struck, she sent him flying backward into a fence post. His spine is injured—bruised or fractured maybe—I can't be certain until the swelling recedes. But right now, your brother can't wiggle his toes. He can't walk."

Rahkki's legs wobbled like noodles, and he had to sit down. *Can't walk?* No, that was impossible. Brauk was always in motion, always springing on his toes, always dancing, or fighting, or running. It wasn't conceivable that he couldn't *walk*. "No. That's not right; it can't be right." Rahkki's eyes bulged, but he saw only Brauk in his mind: Brauk lifting Rahkki onto his shoulders, Brauk racing him to the barn, and Brauk flying on Kol.

"It will be days before I know more, maybe longer," said Brim. "And healing will take time, perhaps several months."

Several months! Rahkki squatted, unable to breathe.

"Brauk must rest and stay positive." Brim's wrinkles danced across her face as she spoke. "Your brother believes he'll heal in a few days. He won't accept a thing I tell him, and he's leaning on his anger for strength; but anger won't help him with this." She nodded toward Brauk's limp legs, and then she left Rahkki alone with his brother and joined Darthan outside the shed.

Rahkki crawled to Brauk's side. He wanted to lie beside him, but there was no room on the cot. He took Brauk's hand, tracing his calluses, prodding his strong fingers, and wondering at his trail of scars. Brauk had the grip of a python, and he often won silly contests with the other Riders—squeezing their hands until they cried out or hanging from a tree branch longer than anyone else. Rahkki hugged his brother's forearm and kissed his palm.

Brauk blinked, his eyelids mere slits. "If you're going to practice kissing, could you use your own hand?"

Rahkki sputtered into a weak laugh and gripped Brauk's palm tighter.

"I can't sit up," his brother said.

"Don't try," Rahkki said. "Just rest." He took long, slow breaths, stuffing his grief where Brauk couldn't see it.

"What happened to that viper, Sula?" Brauk asked, his voice low and his words slurred. "Did the queen sell her?"

"No," Rahkki answered. "She's holding a contest. Whoever can ride Sula gets to keep her." *And if they can't, the queen will feed her to Granak*—Rahkki couldn't bear to think about it.

Brauk groaned and closed his eyes. "Sula's going to kill someone, or worse." Then his breaths slowed as he drifted into deep sleep.

Rahkki clutched his short hair. Sula had perhaps already done the worst; Brauk just didn't know it yet. Why had his brother interfered? He should have let Sula kick Harak. Rahkki shook his head, no; Brauk was protecting another Rider, something he did without thinking.

Brim and Uncle entered the shed. "Come outside with me," said Uncle Darthan. Rahkki stood and followed his uncle while the animal doctor tended Brauk. "Brim told you about your brother?" he asked.

Rahkki nodded. "It's not fair. Brauk was trying to help."

Uncle faced the rising sun, exhaling. "You don't want life to be fair, Rahkki."

"I don't?"

Uncle shook his head. "No, because who decides what is fair—the queen, the giants, Granak? What is fair to one is not fair to another. Fairness is a sentiment that will sprout bitterness in your heart."

"But if Brauk can't walk . . . it will kill him," he said quietly.

"Only if he lets it," said Uncle.

"When will you tell him?"

"Soon," said Uncle, "but not today."

"Brim said the numbness might be temporary."

Darthan smiled. "Life is temporary, Rahkki." His uncle pointed toward the arena. "They're about to begin the contest for Sula. Did you enter?"

"No." Rahkki blushed. In the cozy light of morning, he felt like a coward.

"The queen wants it over with before the feeding of Granak later. Why don't you go watch? Brauk needs to rest."

"Are you sure?"

"Yes. Here, take this with you." Darthan walked inside and returned with a wooden bowl. Inside was a mixture of rice that was soaked in goat's milk and spiced with nutmeg.

Rahkki took his breakfast and walked to the arena. He arrived to a smaller crowd than had appeared the day before. Most of the clansfolk, especially the mothers and elders, did not want to watch the contestants attempt to ride Sula, certain she would destroy them. So it was young, single, and childless folk who were attending today, along with the wealthy merchants and traders who planned to wager on the odds.

Sula was already standing in the ring with Tuni, dancing nervously on her hooves. Her coat was sleek and shining silver; her white mane and tail were braided with feathers, bells, and colorful beads. She was tethered to a tree so she couldn't fly away, and the Headwind had attached reins to her halter. She wore no saddle, no bit. Whoever rode her today would have to do it bareback.

The contestants rolled on the balls of their feet, anxious to get started. They were young, mostly teens and apprentices.

Mut and Koko met his gaze, each looking fierce and eager. This was probably the only chance they would ever have to own a Kihlara Flier.

Rahkki watched Sula stare down the contestants, her eyes flat and black, like a snake's before striking, and he knew like he breathed air that *none* of them would be able to ride her.

And if they couldn't, the queen would feed her to Granak.

The morning bells began to ring. "Last call for names!" shouted the auctioneer. "Who wants to win this wild braya?"

Before he could stop himself, Rahkki threw up his hand. "I do."

39

THE CONTENDERS

EVERYONE TURNED TO STARE AT RAHKKI: THE queen, the contestants, the bettors, and the spectators.

The auctioneer gaped, raking his eyes over him as though there must be more to Rahkki than met the eye. Then he glanced at the queen, and she nodded. "All right," called the auctioneer. "We have thirteen contestants." He introduced all thirteen, ending with "Rahkki Stormrunner, Rice Apprentice of the Fifth Clan. Now step out of the arena, please," he instructed. "You'll ride in the order you were announced. The mare will remain tethered until a contestant has control of her. On the queen's signal the tether will be cut. The first one to fly her to the clouds and back keeps her."

In the pale morning sunshine, the wealthy folk who'd pitched the plushest shade tents gathered around a communal table. They were mostly merchant traders, generals, and royal advisers. Their stewards held their sacks of coin, and as the odds on the first contestant were announced, the betting began.

The folks watching on the grass were friends and relatives of the contestants or curious bystanders. They had grim expressions and crossed arms. Since Uncle Darthan had refused Brauk any visitors, a rumor had spread that he'd died. A Kihlara steed that killed a Rider was a bad omen—bad luck—and the contestants' families were not pleased. But the contestants themselves looked hopeful. An unlucky Kihlara was preferable to *no* Kihlara—and for those without means, like Mut and Koko, Sula was their only chance to touch the clouds.

Rahkki found a spot on the grass next to the teens who'd come to cheer on Mut and Koko. "Isn't that your wildling mare?" one asked.

"She's not mine," Rahkki replied, keeping his eyes on Sula.

Mut looked down at him. "You sure there's no size

limit to ride her?" His friends laughed.

Rahkki finished his breakfast, ignoring them.

Mut was the first contender. He strode into the arena full of spit and swagger.

"Two to one," the auctioneer barked.

Rahkki noted the low odds. It meant they thought Mut could ride Sula, but he doubted it. The boy was too large to control his own weight if she tossed him.

Tuni held Sula steady, but Mut grabbed her reins and shooed Tuni away. A long rope extended from Sula's neck to an ancient tree, tethering her but giving her room to run and glide. The queen wouldn't risk her flying away by herself.

Mut leaped onto Sula's back, and Tuni shuffled out of their way. The silver mare staggered a few steps and then stood frozen. The tent folk exchanged excited murmurs. Mut flashed a big smile to his friends and kicked Sula in the ribs.

She lowered her head and bucked him off, launching the big kid thirty lengths with cool calmness. He landed with a grunt. "What?" Mut said. "I wasn't ready."

"Next," roared the queen.

Coins flew as the odds changed on all the contestants,

and the queen smiled sweetly. Her auctioneer was collecting and paying out the bets, and as the odds rose, so did her profits.

Mut returned to his friends looking about a head shorter and with a sour expression on his face. "I wasn't ready," he repeated as his friends patted his sore back, making him wince.

Sula easily threw off two more hopefuls with the same halfhearted buck as the first. Koko was the fourth contender. She was small and strong and able to ride through the bucks. Sula changed tactics and reared, then spun around in a fast circle. She wasn't trying to hurt Koko, just unload her; but when the excited girl remained attached, Sula took to the sky. "Cut the tether," Koko cried in excitement, but the queen raised her hand.

"Not yet," she commanded.

Sula flew low, just a winglength over the arena, gliding in a wide circle. She flapped hard, gliding faster and faster until Koko's eyes whirled in her head. Then Sula angled her wings, braked hard, and ducked. Koko sailed off her back, blond hair streaming, and hit the dirt with a dull thud and a sharp squeal. She earned a few admiring nods as she staggered out of the gate.

A skinny boy, older than Rahkki, whistled. "Did you

see that speed?" he said to no one in particular. "And in such a tight circle. Sula will make an excellent Flier."

The boy might as well have been eyeing a juicy buffalo steak the way he salivated over the mare, and Rahkki's anger flared. *That's* my *winged horse*, he thought, but of course, she wasn't.

The skinny boy was also the next to ride. He approached Sula slowly and offered her a treat. She snubbed it, which didn't surprise Rahkki. Then the boy slid onto her back, and for a moment Sula held perfectly still. Dead silence fell on the arena, and Rahkki could hear his heart thudding. Then Sula turned, snatched the boy's belt in her teeth, and tossed him aside like an annoying piece of tack.

The bettors and the remaining contenders burst into loud laughter and applause. Even the queen managed a chuckle, and the odds in the tent changed again.

Sula dislodged the next six contenders with equal aplomb, and Rahkki grew nervous. What would Sula do to him? He squeezed his fingers into fists, noticing the clammy feel of them. There was one contender left before it was Rahkki's turn, an adult male. He was tall and fit. Rahkki recognized him—he was a horse breaker—a man used to untrained steeds. He strode to Sula's side, grabbed her mane, and heaved himself onto her back. She lifted off and flew a fast circle, then halted suddenly, but the young man held on, handling her firmly but gently.

Sula whinnied and flew a loop. The man tightened his long legs and rode it out. Rahkki chewed his lip.

As Sula bucked and whirled in the sky, the horse breaker counterbalanced her movements.

"They're a good pair," said the skinny boy, leaning on the rail.

Rahkki felt sick at his words, but he agreed, at least somewhat. They were a good pair, except that the young man's height would be a problem for Sula in the long run. He was too tall, too heavy. He could ride her, but could he really pilot her for life? Rahkki thought not. He'd break her down.

"Shall I cut the tether?" the auctioneer inquired.

Lilliam nodded.

Just then Sula pinned her ears and flew straight up, as high as the rope would allow, and then straight down, hurtling at a breakneck speed toward land. Her tail waved behind her like a banner, her bells jingled in the wind. Just before striking the dirt, she pulled out of the dive and barrel-rolled wing over wing across the arena, dumping her rider onto the sand.

Free of him, she halted her spin and hovered with

perfect balance, clearly unfazed by her incredible display of agility—which was beyond the capabilities of the Kihlari steeds. The tether twisted behind her, a tangled mess.

As the queen, the gamblers, and the contestants gaped at her, Sula landed and preened her feathers, letting them stare.

Rahkki's heart overflowed with pride. Sula was magnificent in the small things as well as the big things. And as he'd predicted, no one could ride her.

But now it was his turn. He entered the arena and stood in the center, wiping his sweating palms on his trousers.

Queen Lilliam drummed her fingers on her bare arm, pondering him and the mare as the gamblers settled their wagers. Just then I'Lenna approached the arena from Fort Prowl, riding her new winged pet bareback. Firo looked confused, but she walked obediently. I'Lenna's smile was radiant, and when she noticed Rahkki, she waved.

The queen glanced sharply from her daughter to Rahkki, and the crown princess quickly erased her expression, looking as blank as a mat of reeds. Lilliam turned to the auctioneer. "Odds, please."

"Twenty to one," answered the little man dressed in black.

The small crowd erupted. No contestant had faced such high odds. The tented folk crossed their arms and shook their heads. "Will anyone wager on the boy?" the auctioneer asked, glancing at the spectators.

"I'll bet two jints," Koko said, looking competitive. If she couldn't win the mare, maybe she could win a bet.

"You'll lose two jints," said Mut, and his friends laughed.

"I'll wager on him," said a voice.

Rahkki gasped as Uncle Darthan stepped out of the shadows. "Two full rounds," he said, holding up two stamped coins of the realm, each worth one hundred dramals.

The auctioneer shook his head, and the tent folk gaped at the rice farmer.

"Uncle, no," Rahkki whispered. It was too much.

"You think *he* can ride her?" Queen Lilliam asked.

"These rounds say as much," said Darthan, turning them so their metal surfaces reflected the morning sun. Those coins represented his uncle's life savings. If Rahkki failed, he'd throw the entire Stormrunner family into worse poverty. Lilliam's eyes brightened as she seemed to come to the same conclusion. "I'll take that bet."

The spectators went from admiring Sula to appraising Rahkki.

"But I . . ." He glanced at Darthan—had his uncle lost his mind?

"You what?" asked the queen. She drew her tongue across her lower lip, slow and careful, like she was tasting the wind, and Rahkki jolted—stung by a distant memory of the night his mother died. He followed it, and it didn't vanish this time. He was sleeping with his favorite toy, a stuffed Kihlara doll, and no blankets because it was a hot night. A figure had entered his room. "Momma?" he'd called. But it wasn't her. It was Lilliam. He was only four years old, but he remembered that she'd licked her bottom lip, just like she was doing right now.

Rahkki tore his eyes from her mouth and stared into her blue eyes. They flamed at him. *She knows I'm remembering*, he thought, panicking. His mother, Reyella, had barged into Rahkki's room and shoved the queen aside just as Lilliam's small hands were closing around his throat.

Reyella had snatched Rahkki from the queen and thrown him out of the room. And there was Brauk, who was thirteen, waiting on Drael's back and still dressed in his sleeping gown. He snatched Rahkki's collar and yanked him up behind him, and then they'd galloped the winged steed down the stone hallways of the fortress and crashed through a shuttered window, flying away.

But Rahkki had looked back and seen the impossible. He'd watched his mother leap into his fireplace and vanish. Lilliam tried to follow, couldn't.

There his mind went blank. He couldn't remember how his mother disappeared, where she went, or where Drael had taken him and Brauk. The following two years of his life were a black void.

Queen Lilliam clapped her hands together, startling Rahkki. "Ride that braya or exit this arena."

Rahkki nodded, his legs shaking.

Queen Lilliam believed he'd fail, but Rahkki couldn't think about that. His thoughts were swirling with fear, rage, and grief. *Was his mother still alive?* If so, where was she and what had happened to her unborn baby? And if she'd escaped through the fireplace, why didn't she come back for him and Brauk?

Lilliam tapped her engorged belly impatiently. "Well," she prodded. "What are you waiting for?"

❧ 40 ❧

FLIGHT

ECHOFROST HAD PRICKED HER EARS WHEN SHE saw Shysong trotting toward the arena ridden by Princess I'Lenna. She whinnied to her friend, ignoring everything else around her. "How are you?"

"I'm well," Shysong whinnied back. "But I don't like Fort Prowl. Fires burn in every room, including hers." She nodded toward the princess. "And she spent hours braiding and unbraiding my tail last night. What's happening here? I thought the auction was over yesterday."

"I haven't sold yet, and now they're harassing me. Seeing if anyone can ride me."

Just then Rahkki touched Echofrost's shoulder, distracting her. She looked down. The cub was shaking. His golden eyes were light, almost yellow. What was he doing in the arena?

"Easy, Sula," he whispered, and he reached out to touch her mane.

She threw her head skyward. *He means to ride me! No, not you too*, she thought, and she reared away from him.

The queen laughed, showing her small white teeth.

Rahkki rested his hands at his sides and stared up at Echofrost. "Please," he begged her. "Or they're going to kill you."

Echofrost felt sick, betrayed. Rahkki knew she didn't like to be touched, let alone ridden like a land horse.

But something was off, and she paused. Everything about Rahkki's posture and scent told her that he did *not* want to ride her. Was the cub afraid to fly? And if so, then why was he trying to win her?

Rahkki reached for her again, and she instinctively flinched.

The queen's grin broadened, and Rahkki's fear increased.

The Landwalkers at the table stood up, excited. The people in the grass also stood, whispering to one another.

Quicker than she thought possible, Rahkki pulled

himself onto her back. Instinctively she bucked, but he moved with her, speaking the soft words he thought soothed her.

The queen laughed at Rahkki again, and Echofrost's anger exploded. Lilliam *wanted* her to buck him off, to hurt him; and Echofrost realized that the queen had set up this contest knowing that no one could ride her. It was sport, an amusement. This was a test—like when young pegasi raced. Well, Echofrost would show the queen and her clan that Rahkki was stronger and braver than any of them thought.

Echofrost bent her head, willingly giving into the reins.

The spectators ceased talking.

Rahkki clucked to her and squeezed her sides. She broke into a slow trot. He turned her in circles and backed her and cantered her. She paid close attention to his gentle pressuring, letting his soft hands and legs guide her. When he pulled up the reins, she flexed her wings and sailed off the dirt. Again, following his prompts, she flew in pretty, controlled circles.

"How's he doing that?" Mut asked, his mouth agape.

Koko threw down her sweat cloth, shaking her head.

The queen pursed her lips, and I'Lenna grinned.

Tuni stalked toward the tether. "Satisfied?" she asked the auctioneer. He glanced at the queen. Her skin had paled, her blue eyes looked black. She nodded. Tuni cut the tether.

When the rope snapped, Echofrost blinked in shock. Again obedience had helped her rather than hurt her. "I'm loose!" she whinnied to Shysong.

The blue roan flared her wings, startling the princess.

"This is our chance," Echofrost neighed. "Let's go! Now!"

"But the princess?"

"Shrug her off!"

Echofrost leaped off the sand and blasted toward the clouds.

"Whoa, slow down," Rahkki said, tightening his grip.

Shysong bucked and tore after Echofrost, but the princess hung on, wrapping her arms around Shysong's neck.

The two mares hurtled straight up with their young riders hollering to each other. Below them, the arena erupted into chaos. In seconds the alarm bells were ringing, and, too late, Echofrost realized how things looked to the Landwalkers—like they'd kidnapped the queen's daughter.

"You were supposed to unload her!" Echofrost whinnied.

"I tried," Shysong answered. "But I was afraid I'd hurt her if I bucked too hard."

Echofrost glanced down. The Kihlari roof was beginning to open, and the Sky Guard would be on them in moments, but if they didn't keep flying, she doubted they'd ever get another opportunity to escape.

"Head to the heights," she whinnied, forgetting all about Rahkki, who weighed next to nothing.

Surging higher, Echofrost and Shysong darted into clouds that were huge and billowing, offering them cover. Far below, the Landwalkers scurried like mice. Inside the barn, Riders quickly buckled saddles onto their mounts. "Higher," Echofrost neighed.

"But the princess can't breathe," whinnied Shysong, pausing to hover.

Echofrost glanced over her shoulder. Rahkki's small face had drained of color, his fists were bleeding from holding on to her mane, and his golden eyes lolled in his head. His breath puffed out in streams of white vapor chilled by the heights. She was going to lose him. Blast it! His weakness was now her weakness. "Drop down!" she whinnied.

The mares plummeted toward land, quickly reviving their riders. Rahkki leaned forward, mouthing words to Echofrost that she didn't understand. He tried to steer her by tugging on her mane and pressuring her with his legs. She ignored him.

"Here they come!" Echofrost brayed to Shysong. The Kihlari army was after them, with Tuni and Rizah in the lead.

"What now?"

Echofrost wondered the same. Then she remembered the Kihlari's clumsy agility. "To the trees," she whinnied, angling her wings. She dropped altitude quickly, feeling Rahkki's body lift slightly off her back.

Behind them, the Sky Guard whooped. Their mounts flew with flat necks, and their tails whipped in the wind. They soared over the village, and the Landwalkers shouted in excitement, watching the tame steeds chase the wild ones. Echofrost dipped lower once she passed the village, and her hooves skimmed the grass, but they were flying too fast to let the cubs off without killing them. "It's because of the princess," Echofrost whinnied. "They won't stop until they get her back."

"Well, we can't slow down; they'll catch us. And if I buck her off at this speed, she'll break her neck."

Echofrost glanced back—the Sky Guard was right behind them.

The palomino pinto Rizah gnashed her teeth. "By Granak, Sula!" she whinnied. "Put the kids down before you kill them."

Echofrost tucked her tail and whinnied to Shysong. "We'll lose the army in the jungle. Are you ready to fly faster than you ever have?" Ahead was the rain forest where the Gorlan giant had attacked Echofrost.

"I'm ready," whinnied Shysong.

The two mares bolted into the trees.

41

THE CHASE

RAHKKI ENTWINED HIS FISTS AROUND SULA'S mane. Her muscles bunched and expanded as she charged into the dark woods. She flew close to the ground, her neck stretched flat and her wings pinned to her sides like the fletchings on an arrow.

He drew in his elbows and knees as they blew past trees in a blur. Sula's body twisted, sometimes sideways. She dodged banyans and palms, rubber trees and Kapoks, her wingtips grazing against the damp leaves. Displaced branches thrashed Rahkki's back and tore at his clothes; the wind stung his face. He gripped her tight and gulped, his heart walloping.

To his right, I'Lenna hunched over Firo. Her long

hair had come unbraided and the feathers she'd tied to her wrists twirled in the wind, making I'Lenna look part flying horse, part girl. Firo's black-edged blue wings were also pinned, flapping occasionally to increase speed and then angling back as she rocketed between the trees.

I'Lenna risked a glance at Rahkki. Her cheeks had flushed bright pink. Her scream was breathless. "I want off!"

"Watch out!" he cried.

Firo swooped to avoid smashing into a massive trunk, and I'Lenna clutched the mare tighter to avoid slipping off her.

The Sky Guard surged into the forest. Tuni hollered, "Stop the mares, Rahkki!"

A helpless chuckle rose in Rahkki's throat. *As if I could!*

Sula surged forward. Rahkki had ridden many horses, but Sula's strength and speed were unexpected for her small size. He wrapped his arms around her silver neck, feeling the bite of her flowing white mane against his cheeks. Her lean muscles rippled, and her wings shaped the wind. She swerved and ducked, startling birds and exciting the monkeys, and Rahkki threw up a silent prayer to the Seven Sisters.

The Sky Guard spread out, attempting to pass the mares and surround them, but they were heavy with armor, and they lost speed dodging the trees.

"Faster!" Tuni ordered.

The Fliers pinned their wings, imitating Sula—a mistake. Rahkki heard explosive thuds as some Kihlari crashed into trees, flying too fast to navigate. They splintered through the branches and fell to land.

Tuni kicked Rizah, sailing closer. "I'm coming!" she shouted to Rahkki and I'Lenna, hoping to rescue them.

A low branch, too thick to avoid, appeared ahead. Sula dived under it, making Rahkki's belly somersault. The branch scraped against his scalp. "Stop chasing us!" he shouted back to Tuni. Sula would slow if she didn't feel threatened, and maybe then she'd let him off.

Tuni flew over the same low branch and lost speed, but did not give up. She dug her heels into Rizah's sides and urged her faster, but the shouts and whinnies of the Sky Guard had faded behind them.

Sula and Firo, feeling pressured by Rizah, increased their speed another notch, which Rahkki hadn't thought possible. His gut twisted into a hopeless knot, and his breath came so fast he felt dizzy. Sula's mane tangled tight around his hands, cutting off his circulation. His injured side throbbed, and his head ached. And nothing about this crazy ride was helping him conquer his fear of heights. It was only I'Lenna's presence that kept Rahkki from screaming like a tot.

"Where are they taking us?" I'Lenna shouted.

"I think they're escaping," he shouted back. "We're just along for the ride."

"So they'll let us go?"

"I think so."

He yelped as Sula surged up and over a small tree, and his body bumped on her back. Then Rahkki spotted gray shapes walking ahead of them. "Elephants," he warned. These were wild elephants, not the ones tamed by the Gorlanders, but their swinging trunks and tusks were dangerous.

Sula cut a sharp left. Firo ducked, following, and I'Lenna slid to one side. "I'm falling!" she screamed. Firo quickly adjusted, and I'Lenna pulled herself upright. They soared past the elephants, and the beasts trumpeted piercing alarms that traveled for miles.

Tuni and Rizah sailed straight into the herd and the pinto balked, almost throwing Tuni off her back. But their momentum was lost as they slowed to circle the elephant herd, and the wild mares pulled away, gliding deeper into the rain forest. As Tuni disappeared behind them, Rahkki faced forward.

After many dizzying minutes, Sula and Firo finally slowed and nickered to each other, and Rahkki was sure they were talking. They flew on for many long miles, but as Rahkki had predicted, the brayas relaxed now that they weren't being chased. Sitting up, he stretched his back. I'Lenna also sat taller and wiped her watering eyes. "Look," she said, her voice carrying on the wind.

They were gliding over a full and winding river that was clear all the way to the bottom. Bright fish schooled and larger ones swam as slow as sharks. Alligators napped on the shores, and insects filled the air. The mares dropped lower and let their hooves skim the water, cutting long ripples.

Ahead the river dropped into a flowing waterfall. The mares bent their wings and dropped with it, buzzing over the edge and down, falling like stones. Rahkki's belly fluttered as they dived hundreds of lengths toward the glimmering pool at the bottom. Fresh spray soaked him, and I'Lenna kicked her feet, ringing the bells on her ankle charms. "We're flying!" she chortled.

The mares gently pulled out of their dives and banked, heading east. Straight ahead fluttered a kaleidoscope of butterflies, thousands of them. "Watch out," he cried. But Sula and Firo flew straight into them. Rahkki glanced at I'Lenna. With colorful wings enveloping her, the blue sky shining above, and the lush green foliage flashing below, she looked as serene as a storybook illustration. Rahkki felt airsick.

They soared out of the ball of butterflies and cruised over a grassy field that was dotted with grazing lowland gorillas. The troop's oldest male, the silverback, stood on his hind legs and watched them fly by with curious eyes.

Next they glided over a flat reflective lake and scattered the fowl there, but not before Rahkki caught sight of their reflection: two winged mares, wild and wind tangled, their feathers glinting in the sun, with two children sitting astride them riding bareback, their clothing torn, their legs pressed tight, and their eyes bright, looking just as wild.

He caught his breath and watched the world pass under his feet, blurred and beautiful. I'Lenna studied the terrain and the animals, as well, appearing equally awestruck. She turned her head toward him and grinned. They entered another forest, and then suddenly, Sula and Firo lifted their noses and shot to the tops of the trees. Rahkki felt the porridge he'd eaten earlier rise in his throat. He swallowed it back down, gagging.

383

The mares flared their wings and braked, hovering above the treetops. Here the wind filled Rahkki's ears and blew his short hair straight up. The horizon shrank, and he could see all the way to the ocean. He closed his eyes and breathed through his nose.

"Look at those huge nests," I'Lenna said, pointing down.

Rahkki opened his eyes and, sure enough, right below them were the largest nests he'd ever seen. Sula and Firo landed in the biggest one and folded their wings. They turned their heads and stared at the kids, and Rahkki knew exactly what they wanted. "Get off," he said to I'Lenna. They slid off their flying horses and collapsed at the bottom of the nest.

"Are we resting here?" I'Lenna asked.

Sula dropped her muzzle into Rahkki's hands. It was the first time she'd sought physical contact with him. He stroked her nose and then he tensed. "Oh no," he said.

"What?" I'Lenna spun in a circle as if something might be lurking near.

"They're leaving us. Sula is saying good-bye."

"What!"

And with that the two mares lifted off and soared away, flying east.

42

THE NEST

RAHKKI AND I'LENNA CRAWLED TO THE EDGE OF the Kihlara nest and looked down. They were at least a hundred lengths above the rain forest floor. I'Lenna reached toward Firo, who was gliding into the blue cloud-filled sky. "Come back!" she pleaded to her winged horse. "Firo! Please come back."

The tree swayed, impacted by the breeze and the quick departure of the mares. Rahkki leaned farther over the nest wall and heaved, splattering the leaves below with porridge. He sat back and wiped his mouth. "Sorry about that."

"What sort of nest is this, do you think?" asked I'Lenna, too upset at being abandoned by her new pet to care about his retching. "What if its owner finds us here? What if it's a raptor?"

Rahkki inspected the nest, which was flat on the bottom and gently curved on the sides. It was strewn with Kihlari feathers. "I think the wild herd made these nests."

I'Lenna wiped her eyes, sniffling and holding the feathers in her hands. "I didn't know the Kihlari could build nests. But how do we get down?"

The thought of climbing down the tree sent a fresh wave of panic through Rahkki. "I'm not sure."

She cupped her chin. "I think we're stuck here."

"Yes, but we're safer from predators here than on the ground. The mares know that."

"You think they put us here to *protect* us?"

"I do."

I'Lenna, still breathing hard from their blistering ride, turned her wide dark eyes to his. "So they're really not coming back?"

He shook his head. "I don't think so. They're free now. Truly free." He smiled weakly, glad that Sula had finally gotten her wish, but sad that I'Lenna had lost her birthday present. It struck him also that Darthan would lose the money he bet if Rahkki didn't return on Sula's back. Darthan had believed in Rahkki, but the queen had been right about him—he couldn't control Sula.

"I was so happy," said the princess.

"I know." He patted her hand, not knowing what else to do. "The Sky Guard will find us," he said, feeling hopeful.

Rahkki scouted the sky around them. He could see all the way from the clear ocean in the east to the black-sand coast in the north. Smoke from the Fifth Clan rose in the distance, but the village was many miles away. He and I'Lenna were so high that birds flew below them, and a troop of orangutans played in the lower branches of nearby trees. The rain forest floor was invisible, shrouded by leaves. The air was thin, and it seemed that if they reached up, they could touch the clouds. The nest swayed gently, like a boat in the ocean.

"If they don't find us today, we'll have to spend the night here, won't we?" I'Lenna said, but she was calming down.

Rahkki stared at her. I'Lenna was bloodborn like him, a direct descendant of the Sandwen clans' founders. But she was more precious than he because she was a female, and only females could inherit crowns. Suddenly a different sort of panic besieged him—Rahkki was the only clan member around to keep the crown princess safe.

She leaned over the edge again and Rahkki pulled her back. "Please don't do that," he said. "You could fall."

She drew up her knees and huddled, looking cold even in the ferocious heat of late morning. That's when Rahkki noticed her bleeding lip. His eyes trailed down. She was dressed in a bleached doe-hide dress that was trimmed in black rabbit fur. The stitching was immaculate, and the sinew the seamstress had used was dyed pale blue. Outlines of orchids were embroidered across the bodice of the dress, and her belt was fashioned from soft black leather. The outfit was torn and streaked with dirt, ruined. She wore only one sandal; the other must have fallen off during their flight. Red welts streaked her legs and arms, and her hair hung in tangles. "You're hurt," he said.

She shook her head. "No, I'm fine."

They sat awhile, thinking and recovering. She reached into a small pocket sewn into her dress and pulled out a hard white candy. "Want a peppermint?"

Saliva flooded Rahkki's mouth. A peppermint cost a dramal, and they were sold across Cinder Bay in Daakur. He hadn't seen or tasted one since I'Lenna had hidden a piece under his pillow when he was nine or ten years old. But he still remembered the exquisite taste: sweet and minty. Of course he wanted it. "Does a fish drink water?"

She laughed, closing her fist around the sweet and drawing it closer to her. "Hmm, I don't think a fish actually drinks water. It *breathes* water. I guess you don't want it."

Rahkki leaned forward, meeting her gaze. "Does a dog chase a stick?"

"My dog doesn't. Too lazy." She raised her hand as if to throw the peppermint out of the nest.

Rahkki wiped his lips. He was actually drooling! He inched closer. "Does a winged horse fly?"

"Not the ones at the Ruk." I'Lenna laughed and cranked back her arm.

Rahkki caught her wrist in his hand. "Does a pig love slop? Does a soldier eat rice? Does a boy trapped in a Kihlari nest want a peppermint? Yes, and yes, and yes!" He lunged for the candy and I'Lenna dodged him. They tumbled and laughed, delirious and tired after the terrifying ride. He was smaller, but stronger. He pinned her down, but as soon as he had her trapped, he let her go.

She sat up and pointed at him. "There are feathers all over your hair."

"Yours too," he said. He let his eyes drift away from the candy. He wouldn't beg her for it.

She grinned and took his hand, dropping *two* pepper-mints into his palm. "You can have mine too."

He stared at the white candies. They weren't just treats; they were the life he'd lost—wealth, goodness, and sweetness—and she was sharing them. No, not sharing. She was giving him *her* share too. "Are you sure?" he asked.

"Does a hen lay eggs?"

Rahkki snorted. "Not an old hen."

"Ah, Rahkki!" She sat back and straightened her hair, pulling out the loose feathers.

He placed both candies on his tongue. Why save sweetness for later? He knew how fast it could be lost. "I'Lenna?" he asked, thinking of his mother. "You've been in my room at Fort Prowl. Is there anything strange about the fireplace?"

Her lips twisted, half frowning, half smiling. "How do you know I've been in your room?"

"The last time I had a peppermint, I woke up with it stuck to my ear. Either you put it under my pillow, or the *kaji* spirits are real."

She grinned. "Yeah, that was me."

"So what about the fireplaces in the fortress? Are they . . . magical or anything?"

She sat taller, thinking hard and studying his face.

Then she seemed to come to a decision. "If I reveal my secrets, I'll have to kill you."

He leaned closer to her. "You do know something then?" His heartbeat skittered.

She rolled her eyes, giving in to him. "Some of the fireplaces in the fortress have false backs that conceal doors, like the one in your room."

"Doors?" he mouthed, breathless.

"Yes. There's a trigger that opens them, but even my mother doesn't know the secret to finding it." Her eyes brightened as she spoke. "There are tunnels running through the interior walls of Fort Prowl, a maze of them. They lead out into the jungle, and they're how I get around, how I sneak into kids' rooms, and how I get out." She ripped a bur off her sleeve and flicked it out of the nest. "There. Now you know."

"What about my *old* room, where I lived when I was a prince. Isn't that your room now? Does that fireplace have a door too? And how do you know about the tunnels? Who told you?"

I'Lenna frowned. "Why all the questions? I told you how I get out; that's all you need to know. What does it matter if your old room has a false door or not?"

Rahkki was caught off guard by the question, though

it was a perfectly reasonable one. He decided that since I'Lenna had shared her secret, he'd share his. "Do you promise not to tell anyone?"

She squinted at him. "Do I look like a snitch to you?"

Rahkki shook his head, feeling excited. "I think my mother escaped . . . that night when, well, you know." It was difficult to bring up the assassination without sounding bitter, and it wasn't I'Lenna's fault that her mother was evil. "Anyway, I saw Reyella disappear into my fireplace."

I'Lenna's body went stiff, and her tan cheeks flushed. "If your mother's alive, then my mother's not the true Queen of the Fifth."

Rahkki swallowed. He hadn't meant to scare her. "I don't care about the throne, I'Lenna. I just want to find my mom."

Her eyes bored into his. "My mother's position is fragile enough already."

Rahkki leaped at the chance to warn her about the secret meetings. "I've heard," he said. "Your family isn't safe. Some are plotting—"

I'Lenna snorted, interrupting him. "I know all about it," she said. "More than you'd guess." Her eyes snapped to his. "But who told you?"

"My brother."

"Land to skies!" I'Lenna let out her breath. "I'm sorry about your mom, Rahkki, but I can't help you. That would be . . . *treason*." She whispered the word. "My mother would kill me, and you know, I'm not saying that figuratively."

"She wouldn't—"

I'Lenna held up her hand. "I can't even talk to you about this. I'm sorry. And I'm sorry about your brother. I heard he's injured."

Rahkki sank into the nest, feeling overwhelmed. "Brauk will heal," he said, but the words felt like lies. His thoughts turned back to the fireplace. He'd need access to Fort Prowl to investigate that, to find any clue about what had happened to Reyella and where she might be now. "So there's a trick to opening the false doors. Can you at least tell me what it is? I'll do my own investigating. I won't put you in danger."

I'Lenna smiled, her expression rueful. "Ah, Rahkki, it's not me I'm worried about. You're the one in danger if you start snooping around in those tunnels. I'm trying to keep *you* safe." Her sharp brown eyes searched his as though willing him to trust her.

But he wanted to know more, and he stared back at

her, his eyes pleading. "I miss her," he said simply, referring to Reyella.

I'Lenna grunted, and her usually cheerful face turned solemn. "I don't know anything about your mother, Rahkki, only about mine. And I can't say another word."

They each sat back and exhaled, realizing they'd reached an impasse. The heights were silent. No insects flew this high, and the noises of the jungle seemed distant, blown off by the wind.

After some time passed, I'Lenna crossed her legs and sat tall. "So, Rahkki Stormrunner, what do we do while we wait to be rescued?"

Her skin had paled, and he guessed she was as hungry as he was. He opened his satchel and removed dried jerky. He divided it between them, then spotted his bag of stones and game board at the bottom. He pulled them out, grinning. "We'll play."

I'Lenna tucked her hair behind her ear and grabbed a pile of feathers. "For betting," she said, smiling back.

Rahkki laid out the small wooden playing board and dropped four stones into each cup. Then he bowed with a graceful flourish. "Princesses go first."

ᏣᏗ43ᏣᏗ

BROKEN PROMISES

WHEN ECHOFROST HAD SEEN THAT THE STORM Herd nests were empty of pegasi, she was crestfallen. But seeing the nests gave her the idea to leave Rahkki and I'Lenna there, where they'd be safe until the Sky Guard found them. She and Shysong had landed in the largest one, and Echofrost was glad when the cubs had slid off so quickly, because they'd each clung like foxtails during the flight.

"Do you think the Sky Guard will find them?" Shysong asked, looking worried.

"Of course . . . eventually." Guilt about leaving Rahkki behind and concern over Storm Herd eroded all Echofrost's pleasure at finally being free.

"So where do we look for our friends?" Shysong wondered.

"Hazelwind mentioned that they graze twice a day now because they ate all the leaves around the nests. Let's fly higher and look around. Maybe we just missed them."

Echofrost dropped her muzzle into Rahkki's hand and let him stroke her face. This was good-bye. She watched his golden eyes round with horror. *He knows I'm leaving,* she thought, again feeling a stab of guilt. "I'm ready," she nickered to Shysong.

The mares tipped their noses to where the blue sky turned black, leaped out of the nest, and surged into the rocketing wind currents of the upper altitudes. Behind them, the princess shouted and Shysong tensed. "I'Lenna's scared. She's calling me."

"She's safe," Echofrost insisted, but Rahkki's sad expression tugged at her and she snorted, still surprised that she cared about him. "We *have* to leave them," she whinnied.

They flew in a widening circle, scanning the terrain. "Look there!" whinnied Echofrost. Far below, on an open grazing plain, was a smattering of large, bright pegasus feathers and evidence of charred grass. The feathers appeared mashed into the green foliage. Echofrost's first thought was that Nightwing the Destroyer had flown from Anok to hunt them down. She stared at Shysong.

The roan mare squinted at the apparent destruction. "Oh no!" she whinnied. "You don't think—you don't think it's Nightwing!"

Echofrost grimaced. "Let's see." Nightwing often used his silver fire to burn pegasi to death. Had he killed Star in the Flatlands and then somehow followed them here? Her heart thudded painfully in her chest.

The two mares flattened their necks, pinned their wings, and dived toward the field. It was located south of the nests. They circled the meadow first but sensed no immediate danger. They fluttered down and landed.

"It's not Nightwing!" Echofrost whinnied. She pointed to massive sets of footprints. "It's giants." But then the impact of this struck her, melting her relief. Giants ate pegasi—at least that's what the Kihlari steeds believed.

"There was a fight here," Shysong nickered, sniffing the ground and examining the feathers. "I smell blood."

Echofrost trotted around the meadow, also sniffing and examining the tracks and trampled foliage. She recognized the feathers of her closest friends—Hazelwind, Dewberry, Graystone, and Redfire. The entire herd had battled the Gorlanders here, but there were no bodies left behind. Had they all survived? She took a breath and swiveled her head. "Where did the fire come from?"

"Maybe the giants lit a fire."

"But these are scorch marks, like lightning strikes."

"There hasn't been a storm," said Shysong.

"I know," said Echofrost, confused. "But some of the feathers are burned too. This all happened at once—the giants used fire somehow to attack our herd."

"No," cried Shysong, pointing east. "Not to attack them, to *catch* them!"

"What?"

"Look at all the hoofprints."

Echofrost followed the direction of Shysong's wing and then noticed the long trail of hoofprints mixed with Gorlan footprints that led out of the meadow. She blinked at them, her emotions thundering. "Storm Herd left by hoof, not by air. That means they're captured."

"This can't be happening," Shysong whispered, her sides heaving in the hot sun.

The mares lifted off and followed the prints, skimming the beaten trail. It was leading them toward Mount Crim. Echofrost flicked her ears, listening for the sounds of giants, of Storm Herd, or of the Sky Guard army; but the jungle was quiet beneath the merciless sun.

"Why do the giants want so many pegasi?" Shysong wondered. "I don't believe they're taking almost a hundred and forty of them back home to *eat*."

"Well, Gorlanders are big," Echofrost said, shuddering. "They must need a lot of food."

"But Rizah said that winged steeds are sacred to the Sandwens. Maybe they took our friends to bargain with the clans."

"That's possible, but what do the giants want?"

The mares answered the question at the same time. "Farmland!"

"This might give them the leverage they need to win back the land the Sandwens stole from them so long ago."

"I doubt Lilliam will trade anything for our herd. She despises us."

"But she likes that other stuff—those coins the Sandwens collect. Our herd is worth a lot of coins."

"True," Echofrost said, thinking as she soared faster east, toward Mount Crim.

Then Shysong slowed. "Look," she whispered. "There they are."

Echofrost followed her gaze, her eyes telescoping into focus as they homed in on the giants. Then she spotted them—her friends. They were tethered to the elephants and marching toward the base of the huge mountain ranges. A handsome buckskin stallion caught her eye.

"Hazelwind!" Echofrost whinnied.

The giants halted their march and turned, looking up. They pointed at the mares and grunted in excitement.

Hazelwind turned his head and saw them too. He strained against his tether but could not fly away. The huge Gorlanders were leading the Storm Herd steeds by ropes cinched around their necks, every one of them captured. Echofrost counted over six hundred giants. She swooped toward Hazelwind.

He reared and shook his head at her. "Don't come any closer," he neighed. "They have fire!"

She paused, hovering. Then a group of giants that were carrying large cages stopped and opened them.

Hazelwind's eyes rolled. "Go!" he brayed.

"Do what he says," Dewberry whinnied.

From above, Echofrost noticed that the mare's belly had spread wider. If the pinto wasn't sick, she was pregnant. *Pregnant!!* Dewberry's words came rushing back to Echofrost: *I've never felt better. Bumblewind will live on with Storm Herd.* Joy and terror collided in Echofrost's heart as she suddenly understood—her brother had sired

a foal before he died! Echofrost was going to be an aunt—
but Dewberry was captured!

Just then, Graystone reared and was choked by his
rope, his words cut short. Echofrost noticed the large gash
in his flank from fighting the soldiers at the farm. "How
did they catch you?" Echofrost asked. It was impossible to
believe what she was seeing: her winged herd in the hands
of giants.

"That's how!" neighed Redfire, nodding toward the
cages.

While Echofrost watched, hundreds of winged bats
poured out of the cages. They swarmed toward Echofrost
and Shysong, splitting off to surround them. But no! They
weren't bats. They were miniature dragons, long and flat
like baby alligators. Their red, orange, and yellow scales
glinted in the sunlight. Black barbs spiked their tails, and
they had needle-sharp teeth, like wolf pups. She and Shysong watched them come, unsure what to do.

"They breathe fire," Hazelwind warned.

"They what?" cried Shysong.

But soon the mares understood when the tiny colorful
dragons opened their mouths and roared streams of blue
flames.

"Go!" Hazelwind brayed.

Echofrost's thoughts sped. These were the fire lizards called *burners* that lived near the volcanoes. The giants must have trained them like they trained the elephants and their saber cats. *Had they used the burners to set fire to the hay barn too?* she wondered.

The burners caught up to Echofrost and attacked, shooting flaming tendrils at her and Shysong. There were hundreds of them moving as one creature, like a flock of sparrows. She twisted away when a few of her feathers caught fire. "Blast it!" she cried, flapping hard to extinguish the puff of flame.

Shysong flew in to help. They kicked at the lizards, knocking some out of the sky. The burners chirped and hissed, and small glittering frills fanned from their necks.

"They're like our sky herders in Anok," Hazelwind neighed, watching the battle from the ground. "They're trained to push you where they want you to go. They will drive you toward land and then you'll be caught, but if you just fly away, they won't know what to do. So go!"

"But—"

"You're no good to us captured."

His words stung her heart. "Retreat!" she whinnied to Shysong.

The two of them turned and sailed away as fast as they could, their burned feathers smoking. And Hazelwind was correct, the burners didn't follow them. The mares cruised higher and watched from the clouds. The Gorlan horde whistled for their burners and collected the miniature dragons back into their cages. Then they tugged on their captured steeds and resumed their march toward Mount Crim.

Echofrost's body trembled, and her thoughts swept across her mind like a wildfire. All the promises she'd made rose up from her gut, mocking her. She'd sworn to rescue Shysong—and she'd done it—but she'd failed miserably at the superior goal: to live free! Now all of Storm Herd was captured, including her brother's coming foal. "I've failed at *everything*," she roared into the wind. Then she swore a new oath to Hazelwind, to Dewberry, to all of them. "I'll save you," she brayed. "I promise."

Whether they heard her or not she didn't know. They were already out of sight, blocked by the swaying branches of the jungle.

Echofrost sobbed, her broken promises trailing her like shed feathers.

Shysong rattled her wings. "Our entire herd is caught!

We'll need an army to free them."

Echofrost cleared her mind, trying to think. But then Shysong's words sunk in. "An army?" Echofrost repeated. "We have one!"

Shysong gaped at her. *"Where?"*

"The Sky Guard! All Kihlari are sacred. The Fifth Clan will rescue Storm Herd once they find out what's happened."

"But how will they find out?" Shysong asked.

Echofrost glanced back toward the nests. "We'll show the cubs and then fly them back to the Fifth Clan so they can tell Tuni and the queen."

"You mean you want to go back?"

The wind tossed Echofrost's mane into her eyes. "Of course not," she said, her throat tightening. "But there are two of us against how many giants? We can't help our friends by ourselves."

Shysong faltered, dropping altitude.

Echofrost followed her. "We don't have time. We have to act. I'm getting Rahkki." She turned and flew toward the nest.

"But we can't control this plan, Echofrost. How can we be sure we'll *all* end up free—and not just captured by the Sandwens again?"

"Control?" Echofrost snorted. "When was the last time we had any? This is our only shot. The alternative is that all of Storm Herd will be lost."

Shysong threw her a dark look, and Echofrost felt her ears grow hot. All this was Echofrost's fault, and that's why she had to try and fix it. She exhaled, long and slow. "If I return with Rahkki, I'll belong to him. We'll be Paired into the Sky Guard. When they free Storm Herd, I'll be with them."

Shysong exploded. "We just escaped that place!"

"I don't expect you to join me," she nickered.

Shysong tossed her head, simmering. "I'm not staying in the jungle *alone*."

"Then come with me. I'Lenna and Rahkki won't hurt us. We'll be safe."

"Safe?" Shysong sputtered. She stared at Echofrost. The clouds drifted around them, the land contracted far below their hooves, and the wind jingled the bells in their tails. Feelings shot between them like lightning bolts. Echofrost chewed her lip, afraid that Shysong would abandon her. She wouldn't blame the mare if she did.

Finally Shysong uncoiled her tense legs. "Okay, I'll go with you."

"You don't—"

"No. I want to. You're right. We can't save them on our own. We need weapons, armor, and numbers. The Sky Guard can give us that."

Echofrost nodded, and the mares soared back to the nest together. The Landwalker cubs were still there, sitting in the base and playing with rocks.

The mares dived down, and Echofrost's wings blew back Rahkki's shaggy hair. He glanced up. "Sula!" His face cracked into a wide smile, and Echofrost felt a small tug at her heart. He trusted her, and she'd left him in a tree so tall that he couldn't get down. She felt guiltier about this than she liked to admit.

She and Shysong landed in the nest, and the Landwalker cubs threw their arms around each steed's neck. Echofrost let Rahkki hug her, realizing she'd scared him half to death, and knowing he didn't deserve it. Not after he'd tried to save her from the giants, stood up to the queen for her, and saved her from starvation too. "Climb on," she nickered, kneeling down.

He didn't understand the words, but he understood her intent. He climbed onto her back and I'Lenna hopped onto Shysong.

"Thank you, thank you," the princess purred to her mare. She kissed the roan's neck several times, and

Shysong pranced, looking uncomfortable.

"Now let's show them what happened to our friends." Echofrost and Shysong lifted off, being much more careful this time with their passengers, and they flew toward Mount Crim.

44

SULA

"WHY DO YOU THINK THE BRAYAS CAME BACK?"
I'Lenna asked, shocked but thrilled.

"They felt guilty for ditching us," Rahkki guessed, raising an eyebrow.

The princess giggled. "I doubt it. Maybe they *like* us."

"That's even harder to believe," Rahkki said, chuckling. Even though he was flying again, high above the jungle, relief coursed through his veins. Sula was protective—she'd tried to defend him from the queen's soldiers and she'd made sure he was safe from predators by leaving him high in a nest. He felt safer flying on her than he usually felt in the sky, but he still avoided looking down. Beads of cloud moisture had gathered on her feathers, making them sparkle, and her salt-white mane flowed against her darker silver coat. Rahkki inhaled to calm his nerves and attempted to guide her toward his home, but Sula, as usual, ignored him. "Where do you think they're taking us?" he asked I'Lenna.

She swung her heels, a look of pure bliss on her face. "I don't care."

They soared through the clouds, and then suddenly dropped altitude. Sula nickered meaningfully at Rahkki, swiveling her head toward him. He stroked her neck. "What is it, girl?" Sometimes, like right now, Rahkki wished he *were* a Meld.

She nickered again, more insistent, and he followed her gaze. Marching across a clearing below them, Rahkki spied hundreds of Gorlanders. They'd lassoed the wild herd and were leading them toward Mount Crim. "I'Lenna! Look down!"

Pulled from her reverie, she did as he asked. "Bloody rain," I'Lenna whispered.

The caravan of Gorlanders and Kihlari slowly vanished into the trees. "This is why the mares came back," Rahkki said, sitting taller, "to show us that their friends got captured." His thoughts tumbled. "Sula needs us to help them."

I'Lenna narrowed her dark eyes, nodding. "All right. But how?"

Just then the wild brayas banked hard and glided back toward the Fifth Clan settlement.

"Correction!" he said. "She wants our *clan* to help them."

"Then we'd better hurry." I'Lenna, who'd been riding Firo with one hand on the reins and the other twirling a lock of her sun-streaked hair, leaned forward and dug her heels into her pet's ribs. "Yah, Firo!" The roan mare shot forward.

Sula surged after her and Rahkki slid toward her tail. He snatched his braya's mane and yanked himself forward. Then he leaned over her neck, copying I'Lenna. "You were born to fly!" he shouted to her.

The princess laughed, her voice ringing like the clan's morning bells. "So were you, Rahkki!"

The mares had risen and were now flying with the lowest clouds. The mist dampened his hair and it felt good, a refresher from the sun's burning heat.

"The Gorlanders must have used their little dragons to drive the herd into a trap. Poor things," I'Lenna said as they glided closer to home.

Rahkki rode silently, feeling tired. Sula's wings

carved the wind with a grace and power that exceeded Kol's. If he were to compare them to their ground-dwelling counterparts—Sula was a racehorse and Kol was a plow horse.

As Rahkki was musing, Sula's right wing suddenly seized and twisted. "Uh-oh!" he cried. Rahkki was pitched hard when her body rolled onto its side. Her hooves thrashed the sky.

And then he was weightless.

Falling.

"Rahkki!" I'Lenna screamed.

The boy and the winged mare plummeted toward land. His tunic fluttered around him, his lips and cheeks pulled away from his teeth, and the wind stole his breath. The planet seemed to swell as he raced toward it. If there was a thought in Rahkki's head, he couldn't find it.

Sula threw out her wings with a loud snap against the wind. The cramp passed and with gritted teeth, she pushed into the current and spun herself right side up.

Rahkki whizzed past her.

Pointing her head down, she dived after him, flapping to catch up.

Rahkki grasped at nothing, his arms cartwheeling.

Sula caught his tunic in her teeth. It ripped off him.

She let go and it flapped away like a distressed bird. She passed him, dropping in a controlled dive. He spotted her rippling white mane and tried to grab it. Missed.

She angled her body beneath him and slowed her descent as he reached her. She meant for him to land on her back, so he spread his legs. They collided and he slammed onto her spine, crotch first. White-hot pain shot through him as he grabbed a fistful of her mane. By instinct, he tucked himself up under her wings and lay over her neck, hugging her.

"Rahkki! Are you all right?" I'Lenna shouted, her voice warbling.

He nodded once, but couldn't speak. Waves of pain and nausea washed over him, and all he could think was: *Don't pass out, don't pass out.*

Echofrost leveled out, her heart pounding, and slowly caught her breath. A moon ago, she'd have let this cub fall to his death—now the sight of him falling had driven her to rescue him. How had that happened? All she'd wanted was to live in peace. Well, she had no time to ponder it.

With Rahkki secure on her back, Echofrost turned to Shysong. "The kids have seen our captured herd. Now let's get them home," she whinnied.

The mares flew back to the Fifth Clan. As they glided over the Kihlari barn, Echofrost thought about the three hundred ferocious pegasi inside. She'd gone from fearing them to needing them. They were her only hope of saving her friends, and her brother's foal, from the Gorlan horde.

Echofrost glanced over her shoulder at Rahkki. The boy was pale and grimacing in pain. He'd struck her back hard, bruising her spine and himself, she imagined. He was clearly not a fighter like Brauk or Tuni, but of all the Landwalkers on this blasted continent, he was the only one she trusted, the only one she liked, and the only one who'd fought to protect her. She could teach him to fly— she'd have to.

She and Shysong flew over the fortress, and then the village. The clansfolk erupted from their huts, shouting up at them. Echofrost hovered over the arena, but no one was there. She waited. Soon the spectators returned, running to see if the wild mares were returning their princess. The tented folk emerged, their mouths agape, and then the auctioneer, and lastly the Sandwen queens appeared. The Sky Guard army was still saddled and circling over the jungle. They spotted the two mares and darted back, hovering near them.

Echofrost and Shysong soared toward Lilliam.

"What sort of stunt is this?" the queen shouted at her daughter.

Shysong landed, and the princess slid off her back. "I followed them," I'Lenna explained, nodding toward Echofrost and Rahkki, who were still hovering overhead, "to make sure they came back."

The queen crossed her arms, scowling at her daughter's ruined dress, torn skin, and bleeding mouth.

"And we bring news, Mother!" I'Lenna added.

"Not now," Lilliam snapped. "Take your winged pony back to Fort Prowl and clean yourself up." The queen's eyes glittered like ice shards. I'Lenna led Shysong quickly away.

Echofrost sailed toward the arena and landed gracefully on the sand. Rahkki's injured body slumped forward and then slid off her back, landing in a crumpled heap at her hooves, unconscious. He had bloodied hands from holding her mane so tight and a bare chest from losing his tunic, and long welts across his bare skin. With his dark lashes shadowing his cheeks, he looked small and young and fragile.

"He did it," Mut cried in disbelief. "Rahkki rode that mare to the clouds and back."

The spectators and the tented folk cheered.

"'E slayed three giants once too," Koko added.

Mut smacked her arm. "No, he didn't."

"I ain' lyin'," she said, and smacked him right back.

The auctioneer approached Rahkki to help him up, but Echofrost stamped her hoof, threatening him back. She didn't know this Landwalker and didn't trust him.

Then Tuni approached Rahkki, and Echofrost let her. The Headwind fussed over him. "He's fine," she said. "He just fainted."

"May I pronounce him the winner?" the auctioneer asked the queen.

Lilliam's eyes darted toward the spectators—the tented folk, the other contenders, and the visiting queens; they'd all watched Rahkki successfully ride the mare, and they were waiting eagerly for a triumphant pronouncement. Finally the queen offered a stiff nod.

The auctioneer strode to the center of the arena and raised his hands. Everyone quieted. "We have a new Pair," he rumbled with a flare of showmanship. "Rahkki Stormrunner of the Fifth Clan, bloodborn son of the Sacred Seven, rode this wild Kihlara mare called Sula to the clouds and back, completing the challenge."

Echofrost flicked her ears forward, listening to the

Landwalkers' cheering. She peered at Rahkki, wishing he'd wake up so he could tell everyone about her captured friends. The pegasi were sacred and valuable to his clan; she was counting on them to be outraged.

The auctioneer continued. "The binding ceremony for new Pairs is tomorrow. Congratulations, Stormrunner." He spit on his hand and turned to shake Rahkki's, but the boy was still lying in the sand, out cold.

Next the man called Uncle leaned against the rail and cleared his throat. Lilliam hissed under her breath.

"We have a wager to settle," Darthan said.

Echofrost watched the queen clutch her belly and pull her flowing silk cape around her shoulders. "Tomorrow," she said, standing up. "I'm not feeling well, and I have a dragon to feed." She was so pale now that only her glossed lips held color. Her armed guards followed as she swept out of her tent, climbed onto her stallion, and flew toward the land soldiers who had gathered outside the arena.

Echofrost stood protectively over Rahkki's body and closed her mind to thoughts of freedom and escape. *I am no longer Echofrost of Storm Herd*, she told herself, changing her identity and with it changing the course of her life. *I am Sula of the Fifth Clan, Kihlara Flier in the Sky Guard army, and Rahkki Stormrunner is my Rider.* She repeated this over and over in her mind. She'd need to believe it in order to accept what was coming next: wearing a saddle and armor and a bit, and letting a Landwalker ride on her back. But she would do anything, *anything* for her herd.

She glanced toward Mount Crim in the distance, where the Gorlan giants had taken her friends. "Hold on, Hazelwind," she nickered softly. "I'm coming for you and Storm Herd, and I'm bringing an army. Then we'll go. And this time I won't fail. I promise."

ᏟᎡACKNOWLEDGMENTSᏟᎡ

THANK YOU FOR READING AND I HOPE YOU enjoyed the story! My characters would like to thank you also, for allowing them into your imaginations. We are honored you chose to journey across the Dark Water with us.

If you'd like to further immerse yourself in the Realm, try playing "stones" with your friends. This Sandwen strategy game is based on Mancala, an ancient system of play that involves capturing your opponent's stones, seeds, or beans. Rules can be found online. You can make your own playing board or buy one at a toy store. Try it with a sibling, friend, parent, or book club—best enjoyed with peppermints!

And for those of you who've read the first four books in the Guardian Herd series, beginning with *Starfire*, I'm thrilled you're joining me in these new adventures. For those of you who are curious about Anok and the pegasi who live there, I invite you to visit the Guardian Herd website. Here you'll find games, quizzes, a herd glossary, giveaways, printable trading cards, interviews, FAQ, stunning fan art, pictures of the characters, and more!

Without further ado, I'm pleased to announce that I'm writing the Riders of the Realm trilogy with many of the same incredible people who I worked with on the Guardian Herd series: my agent, Jacquie Flynn, and the talented folks at HarperCollins Children's Books. Their belief in my stories has inspired me more than words can express.

Senior Editor Karen Chaplin remains by my side, traveling with me across the Dark Water. I couldn't ask for a more inquisitive, enthusiastic, and supportive co-adventurer. Illustrator David McClellan is with us, documenting the new world with his incredible sketches and paintings.

Book Designer Heather Daugherty continues to

inspire, casting the words and the art into beautiful physical books. Megan Barlog from Marketing, Andrea Pappenheimer and Kathy Faber from Sales, Olivia Russo from Publicity, and Patti Rosati and Molly Motch from School and Library Marketing lend their creative dedication to bringing these stories to you, the reader. Senior Production Editor Jessica Berg and Copyeditor Andrea Curley are at the rudder, steering the prose and the plot into alignment with all that has gone before. And Editorial Director Rosemary Brosnan plots our course, ensuring no one gets lost on the way.

Special appreciation to the authors who've encouraged and helped me thus far, especially Peter Lerangis, Anne Greenwood Brown, Kristin Kittscher, John Kloepfer, Anne Nesbet, Jenn Reese, Lindsay Cummings, Sarah Prineas, Sage Blackwood, Angela Lam Turpin, A. E. Conran, Jill Diamond, and Esther Ehrlich.

To the booksellers, teachers, and librarians—thank you for hosting in-house events that allow authors like me to meet readers. These experiences are priceless.

Much love to my horses, past and present, and to my pets. You talk to me without speaking and love me without judging.

And to my husband, children, family, and friends—
thank you for understanding that I live in two worlds.

Wishing you wings,

Jennifer